The Scholar's Sanctum

Chris Delude

Published by Chris Delude, 2025.

THE SCHOLAR'S SANCTUM

First edition. November 12, 2025.

Copyright © 2025 Chris Delude.

ISBN: 979-8998673627

Written by Chris Delude.

The Scholar's Sanctum would not have been possible without the help of so many people. My wife, best friend George, and mom have provided so much substantial feedback on the book itself, but also tireless support when I've received hundreds of rejections, spiraled, burned out, and doubted whether I've ever written a single decent sentence in my feeble existence.

My life is also filled with less literate people who haven't done an ounce of work for *The Scholar's Sanctum*, but have enriched my life so much that I feel like I wouldn't be capable of writing this without them. My friends provide me with endless laughs, my dad gifted me with the best sense of humor, and my brother will forever inspire me to do cool stuff with my life.

Words cannot express my gratitude toward you all.

CHAPTER 1

"Welcome and enter!" I hear Professor Lewis sing from behind his office door.

I'm slightly out of breath from jogging up three flights of stairs to the Ancient Studies department, but I roll my eyes and let myself in.

"Cleo, my boy!" he announces, leaning back in his chair. "Please, take a seat. To what do I owe the pleasure?"

I sigh, sitting down. After three and a half years of working on the same PhD dissertation, it's awkward to tell my advisor that I still have nothing to report. In a way, our grant was set up to fail from the beginning; Rockwell University was awarded millions of dollars by the National Institute on Aging to find a cure for dementia. How, anyone would ask, are two crusty Ancient Studies scholars supposed to formulate such a cure? We won't. But there's evidence that healers in India found effective treatments over three thousand years ago, and it's our job to uncover what they knew.

The Indian science of ayurveda, translating to "life knowledge," is their understanding of medicine and wellness. It has been cultivated for thousands of years and, fortunately for us, was documented in the third century. Unfortunately for us, the British burned these libraries and persecuted the masters of this information when they colonized India. Almost everything was destroyed or lost. A few primary texts survived, the most relevant of which is called the *Charaka Samhita*. Here I learned about the herb Brahmi, which has numerous medical applications including the improvement of memory. In recent years, the effect of Brahmi in dementia patients has shown preliminary benefits in western research, but it is believed that there is still more we don't understand about its potential. That's what happens when you burn down a civilization's libraries...you tend to lose a few things.

To date, my research into the subject has been exhaustive and unfruitful. I've re-translated the *Charaka Samhita* several times, done infinite online searches, scoured Rockwell's library and countless others for information about ayurveda...only to come up empty. In the chair across from Professor Lewis, I prattle through the limited progress I've made and where I'm left stranded.

"I beg you not to get discouraged, Cleo. You're really finding yourself as a historical researcher in this work, but I caution you to not get lost in the shuffle. It's taken me three decades of research—and five best-selling books!—to get where I am today. You might not know this, but I wasn't always thought of so highly. In fact, many of my early colleagues believed I was mad for suggesting that we should 'taint' ancient studies by modernity and popular interest. This intersection may seem obvious to you now, but that's only *because* I have made it obvious for the department. Do you understand what I mean?"

"Absolutely," I say, nodding.

Professor Lewis is very easy to understand as an advisor because he's repeated this exact sentiment over a dozen times. His favorite pastimes include tousling his windswept salt-and-pepper hair, flirting with co-eds, and convincing the world that he's a radical pioneer of his field. If you forget, just look at the publications and awards he has framed around his office, bathing himself in his accomplishments. I make the mistake of glancing at my distorted reflection in one of his framed plaques, and see the unfortunate effects of my study habits: my stringy dark brown hair is getting too long, the stubble on my chin could use a shave, my pale skin is desperate to be let outside of the library, and the bags under my eyes are begging for about a year of uninterrupted sleep. Sucks for them.

Professor Lewis clasps his fingers over his desk, glancing at me. "I'm certain that we've discussed this before, but remind me what your long-term goals are? What career aspirations do you have once this work concludes?"

My gut says *stay at Rockwell University forever*, but that's not the kind of answer your advisor wants to hear. I would do anything to get tenured here, but professors are expected to acquire their initial teaching positions outside of their alma mater. The idea is that doctoral minds will go off into the world and be enriched by other academic cultures.

"I'd like to receive an Assistant Professorship at a competitive Ancient Studies department in New England, preferably Massachusetts. Then, ideally, I'd like to return to Rockwell after a few years of experience. The culture and rigor here are exactly what I'm looking for."

Professor Lewis gives me the slightest wink. "I would accuse you of flattery, Cleo, but I believe your sincerity to its core. If I could take credit for anything at all in my humble leadership, it would be my ability to inspire true passion in the minds of already budding curiosity. This alone is what fuels our capacity to sift through tedium, tirelessly and often without immediate gratification. That said, I do wonder whether your dedication is still intact, given your decision to publish null results in your final dissertation."

His remark stings. It isn't the ideal outcome for any researcher, but I *can* publish null results—results that say that I didn't find what I was looking for—and still receive a PhD so long as my methods prove to be sound. Funding was invested for me to bark up at a particular tree, but it was ultimately the wrong one. Future dogs will now know to avoid it, however, and there's academic merit to that. After three and a half years of only the slightest progress, I decided (with a very unenthusiastic blessing from Professor Lewis) to go this route. Clearly he's still not over it.

"I'm just hoping to get some additional guidance on where to search, Professor," I say, desperate to indicate that I am still trying. "I've exhausted all existing resources and referential texts that we we've found—"

"Ahh, but there is always more to find. I would suggest going back to the text that I recommended to you in September, by the Western historian Albrecht Rondurer. He was quite influential, and has shaped Ancient Studies—and myself, believe it or not!—in more ways than can be counted. It will be your north star for—"

Professor Lewis' phone suddenly rings. He flashes me an apologetic smile that gushes *"I'm just too important for my own good, I simply must take this!"*

Fucker. Not a single question answered. And that Albrecht Rondurer guy? He was a hack historian and racist as hell; he bought himself several native concubines from every country he "observed."

Resigned, I leave Professor Lewis' office and re-enter the aging, stale corridor of the Ancient Studies department. I wave to the handful of other graduate students who are holed up in the study area. I worked in there at the start of my PhD, hoping to cultivate a camaraderie with others who dedicate themselves to such niche areas of study. The unfortunate reality is that everyone there is too stressed and burnt out to talk about anything else. Deadline pressures, publishing, competitive funding, professor tracks...all of it poisoning them against the subjects they used to love. The only way they survive this pressure is by complaining with each other and feeding into each other's anxieties in perpetuity, and that just wasn't productive for me.

I deal with my dissertation stress the only way I know how: I cross the campus lawn, enter the arched library doors, and navigate my way to my favorite study room for the next seven hours. The dusty radiators are busted, so this room is always swelteringly warm. The precious undergrad cherubs literally can't take the heat, which leaves the beautifully antiquated space to me. The walls have a green and white damask wallpaper bordered with dark mahogany paneling. Antique carpeting is faded and worn from centuries of students throughout the university's history. A large grandfather clock ticks away, although I can't really hear it anymore after years of it being in my periphery. There's a memorial plaque on the wall that commemorates wealthy old men who gave funding to the school (try counting the number of William and John donors and you'll lose all belief in human creativity). The study room is furnished with a solid wood table, chairs, and two large wingback chairs, presumably so one William and one John always has a place to read his newspaper.

I absolutely love this place. Not just the study room but this library, this school. It's the place I call home above all else, and I can't say that I'm prepared to leave.

CHAPTER 2

E very train ride I take reminds me of every train ride I've taken.
This is, in part, because I take the train from Framingham to
Brookline seven days a week to get to Rockwell University. I walk
twelve minutes from my apartment to the train station, during which
several inevitabilities occur. I will hear at least one car honk from angry
commuters. I will pass by the sullen-faced man in camo pants as he
walks into traffic with his cardboard sign. The middle-aged Italian man
will be pumping gas for his customers, his lower belly pouring out of
his clothes regardless of whether there's a summer heatwave or a winter
advisory warning. If I'm lucky, I will cross the tracks before the inbound
train arrives. If not, I will hear *bing-bing-bing* and have to wait behind
the red-and-white candy-striped bar that lowers until the train passes.

Today, on my way home, I arrive on the platform five minutes early
and watch the daily latecomers. They clutch their bags in stride, their
breath fogging in the chilled and miserable December rain. The train
arrives with a squeal against the tracks and I board, getting into one of
the last remaining isolated seats. I place my wet backpack on the seat
beside me and shed my coat. Glancing out of the smudged plexiglass
window, my thoughts slowly begin to drift.

I remember being nine, watching out of a train window on an
equally dreary day. I was terrified that my mom and I had left my dad
behind.

"Your father is just a bit busy," she said, fussing my hair. "He's trying
to find work to take care of us. Isn't that nice?"

I nodded, watching her face as she, too, glanced out of the window.
My dad always had a way of weaving his life into and out of ours.
He never outright abandoned us, nor was he abusive or toxic. He was
just...a bit restless, I think. He always had another big idea to get me and
my mom everything we wanted; one initial investment that would pay
back tenfold. A brief move to Delaware or Minnesota, and we would

have our own house that we could heat as high as we wanted! Wouldn't that be special? I would nod. It always started special, until I realized that it was just a different backdrop for the same situation. Sometimes my mom and I went with him, and sometimes they "took a little time off" and he would be away for months.

My mom was never scared of anything, but she had nerves. Sometimes my dad would be on her nerves or wear them down, sometimes her nerves were shot, sometimes they were "just nerves." But they were always there. I'm sure a psychiatrist could have formally diagnosed her nerves as something more legitimate than she allowed herself to express, but we never had the money for that, and I never had the nerve to ask. A shaky cigarette on the porch was about all she could do. I used to resent them both for all of it, especially in my teens. *Get your shit together; you're goddamned adults! How do you keep putting yourself in the same position* every *time, reliving the same mistakes and hoping for a better outcome?* In retrospect, it's hard to know whether they were doing their best, but I believe they both thought they were at the time. It can be hard for people to get out of their own way.

We would make rent for a few months before having to leave. Then for another few months we would stay with my aunt, who would both ease and wind up my mom's nerves in a ritual of bad-mouthing my dad. Sometimes our places were moldy, roach-infested dumps. Sometimes they were real homes, where I might lay awake at night thinking *this is it. This could really be the one.* But neither the awful nor the perfect were permanent. The only consistencies were a few duffle bags on the train and whatever books my mom could find for me to read along the way.

My schooling was always "unbalanced," as one guidance counselor delicately put it. I jumped to different paces, curriculums, and teachers as infrequently as we could manage, but for us that was still at least once a year, often more. I was diligent about learning whatever books I was given, though. Even if it wasn't what the next school system was working through—ancient Egypt, *To Kill a Mockingbird*, the periodic table—I found that it always came up eventually. Being behind in one moment put me semesters ahead in others. I learned and I learned, because the books I had were always there, their text unchanging. When I woke up panicked in some converted attic, I could reach under my pillow and find my bookmark exactly where I had left it. Of course, history was my favorite subject; the past will forever know the beauty of never changing, the allure and comfort of being finished.

My dad never went to college, and my mom only had an associate's degree from her local community college. They didn't expect much from me because of the life that we had, and they assumed that the SAT study manual I slept with was just another fixation. Maybe it was. I can't say that I chose it because I was overly thoughtful about my future—it just felt like another great outlet for consistency. When my score came back as a 2380, my mom had to ask me what that meant. I shrugged my shoulders. I thought it might help me get in somewhere affordable, but I had no idea it would be my ticket to a full four-year scholarship to Rockwell University, one of the most prestigious universities in the country. I brought my two duffle bags with me on my train ride to campus, and for the longest stretch in my life I never had to pick them up.

I feel the train squeal to a stop, night surrounding me.

CHAPTER 3

I push open the heavy glass door, and a bell rings. The warm oven air and rich smell of dough hit me immediately, already thawing my chilled bones. I walk across the tiled floor of Arlo's Pizza Planet, passing by the rows of classic red-and-white checkered tables to get to the largest booth in the corner. Art and Thanh are already there with two boxes of half-eaten pizza in front of them. They nod at me, before Art glances back down to his laptop screen and Thanh shakes his head.

"I don't even know anymore, man," Thanh says.

"What's Thanh worried about now?" I ask, settling myself into the familiar sticky table. I pull out my own laptop and reach for a slice of cheese.

"Darling Thanh is revisiting an old crisis this time," Art says, typing away. His pristinely manicured nails are a blur of electric blue and white swirls. Art works as a freelance social media consultant for a few businesses, but I know at Arlo's he's usually doing something for his own fashion influencer content. When he first started I tried to help promote him, but he routinely gets tens of thousands of views now and he's close to getting sponsors. He doesn't need the help of my seventeen Facebook friends anymore (two of which are seated at this table).

Across the table, Thanh fidgets with his straight black hair, readjusts his glasses...any nervous habit he can think of that isn't smoking a cigarette. He's gone forty-seven hours since his last smoke, and it isn't going well.

"It's the *fudging* pizza, man!" he declares, careful to avoid the curse word. About seven years ago, Thanh watched a video explaining that swearing can negatively alter your brain chemistry, and he vowed to avoid it ever since. "I don't even know if I should be eating this stuff, or anything anymore! They tell you to eat locally because it's better for the environment, but then I read this article—this *peer reviewed* article—that explains how an economy of scale makes it so there's far less waste and resource use in giant, soulless farms than local ones. The carbon emissions of sending ingredients in planes is way less than production itself, so if you have a thousand local farmers producing as much as one mega farm in Argentina, then each of them needs their own plow, their own seeds, their own shipping, their own everything! It's so much more waste and I don't know if I should be eating their local food, corporate food, or just starve because that's the only ethical option anymore..."

Thanh continues on, fuming as a sauce stain rests on his cheek. He's a great guy, but when he's anxious he has the charming habit of questioning everything he believes and crashing out. His mom's been sick for a while and he's struggling to help pay her bills on top of his own student loans. On late nights when he's stressed about it all, he goes on Reddit and doomscrolls any thread that comes in his path. Unfortunately, this stress-reliever can yield the opposite effect; it convinces him that super viruses will wipe us out in twenty years, that most of the coastal United States will be underwater in ten years, and that AI will make ninety-nine percent of the workforce obsolete and there will be a civil war between them and the billionaires that own everything. The validity of any of these statements I can't confirm; they are posted by anonymous users who could be experts in the field or lunatics with Wi-Fi access. But when Thanh's already emotionally charged and in an echo chamber of thought, it can be easy to be swept away by ideas that validate what he's already feeling.

I choose to stay away from all of it: Art's social media world and Thanh's jungle of (mis)information. Instead, I take refuge in the solid, historically validated spaces that I know. Except when it's pizza day and Thanh needs someone to listen...

"...and even if I knew where the cheese came from, how am I supposed to know how they harvested the wheat? The tomatoes? Plus, the pizza here isn't even good anymore; I don't know why we bother coming and why I need to face these demons over *bad* pizza—"

"Heey, watch it," I say, half-kidding. Thanh and Art have been plotting an insurrection against our seven-year tradition of coming to Arlo's Pizza Planet ever since it changed owners. Their slander will not be tolerated.

"Dang, dude, just saying," Thanh responds, glancing around. "This place feels more like a sewer than a pizza joint at this point. Look, there are literal flies by the bathroom!"

I roll my eyes. "Every Chinese food place in Framingham breaks a thousand health code violations, and we still eat there all the time. Grime is the secret sauce, the love behind it! You can't—"

"Settle down, boys," Art cuts in, smirking from behind his laptop. "Yes, our beloved Pizza Planet sucks now; don't bother denying it. However, it is still ours. We can't find a new dirty pizza place every time Thanh has a bad week. Now, if you'll excuse me!" Art stands from the table, his bright pink pants flaring as he walks to the fly-infested restroom.

Thanh glances at me quickly, then looks away. "How are you and Kelsie doing lately?"

"Ehh," I say, not looking away from my laptop.

"I wasn't sure if you two were fighting still. I don't mean to pry..."

He does, but I know it comes from a good place. "We're the same. Relationships just involve compromise sometimes, you know?"

"Yeah..." he says.

I try to ignore the tone in his voice. Instead, I nod my head in the direction of our server. "Who's he playing this week?"

Thanh hesitates for a moment, then laughs, leaning in close to whisper. "I think it's supposed to be, like, an old cowboy or something? He said 'yeehaw' twice when he took our order."

The familiar thirty-something year-old server struts over to us, sporting a thin black mustache, greased hair, and a stiff, squinting glare as if he were keeping the sun out of his eyes. His real name is Carlos, but we call him Pizza Mysterio. He's been an aspiring actor since he started working here six years ago, and every few weeks he changes his appearance and accent to match whatever theatre and commercial roles he's going out for next. He's not very good, but he's a Pizza Planet fixture just like the checkered tables and the neon "Open" sign that's lit even after closing. The new manager tolerates him the same as the old one did; so long as he does a good job with customers and doesn't come in full costume, he can do whatever voices he wants. Except Asian accents. That one was so bad it almost ended in a lawsuit.

Art returns to the table, diving right back into his laptop.

"You editing another video?" I ask him.

"I certainly am. I have a date tonight at eight, but I'm so behind on this New York Fashion Week review. I did a decent job with the analysis, but my god the editing is a bitch."

"You'll figure it out," Thanh says. Neither Thanh nor I know the first thing about Art's fashion hobbies, but I've always been impressed by how ruthlessly he pursues them.

"Thanks bubby," Art says. "My future lover won't be pleased if I show up late, though, so I need to hurry up and get this done. And speaking of romance," he adds, turning to me, "how are you and Kelsie doing?"

Thanh gives him a look to drop it.

CHAPTER 4

There is nowhere to hide in our apartment.

There are four rooms: a bedroom that barely fits a queen-sized bed, a living room that barely fits a loveseat, a kitchen that barely fits a tiny round table, and a bathroom that barely fits a shower. Holes from the previous tenants pepper the walls (varying in size from thumbtacks to fists), although Kelsie has managed to cover most of them with her curtains, tapestries, and Marvel posters.

My contributions to the space happened before Kelsie agreed to move in, and they were mostly damaged furniture that I got for free on Facebook Marketplace. It may seem dingy to some, but I feel truly comfortable here. All I want from an apartment is a roof over my head and a safe place to keep my things, and living frugally allows me to do this. I spend most of my time at the library anyway; I get my dose of gorgeous aesthetic there. When Kelsie first moved in, she liked to tease that my place was "adorably Spartan," but over the past eight months this sentiment has been expressed less generously. Somehow, we manage to squeeze the two of us in here.

"Were you hiding at that pizza place again?" Kelsie asks, sitting on the couch under one of her frilly white blankets.

"I wasn't hiding," I say from the other room, dropping my wallet and keys on my bedroom nightstand. "We've always gone to Arlo's. I'm just busy at school lately, so that doesn't leave room for much else." I take off my coat and hang it on the front hook, running out of ways to settle myself before I have to enter the living room. I take a deep breath. This isn't the conversation I was hoping to have as soon as I stepped inside.

"But you make time for them," she says.

"I do," I agree, "and I make time for you, too. We went to your parents' house all last weekend, remember?"

"It was their anniversary! Of course we had to go. And you were working half the time we were there, I wouldn't exactly call it 'quality time.'"

I sit on the far edge of the couch, half-turning to face her. "I can't afford an entire weekend without working on my dissertation. Professor Lewis dumps the whole workload on me, and he's the one who decides whether I graduate or—"

"Yes, you always say how much Lewis is putting on you. But what about *your* choice in all this? With whatever free time you do have, you can choose to make time for us. When was the last time we sat on the couch and watched a movie or something? I keep saying you need to see the new *Guardians of the Galaxy* movie. I saw it almost four months ago and you said—"

We never agree on what movies to watch, so we established early on that we would take turns choosing. She says "this movie is so fucking weird" during half of mine, eye-rolling her way through them so that she can get back to her picks. I suppose I do the same for hers; we watch another Marvel movie every time, totaling fourteen since we started dating. I didn't even know there were that many, and I don't know how there can still always be more.

"I'm sorry," I cut in, lowering myself down on the couch next to her. "We can watch it tonight if you don't mind staying up late?"

Her eyes suddenly widen, excitement erasing whatever fight we were about to dive into. "Oh my god, really?" she says, leaning her head against my shoulder. Her bundled, blanketed body quickly reaches for her laptop to find the movie. "Yes, let's go! I am Groot!!"

I lean in to kiss her, then get up to use the bathroom before it starts. I feel the knots uncoiling in my chest; the tension easing into relief and a mild dread. It's going to be a long and exhausting night that I'll pay for tomorrow, but the momentary peace feels worthwhile. It does feel good to make her happy.

I hear her pause her laptop on the opening production credits.

THE SCHOLAR'S SANCTUM

"Don't want you missing anything!" she calls after me.
I exhale, shuffling back into the living room.

CHAPTER 5

Today is one of those deceptive early winter days. The sun is shining so my heart tells me it should be warm, until I step out of the apartment to a greeting of below-freezing temperatures in nothing but a sweatshirt. It's still beautiful, though. I walk briskly over the crunching lawn, across the road, and past the tired campus security office. I climb the impressive granite stairs, skipping every other step because I'm cold and impatient, and let myself into the familiar library entrance.

"Hi Kathy!" I say to the older librarian at the front desk. "Nice haircut, did you get that this weekend?"

"I sure did!" she says, smiling and showing off her newly highlighted blonde bob. Most students at Rockwell don't usually greet the librarians by name, nor do they go out for drinks with them or attend their eight-year-old grandson's birthday party because they needed a chaperone who could teach the kids how to bowl. But Kathy and I go back to finals week of my first semester of freshman year. I would be in the library every night until she gently knocked on my study room door to kick me out at closing.

"Sleep is as important as studying for retaining information! Now off to bed, you can come back in the morning!"

And then I did. The other librarians who worked in the morning described a young man who was in first thing all week, and it corroborated with her description of the young man who would leave at last call. In my defense, I *did* leave for meal breaks, and I wasn't as close with Art and Thanh yet so I had less recreation to tempt me away. One morning when I greeted the front desk, the librarian said, "Hold on a minute, I have something for you." She rummaged under the circulation desk and pulled out a Tupperware container of homemade lemon poppyseed muffins. "Kathy left them for you," she said, smiling. "With a reminder to take a break and remember to eat once in a while."

I reached out hesitantly, my groggy morning brain not processing the simple, beautiful gesture. "Thank you. I...I'll thank her as well tonight."

That evening at closing time, Kathy knocked on my study room door at the usual hour.

"Enjoying the muffins? I hope they help you stay focused. I can't imagine how you're still working at this breakneck speed."

"They were wonderful," I said, lifting the empty container.

"You weren't supposed to eat them all in one sitting! Good lord, boy!"

I shrugged, handing the Tupperware back. "Lemon poppyseed are my favorite. How did you know?"

"I didn't," Kathy said, turning off the lights behind me as we walked out. "But they're my favorite as well, and I baked a double batch."

"Hopefully you have more self-control than I do," I remarked.

She laughed and ushered me down the hallway. "Off to bed with you now!"

I waved goodnight. Muffin day marked the momentous beginning to our friendship.

Today the library is bustling with anxious undergrads. They have their finals coming up soon, but I struggle to muster any sympathy given that they have a six-week winter break afterward. With them gone, however, I can enjoy a nearly empty library all to myself! Last year's winter break was devastating; they closed the library for two weeks due to "cleaning and repairs." When they opened back up, I couldn't find a single thing that looked fixed (especially not the heating in my study room). Of course, Thanh had some wild conspiracy about the Institute of Museum and Library Services laundering money, but my explanation was far simpler: lazy bastards.

I walk down a spiraling staircase into the Stacks, which house row upon row of bookshelves spaced tightly against each other. As you go down each flight of stairs, the library has more books, fewer people, gets quieter, and ages another thirty years. I, being the antiquarian dweeb that I am, go to the bottom floor every time. The dusty heat, the mildewy book smell, the centuries of old texts...all of it is intoxicating. Breathing it in is like breathing in humanity. Yes, it's just musty paper, but every life that picked up these volumes across centuries has left their mark, and the authors who wrote them left theirs. Each one of us is sharing in a wisdom with thousands of strangers with shared hearts and minds. Multiply that sentiment by the millions of books in this collection, all concentrated and squeezed into one drab space for a perfect purpose.

I turn to enter my study room...crap. Unfortunately, the hot-box is a hotter commodity during finals season. I peak through the window and see a cluster of stressmen with calculus textbooks. I do not envy them. I haven't spent this much time in the library by being a quitter, though. I stalk the Stacks for every other study room possibility and unsurprisingly find them occupied as well. Not to fear. I go back upstairs, past the modern reading room and up to the third floor.

These upper-level floors feature a lot of modern offices and conference rooms for the library staff, but they're usually dead empty. They are technically locked, but if I jam a plastic card in the door frame they pop open pretty easily. My personal philosophy on such door-jimmying activities is as follows: Any public space should remain open to the public so long as you respect it. Libraries are a place of learning, and as such it aligns with their mission statement to allow me, an upstanding member of society, the free use of their conference room at any and all times whenever unoccupied. The only victim in this act is my poor, beat-up childhood library card; after this many years of jamming, it looks like a Rottweiler's chew toy.

I glance around the sterile hallway to confirm I'm alone. There's no sound from inside the conference room, either, so I quickly pop the lock and close the door behind me, leaving the lights off to avoid suspicion. I unload my backpack across the wide wooden table, splaying several books, mint gum, pens, highlighters, chargers, laptop, and headphones (I'm never working without some glammed British rocker bellowing in my ear) generously across the surface. And now...time to dig in!

Left completely uninspired by my meeting with Professor Lewis, I decide to review the challenges I'm facing. I begin with my primary source, the *Charaka Samhita*. It's written in ancient Sanskrit, and any time something is translated there are certain parallels that can't be drawn and cultural significances that won't be conveyed. Perfection isn't possible, so you're left with a series of options that can have incredibly significant implications. Especially when you're translating a medical textbook like this. The second challenge is that the *Charaka Samhita* was written in poetry to facilitate ancient students' abilities to memorize it all. To be clear, this is so fucking cool that it still makes my heart soar—imagine if the American Medical Association changed *Gray's Anatomy* to read like Shakespeare!—but this leaves modern me to make sense of not just ancient medicine, but ancient poetry as well.

Finally, and most interestingly, we know that there is more to the story than what's in these few remaining texts. The *Charaka Samhita* references several other books of wisdom that we don't have access to. One in particular is referenced during all remedies related to memory: the *Prabud'dha Sanskara*, which translates to *Enlightened Rituals*. For years I've been plagued every time I read that name; it's seemingly the lynchpin for my entire work, the missing piece that will be a breakthrough for dementia research. Like most ayurvedic texts, however, it was either destroyed or lost to time.

The initial focus of my grant was to learn herbal ayurvedic treatments that were used to improve memory. Over the past year, I've wondered whether the secret sauce wasn't an herb, but rather some kind of behavioral treatment. Scientific consensus shows that increasing sensory stimulation (such as having a person listen to music, paint, or do brain puzzles like Sudoku) is beneficial for tempering dementia symptoms. Approaches like reminiscence therapy have shown a small amount of success; this is when a person is asked to talk about long-held memories while holding items from their past, such as mementos and photographs. Aerobic exercise, massage therapy and even acupuncture have been known to improve memory as well. In modern rural areas like parts of Missouri, using non-medicinal interventions like these can be important because many people don't have easy access to drug stores, hospitals, or nurses. Ancient Indian civilizations would have faced the same issues.

I shake my head for a moment, realizing that I have a slight headache. I glance at the bottom of my screen and see that I've been here for five hours. I smile to myself; there's nothing quite like the flow state of losing myself in a good text, like Alice falling down the rabbit hole. The conference room is almost entirely dark now. I remove my headphones and reach for my phone, noticing that I have four missed texts from Kelsie.

2:16 PM What time are you coming home?

2:19 PM Trying to figure out dinner plans

3:08 PM Omg I know you're at the fucking library just respond I need to pick up groceries if we need something

3:21 PM I swear to god if you go out with your friends again...

I start typing a message...then delete it. I twist in my chair, cracking my back from sitting for so long. Before I went grocery shopping this weekend, I asked Kelsie if she wanted anything special for dinner so I could pick it up then. There's nothing wrong with her wanting to go again; I just like focusing on work during the week. If I had seen her first message it all would have been simpler, but now I don't know what I should say. Do I defend my friends, even though I had no plans to see them? Set boundaries about working late? Apologize for the late response and just answer her question? I shake my head, standing up. I'll think of a response on the way to the bathroom.

I listen at the door, hearing no footsteps in the hallway, and walk out with the confidence and boredom of someone who received full permission to be up here. At the far end of the hall, one of the newer librarians is talking with a young woman I don't recognize. Her brunette hair is streaked with a line of vibrant scarlet, and she is wearing a shearling tan coat, gray scarf, and has rosy cheeks like she just escaped the cold. I keep my head down so they both ignore me, but just as I enter the restroom I see the scarlet-streaked woman's gaze fall on me. I shouldn't have looked at her as long as I did; I drew too much attention to myself. Usually I'm better about staying invisible, but I guess I was thrown off by the new face.

I'll hurry out of here, wrap things up with work, and take the next train back.

CHAPTER 6

I sling my bag over my shoulder, rushing to catch the last train home. Whoops.

I had meant to just look over a few things and leave, but I spotted a few lines in the *Charaka Samhita* that could have multiple translations, potentially related to behavioral therapies. Another four hours and two stolen cups of librarian lounge coffee later, I was able to chase the bliss of momentary progress.

The train station transforms at night. The concrete and iron world is laced in frost, huddled in darkness. Lansdowne Station is normally bustling with commuters, but at this hour I shuffle my feet down to the cold platform alone. Lights speckle the night sky from the city high-rises. There's a world of anchored opulence up there, looking down on the hundreds of transient men, women, and children that scuffle on and off the trains every day, who have nowhere to go without being ushered elsewhere. I board the next outbound train.

The commuter rail provides a discomfort that's somehow pleasant in its consistency. The yellowing fluorescent lights illuminate the dull, beet-colored seats made of hard clinical pleather. Torn ticket stubs dangle from seat handles. The stifling heat intensifies the concoction of smells: musty air, hot leather, and an occasional assault of perfume. There's a constant rattling, both of the tracks outside and the creaking seats inside, that sounds like cicada bugs chirping on a hot summer's night. Static from attendant's distant walkie-talkies melds with the vague chattering of passengers, orchestrating a white noise that lulls me into my own thoughts.

Moving a lot during my childhood frequently got in the way of things. In the eighth grade when I was living in North Attleboro, a quiet Massachusetts suburb, I made the mistake of asking out a girl that I really liked. Her name was Aisha, and she said yes. She had dark skin with long braided hair that she had beaded at the bottom. We had no money and no rides anywhere, but we were young and needed nothing but each other. She knew of a closet in school where they kept the theatre costumes, and one day she showed me how to pick the lock simply by jamming my old library card—I wasn't going to Dover, Delaware any time soon—into the door near its locking mechanism.

I was too young and inexperienced to do anything but kiss her and feel the outside of her bra, but almost nothing has topped that adrenaline-filled high. We weren't always kissing in that closet, though. Sometimes we would just sit down on a pile of old coats and talk. Talk about how her parents worked seventy hours a week, working construction and cleaning houses. How their landlord threatened to have them evicted unless they paid more rent than they owed, just to fuel his own drug habit. They couldn't afford anywhere else, and they didn't want Aisha to have to move all the time. I understood that. I told her all the places I had been and she was desperately jealous...until I started quietly crying. Then Aisha held me, and we kissed more.

When the theatre kids were practicing, we would walk across the highway to the Emerald Square Mall. We didn't have any money, but that never mattered; we would giggle at the sex objects in Spencer's Gifts and try on fancy clothes at Macy's until some disgruntled worker yelled at us to leave. When we got hungry we did laps of the food court, reconfiguring our coats and hats and glasses in different ways to get as many free samples as we could. I'd walk her home afterward in the dark, and we'd kiss outside her apartment building before saying goodnight. She never let me inside—said she had too many brothers and sisters and the place was a mess. Then I would walk home and tell my mother that chess club ran late today, and did I mention I got an A on my biology quiz? That settled her nerves.

Aisha and I spent a blissful six months together until it was time for me to move again. I had never pleaded with my mom so much to stay where we were. I would get a job, get perfect grades, do extra chores around the apartment. What else could I do? I hadn't felt that connected to another soul in my entire young life. It's not that I hadn't tried to establish roots before...I just hadn't been so damn successful. There were a few momentary flings throughout high school, but I never bothered with close friends or dating after what happened with Aisha.

Until I came to Rockwell. Here, things finally began to settle.

Kelsie and I met in our freshman year. Art—my roommate at the time—was desperate to get me to an off-campus party one night because he was trying to exchange glances with a hot lacrosse player in his communications class. I asked why that meant I had to go, as I was pleasantly enjoying a text about Medieval monasticism.

"Because all of the people worth reading about go into the world and do things, not spend Friday nights reading about them."

I hold up my book. "Not these monks. And anyway, I don't need to be of historical significance. I'm quite content to be a fly on the wall of a peaceful cloister." Yes, I said it to piss off Art, but I still believed every word. The term "The Dark Ages" was popularized because there were not enough historical records to show human progress between the fifth and tenth century, so people assumed it was a period of decline in culture and science. Historians would later debunk this belief—ironically discovering that universities were first established during this period—but the name still stuck. In some small way, learning about history feels stabilizing both for me and those who lived through it. It makes us all more real.

Art disagreed. He rolled his eyes and dangled my sweatshirt in front of me. "Okay, how about you come because friendship is fun, and I'll buy you booze for the next two weekends?" Art's older sister bought him liquor whenever he wanted, and I would have been a fool not to take him up on the offer. Truthfully, it was probably a good idea to get out of the room; I'd been inside all day.

I inserted my bookmark with a smirk, stomped my shoes on my feet, and grabbed the sweatshirt from his hands. "All you had to do was ask."

I recognized Kelsie from a course last semester, and we smiled at each other briefly when Art and I entered the party. It was completely dark in the unfinished basement except for a gyrating green, yellow, and pink lights. It was late winter, but the unheated basement had reached about eighty-five degrees from an unsafe volume of human bodies. I helped Art talk to Kevin in the beginning (although he didn't seem to need it), mentioning that we had been on the same dishwashing shift for our work study job last month. Once they fully started ignoring me, I excused myself as politely as possible: I cupped my hand around my mouth and screamed "BATHROOM!!" over the deafening speakers. I lingered by the keg that was underneath the wooden staircase, watching the horde of students jump, grind, and drunkenly belt the words to "Mr. Brightside." It was fun to watch sociology happen in front of me; mating rituals have incorporated alluring outfits, intoxication, music, dancing, and flickering lights for all of human civilization.

Eventually I did need BATHROOM, and when I made it to the first floor, I was delighted to discover that it was fifteen degrees cooler and had infinitely more oxygen. The kitchen was old and small, and there were a few girls chatting quietly in a circle. I registered that they were staring at Kelsie who was talking nervously into the bathroom door. I walked up to her, both because she looked gorgeous and because I needed to assess whether I'd have to pee in the bushes outside.

"Everything okay in there?"

"Things have...been better," Kelsie said, cracking the door open slightly to peer in. Her face contorted as the sound of retching came through. She looked desperately around the party. "My friend Allie is in there. I tried helping in the beginning, but I don't do well with puke—" Another retching sound, and I watched Kelsie's body tense, face grimacing.

"Do you want me to...?" I pointed inside.

"No, I couldn't have you—"

"Seriously, it's no problem. Everyone's been in that position before; I don't mind helping out." She looked at me gratefully as I knocked and entered.

I can't say that the next thirty minutes were a delight, nor what I expected the night to turn into. Allie didn't make a great first impression and I'm sure I didn't either; I spent most of the time bullying her into drinking water, eating saltine crackers, and aiming into the bowl while I held back as much hair as I could. Once she settled a bit—blinking as if coming back from a possession—I offered to help walk her back to her dorm.

"You live in Clark too?" Kelsie asked, as we made our way out of the party and onto the cold street.

"Sure do!" I said, readjusting Allie's arm over my shoulder. "Speaking of which, remind me to text my roommate when we get back. I'm certain he's busy with some guy in there, but I'll at least let him know I haven't died."

"How thoughtful," Kelsie said, laughing through teeth chatters.

"Do you want my sweatshirt?" I offered, pausing to remove it. "I'm getting a workout here so I'm plenty warm."

"You're sure?" she asked. "That's really sweet of you." She wraps the oversized hoodie over her, looking unbearably cute.

It was a ten-minute walk and the two of us spent the time chatting. It was nothing serious—she told me about how she was an economics major, how her parents had attended Rockwell University thirty years ago and met on campus, how she had gone out with her friends recently and seen the new Marvel movie. I kept asking questions—feeling the wonderment that this beautiful woman was interested in me and the hope that it wouldn't end. When we made it to Clark, Kelsie opened the doors for us. There was a tense moment outside Allie's room where she struggled to remember the combination to get in, but then her roommate opened the door with an eye roll at her compatriot's condition. I unceremoniously plopped her on her bed, and the girls helped Allie take off her shoes ("Why would...they make...the straps so hard?" Allie mumbled. "What kind of psycho makes something like this?").

When things settled, I walked Kelsie down to her own room. We arrived at the door and I swallowed hard, forcing myself to make the move. "Is it cool if I text you tomorrow? If you're up for watching it again, I'd love to see that Marvel movie."

"Oh my god, of course!" she said, face alight.

We messaged the next morning to complain about hangovers, the following day to set a movie date, the day after that about roommate drama...and every day since.

The train jolts—I hear the conductor announce my stop. I have the briefest moment of hesitation before rising from my seat and exiting.

CHAPTER 7

I feel like a moron sneaking into my own home.

I stayed at school later than I should have, though, and Kelsie doesn't do well being woken up. I think through every stealth trap in the apartment—the squealing door, the click of the lock, the jingling of keys. I've lived here for four years and know the place intimately, only needing the digital stove clock to light my way. I take off my jacket, put my wet winter boots by the door, and breathe a sigh of relief when I make it to the bathroom. I close the door behind me, bathing in the light as I wash my face and brush my teeth. I strip down to my boxers and go to the bedroom, head aching from the day and completely exhausted. Sleep is going to feel sooo gooooood.

"Really?" she says.

The word shatters the silence, floating in the darkness beside my half-naked body. My chest tightens. I don't know what to do or say so I just lie down; however I need to respond can surely be done horizontally.

"You come sneaking in here this late on a work night," she begins, "you don't even apologize, you didn't even respond to my texts earlier! I sent like four and I know you read them. Just didn't want to acknowledge your fucking girlfriend?"

Shit. Sometimes I do this thing where I read a text, and in my head I've responded so I mentally cross it off, but I didn't actually type or send anything. I've tried explaining that to her before and it's never gone well, so I don't bother trying again. Shit shit.

"Are you even going to respond to me now? Like, do I have to worry about you sneaking around and...and...fucking someone else or something? There's no way you're just studying this whole time. I've talked to Lauren and Jessica; they don't think it's crazy for me to think—"

"Listen," I say, looking toward the shapeless, berating voice from the other side of the bed. "I'm sorry. I know that doesn't cut it right now and you have every right to be upset. I promise you that I was just studying. You might not believe it—I know I'm weird about work—but my dissertation advisor has just been so unhelpful and I'm really starting to feel the pressure of being behind. I did see your texts and I meant to respond, but I went to use the bathroom and when I got back I was distracted and—"

"But that's just it! You're always distracted! If this was the first time this happened I wouldn't be upset, but I swear you only love those old fucking books! It's like you go through the motions of our relationship, but you..."

All of the same, tired arguments are rehashed. She turns on her bedside lamp at one point, and I see that the walls are entirely bare. Did...she redecorate? I also see the building resentment etched on her features. I briefly think of that girl at the party, seven years ago, leaning in closer to chat in the narrow hallway by the bathroom door. Tonight, she storms out of our small bedroom, leaving me to follow her to continue whatever I was saying. It feels like we're in a play. We walk around different rooms of the house, exchanging monologues of the past, the present, the future. Minutes become hours. Talking becomes yelling becomes pleading. It's deeply unpleasant but doesn't feel like anything abnormal...until it does.

There's a shift in her tone. Suddenly things become quieter, her voice adopting a strange, strangled hollowness that I've never heard before. "I can't keep doing this," she says.

"What?"

"Cleo, don't do this. Neither of us are happy. I've tried and I wish you had—maybe you have, I don't know—but this isn't what it was. I can't even remember what it was, to be honest." I expect her to be angry and bitter. She isn't. She's breaking us and she feels horrible. Why would she break us when it feels so horrible to do it? We had never seriously discussed marriage, but after seven years it just felt like we were staying together forever. What else would we do?

She's crying. I think I'm crying too; I've been crying long before her. I haven't said much in a while—just a lot of apologizing and listening. I'm scared. I don't want this to happen and I don't know what will happen. Relationships take sacrifice, they take compromise. Why are we both crying and why is she saying it's over when we just need to get past this? We're in each other's arms, cradled like infants. We feel the pain of an appendage being amputated—severing seven years of daily texts, brushing our teeth together, navigating road trips, being plus ones to parties, whining about upstairs neighbors, supporting each other after a bad day at work, trying out that new Thai place that just opened up across the street—only to be left with this gaping void, this open bleeding wound that keeps gushing no matter what I say or do and I want it to stop and it just won't stop, please stop.

It was late when I got home, and now it's early. It's four in the morning and my insides are hollow. We're both empty in a sick way. She already had her things packed up and in her car—things I thought were mine and she thought were hers but are probably ours but not anymore. She's going to stay at her friend's place. I have to be back at school in four hours. The door closes behind her. It isn't quiet and it isn't slammed—it's ordinary but final. I collapse into bed and stare at the wall. I gradually watch the glorious sun radiating across a bright blue sky, encouraging the world to conquer this beautiful day.

Everything hurts.

CHAPTER 8

Zero hours of sleep isn't great for productivity or the soul. Only one of those things matters to me at the moment.

Unfortunately, the undergrad gremlins are still taking up my library real estate. I sneak upstairs to the conference room again, but my body tenses almost immediately—this is the hallway where the text went unsent, the beginning of the end for me and Kelsie. I can't unsee the sadness from her face. I get freaked out and leave, heading back down to the Stacks again. I'm too exhausted to meaningfully work, but I can't afford to stop.

I strike a happy medium by pacing every aisle of the library, top to bottom. It feels like a goal. The first step toward motivating myself is to find a good study space, and even if they're all taken, I'll be the first to pounce when one frees up. These cretins can only go so long without their precious food.

Down and back, down and back.

I get some stressed glances from the faces I pass, and even more when I pass by them a third and fourth time. On the main floor I walk by the young woman with the scarlet streak in her hair, wearing the same brown coat as yesterday. I re-route myself entirely, stalking away before another harbinger of last night can creep up on me.

Lap number five provides no study space, but it is undoubtedly interesting. A door that has only ever been closed and locked for as long as I've been at Rockwell is now open. There's an older woman entering it; I believe I've seen her in the library before, but only at a distance. She's pushing a cart with a white cloth covering something, presumably books. My curiosity gets the better of me and I peer over her shoulder to see what's inside the room—nothing but wooden shelves and old books.

"Excuse me," I say, clutching the straps of my backpack. "Sorry, I'm just being nosey. What's in that room?"

31

The woman turns to face me. She has a web of thin gray hair that has been fluffed to imitate volume, a cream-colored sweater adorned with snowflakes, and a scowl of mistrust. "This is the university's conservation room. Students are not permitted inside." She moves to enter through the door.

"Conservation room, as in where you repair old books?"

Her arthritic fingers clutch the door as she's about to close it behind her. She turns to me again, peering through the narrow slit. "That is correct. Rockwell University has one of the oldest collections in the country."

"I've heard that before, I just never knew where your office was! I'm sure you're busy now, but if you're ever free to chat I'd love to hear your thoughts on historical conservation methods. I work with a lot of Indian texts in the Ancient Studies grad program, and the fact that some have survived for millennia shows astounding preservation efforts. I've read that they used everyday kitchen spices—cinnamon, cumin, pepper, and turmeric—as insect repellants for their important works."

Her initial curtness evolves to a curiosity. She looks me up and down, as if considering something. "I would be very open to having that discussion, but a thoughtful answer would require far more time than I have presently; experts in the field have debated the effectiveness of various cultural conservation practices for centuries. If you would be willing, I have another appointment here next Wednesday at nine in the morning. If you meet with me then, you may enter and ask any questions you like. Without touching anything, of course."

The sudden change surprises me, but I can't suppress my excitement. "That would be amazing! Thank you so much..."

"Mildred," she says, nodding. Without another word, Mildred disappears behind the door and closes it. A lock clicks into place.

My mind lifts for the first time today. I go back to my usual study spot and find that it's miraculously emptying; a tired-looking boy shakes his head as he walks off with an organic chemistry textbook. I open my laptop, splay out my materials, and queue my headphones to the debut album from Slade.

CHAPTER 9

A lcoholism is a lot more work than I suspected; so many famous authors and artists throughout history have made it look easy. Every morning I wake up unrested and hungover, with a throbbing headache and every digestive problem under the sun. My body has come to revile alcohol, and the empties left on my kitchen sink are a repulsive reminder of the poison it consumed the night before. The trick with all the greats is that their innards felt just as terrible as mine; they just had the determination to shit their brains out, suit up, and go at it again the next day. Practice makes perfect. Ten thousand hours. Unfortunately, I've only been at it for the last five days.

I'm on the couch with a beer between my knees (I vaguely remember my dad in this position), a plastic handle of vodka in one hand, and my phone in the other. It's a little after one in the morning. I won't be able to sleep but I don't have any worthwhile ways of passing the waking hours. I don't know how I feel about Kelsie, so I've been trying on every feeling. I filter through them not in days but in minutes, in seconds. Sometimes all at once, when I'm feeling frisky. I go through my photos, her Instagram, our messages, our WhatsApp messages from when she went to Paris a year and a half ago. What am I looking for...validation of whatever I happen to be feeling at the time? Memories of the good times? Unadulterated pain?

Looking away from my phone doesn't provide relief because the apartment is essentially vacant. All the battered, secondhand furniture that I found is still lying around, but its backdrop is now a bare beige wall littered with holes and cracks. The tops of the table, dresser, and nightstand are all empty, along with most of the kitchen cabinets and counters. I've realized that I'm merely occupying this space, this shell, rather than living in it. Before I was occupying Kelsie's space, but that didn't feel as pathetic because she was always here to fill it.

The only thing left of her is an ugly stuffed walrus she got me for Valentine's Day two years ago. Even when we were together it provoked mixed emotions: guilt about thinking it was stupid, annoyance that she didn't know me well enough to buy something I would actually like, but also a kind reminder that she cares enough to get me something. Now the walrus mocks me, ashamed of me. I put him next to the vodka handle and some of the condensation got his belly wet, but I don't think he minds. He's an aquatic animal and he's not even real, so what the fuck do I even care what he thinks? I can't look at him but I can't get rid of him either; just because something's unpleasant doesn't mean it should be forgotten. I swat him away and he flies into the corner behind the couch—out of sight for now, at least.

Flinging him reminds me of this geode I found about a year ago. Kelsie came to visit me on campus after work—she used to do that more—and we had a picnic on the lawn. We ate chicken salad sandwiches that she'd made, and when we finished, we went walking on this beautiful wooded path that led to a stretch of lake. I found a geode by the water's edge—purple and crystallized and beautiful. I handed it to her as a small, silly gift because I thought it was beautiful like her. She said, "Cool, thanks!" and threw it in the lake, trying to skip it. I can still see it rippling in the water, its impact spreading further in me and on the water than I would have thought possible. I loved that geode and I loved Kelsie, but when she saw it, she didn't see what I did. She never knew what it meant to me. I know she would have kept it if she did.

CHAPTER 10

I slog through another day of research. And another. I can barely keep the days straight. I can't focus on work, but the thought of going back to the apartment feels even more miserable. I'm shivering on the train platform, and I give a silent nod to pencil kid.

Weekly commuting feels like you're an actor in a sitcom that should have been cancelled eight seasons ago. When you take the same trains, you see the same familiar faces. Pencil kid, for example. He's about twenty years old and jittering in a gray beanie that can't be warm enough. He wears a black backpack, has no chin, and looks like a pencil. Smoking a cigarette by the railing is a pale, unshaven community college professor who has the raspiest voice I've ever heard. He likes to break the unspoken train rule (i.e. don't talk to people), but one day I heard him help a woman who had limited English ability get to the opposite platform to catch her train. That was nice.

The list goes on. Door guy has thick dreadlocks and always sits in the same seat by the door. Tired nurse always comes off a tough shift. College commuter girl gets talked at by the same moderately creepy train attendant, but he lets her ride without paying for a ticket. There are also many guest stars. Although the individual actors may change, the same archetypes keep coming back. There are the 10,000 lifeless drones staring silently at their phones. The sleeping unhoused population, who reach the last stop but don't shift or stir to leave the warm train compartment. The psychopaths who have never heard of headphones in their goddamned lives and insist on watching music videos at full volume. The confusingly hot people, who are, by all accounts, far too attractive to be degraded by the American public transportation system. There should be a service that privately shuttles them wherever they need to go.

Sometimes it's comforting to see familiar commuters each day, but lately the same faces remind me of the same stories, the same existence

I had with Kelsie and what I'm left with now. I can't face this today. It's dark and cold and miserable, which feels comforting, at least; the universe got the memo that we're in our moody-forlorn phase. I bury my hands deep in the pockets of my winter coat and slink my head down to protect my neck from the wind.

"You sneaky bitch!"

I whip my head around. Art and Thanh are on the platform grinning at me. They've never come on the train with me before; it's amazing and a bit alien to see them here. Art walks forward and gives me a hefty hug.

"Darling, when you go through a major breakup, that's something you share with your friends."

Thanh just claps me on the shoulder; he's never been a fan of guy-on-guy intimacy.

"You guys stalked my train schedule just to see how I'm doing?" I try to sound casual, but my voice catches a bit. I know that the three of us are close, but I've never had to rely on them for serious things like this before. Somehow, they found out more than I was willing to tell, and somehow they give a shit enough to do something about it.

"Don't look at me," Art says. "Thanh's the mastermind behind all this."

Thanh shrugs and looks away. "You don't just, like, drop off the face of the Earth. We're your homies, man. At least give us a heads up if you decide to become a recluse; I still need to return that Stephen King book you lent me."

"That was four years ago," I say.

Thanh waves his hand at me dismissively, bouncing on his feet to keep warm. "I've been busy. Also hungry, when the heck is this train getting here?"

Art climbs on top of the wheelchair ramp railing, teetering next to us for no reason. "I believe you said 5:48 PM. Cleo, can you double check?"

I smirk at the familiar ridiculousness of my friends. "It's technically the 5:48 train, but it never shows up on time; all of the delays throughout the day push it out further, so it'll be at least ten minutes late."

"So you just stand here every night doing this?" Thanh asks. "God, no wonder you're so miserable."

"I'm barely miserable!"

"You look terrible and exhausted. Have you even eaten since it happened?" Art asks, jumping down as the train horn blares and the lights come into view.

The question surprises me—I haven't had much of an appetite and certainly no motivation to go grocery shopping, but I didn't expect it to be physically noticeable already.

He pats me on the back, perhaps reading my sheepishness. "Well, dinner's on us anyway, love."

Wheels screech as the train comes to a stop. I find us a three-seater and wedge my bag against the wall; I'm not usually crammed in with other people. "So how did you all find out that Kelsie and I broke up?"

Thanh is busy people-watching; there's a group of old men speaking rapid Vietnamese and playing some card game together.

"I know you like to pretend it doesn't exist," Art says, "but social media is a very real thing. Kelsie deleted a bunch of photos of you on her Instagram and posted some of her with her friends."

"That doesn't necessarily mean..."

"No, but you also didn't show up to Pizza Planet a few days ago. Both of us texted you and you didn't respond, so we figured it was true. You're a garbage texter, but not *that* garbage."

A wave of self-hate hits; my texting is what caused the end of me and Kelsie. I think of her yelling on that night, the hours of fighting, the evidence laid out of every fault and every problem that we've—

"Get out of there, love," Art says, bopping me on the head. "You can't be stewing forever, it's bad for you. Luckily, we've devised the perfect distraction: we're going out clubbing tonight. The Royale has half-priced drinks on Mondays. Don't argue, it's happening. Embrace the lights, music, and sex of it all. The club is where dreams go to rise and fall, like the Roman Empire!"

My gratitude wanes severely. "You know I'm not a 'club' guy! And you can't just make references to ancient civilizations and think I'll agree to anything you say!"

Art shrugs. "It's worked before."

CHAPTER 11

"Canna interes' yeh in sum extrah napkins, laddies?" Pizza Mysterio asks. Bless his heart, the man has fashioned himself into an old sea captain today.

"Yes please!" I say, helping myself to another slice of meat-lovers pizza. God the nourishment feels good.

Art and Thanh are pleased that I'm eating, but clearly antsy to move on to the main attraction. We ordered a pitcher of beer here, and I'm forcing them to nurse it until I'm good and ready. I take a swig of my own beer. Sure, I'm getting drunk just like I was at home, but there's something immensely relieving about our ritual. I spent all of last week swaddling myself in some cocoon of self-loathing, but all that brought was more misery. The mere presence of people—even if we're gathered for a shallow activity—is enough to take me out of my own spiraling thoughts for a momentary reprieve.

"Do we need to change before we go?" Thanh asks. "I don't feel, like, clubby. Does that make sense?"

"You were in on this plan, love," Art says. "How are you possibly caught off guard more than Cleo?"

"Whatever. I have a white t-shirt on under here. I'll just wear that and tie my hair in a headband. Pretend I'm on acid or something—get weird and wild. I'll need to get more drunk for this, though." He nods to himself as if considering, then lunges for the pitcher. He opens his throat and pours the beer directly into his mouth. Art slaps at him while I laugh, but nothing stops him until the carbonation becomes too much to handle. He finally gasps for air and wipes his chin with the extra napkins that Captain Mysterio left for us.

"More stressed than usual?" I ask, patting him gingerly on the back.

"Ehh," Thanh says, grimacing as he holds his hand to his throat. "Mom had a hospital bill come in from four months ago and I'm not sure how we're going to deal with it. Considering organ donation. Anyway, when are we going?"

I glance briefly at Art, the two of us clocking the sudden change of conversation. Thanh isn't one to get personal, and we try not to pry about the serious stuff until he's ready. "Sooner, now," I say, smirking while I pour myself the last glass from a considerably lighter pitcher.

"If that's the case then y'all better get ready!" Art says, raising four vodka nips with a wicked grin.

"I know for a fact that your striped pants don't have pockets," I say. "So where the hell have you been keeping those?"

"Should you accept my generous gift, your question will no longer matter to you, darling. You get the bonus fun," he says, sliding two of them my way.

"I thought you guys were supposed to make me feel better, not poison me." I'm secretly glad to get the extra booze; I'll need the social armor if I'm going to survive the next few hours.

"No bad attitudes tonight, my dude," Thanh says, reaching for his own. "We're raving. End of story."

The bell jingles as we exit Pizza Planet. The night feels cold and I feel cold, but my body is blissfully loosening. I blow air out of my mouth, feeling like a dragon breathing white fire.

Art puts his arm around me. "I am sorry about Kelsie. Life won't seem right for a while and you have every right to be devastated, but things will work out. You just need time. Time and distraction."

Thanh nudges me with his elbow. "We're good for that."

Tears well in my eyes, and the wind makes the feeling ache more. I smile and nudge him back. "How much farther till we're there?"

Art glances at me for a moment, but gratefully answers, "Only ten more minutes."

I swallow. "Any chance we could get one more vodka nip before we go in?"

"Hell yeah!" Thanh says, pointing to a liquor store on the corner. We all sway and laugh, almost walking into someone paying a parking meter. We slide into the store and buy our bonus treats from a tired, unshaven clerk. For some reason it's more fun to go into a liquor store when you're already drunk, like a kid in a candy store already bouncing on a sugar high.

After a few minutes of walking, we hear faint bass reverberating from several blocks away. The shine of seductive lights spills out of The Royale, and a long line of glittery women (who are not dressed appropriately for a New England winter) decorate the sidewalk.

"Kelsie would hate this place," I say, not knowing why I say it.

"There were a lot of things Kelsie didn't like," Art says, and Thanh tries to stifle a laugh.

My brain isn't processing what's going on. We're standing in line behind the glittery women, and two of them look back at us with open disdain. "What do you mean about Kelsie?" I ask. "She didn't like certain things, but she was amazing. You guys always liked her."

"Yeah," Art says. "Especially when she made you happy."

The phrasing seems strange, but my mind is blurring.

"Uh huh," Thanh mutters, peeking in the tinted windows to scope out the place. I pretend to join him and ignore the nagging hollowness.

The line inches closer. We're only a few people away from the bouncers now. This feels like a mistake.

"I've got your cover fee, man," Thanh says, shouldering past me.

"Thanks," I say. We're next now. My ID is ready in my hand, and with every step my chest tightens. I'm grateful for my friends coming to me. They are trying to make me feel better, and maybe this is better.

"All set," the bouncer says, handing me my ID with one final stare-down.

In the entryway, there's a large, abstract modern art piece dangling from the ceiling, which surprises me for some reason. The room is dark and reeks of perfume and spilled beer, which does not surprise me. We've just walked in and I already can't hear when Art mouths "THIS WAY!" Thanh stops at a sleek, modern-looking white bar while I follow Art, squeezing our way between a crowd of guys in expensive-looking blazers. A group of beautiful women in short dresses walks over to them, laughing and wrapping their arms around some of them. It would take triple the alcohol to make me forget Thanh's initial dress concerns; I'm wearing thick jeans and a puffy winter coat. I feel greasy from school and pizza, and ugly from life.

"I am an assault to these happy, glamorous lives," I say, but Art can't hear me. No one can. He has me by the wrist, guiding me further into the mob of bodies, the wall of bass rumbling the room. We sneak up a narrow staircase that's overflowing with people going in and out.

At the top, we emerge into an industrial-looking open floor plan. It is entirely filled with people. A current of humans is moving and jumping toward the center, while those in the back are standing with drinks, screaming to each other, and making out. Art loves dancing, so he pushes us in with the bodies in motion and I force myself to dance too. I smile and shout until my voice is hoarse, not really knowing why I'm doing it other than that it feels appropriate for the setting. I want to want to be here. Eventually, Thanh manages to find us in the crowd and sloshes a beer into my hands, spilling it onto the sticky floor and several shoes. I shout, "THANK YOU!" and mean it.

The three of us go wild. I think they feel wild while I just act wild, which may or may not be different. The mob makes room for Art as he dances, wiggling his legs and shoulders like Jell-O. He becomes the nucleus of the crowd, dancing with men and women, bringing in the shy, lifting up the bold, teasing me into the thick of it as much as he can. I can usually count on Thanh to match my awkwardness, but tonight he's a different man; he and a woman he just met are in the center of the dance floor grinding with their eyes passionately locked. I've never seen him like this before. I wonder what has come over him so quickly...until I realize it's been over an hour.

The deepest wave of exhaustion hits me. I look at the faces around me—bursting with excitement, eyes wide, shouting, laughing, jumping, feeding off their own mania—and wonder how the hell I'm mingling with them. Is that what I was pretending to look like? I'm getting bumped into—jostled every which way. I feel the heat radiating off everyone, their sweat sticking to me. I don't know whether to be more disgusted by them or myself. I yell an excuse about getting another drink downstairs, but the guys are far too entangled to notice. On the staircase there's a fresh batch of excited, eager bodies going the opposite direction, pushing their way up to join the already swelling crowd up there. Can't they see there's no room? That there's nothing up there for them?

I finally make it downstairs, relieved that there's enough room to walk without feeling four others pressed against me. I pass the glamorous couples and wait for what feels like twenty minutes to be served at the bar. I ask for a vodka cranberry because it seems healthy. I'm drinking it fast and I'm still swelteringly hot. I feel disgusted by myself, by everyone in here...

"Hey," a woman says to me. She's leaning against the bar, wearing a metallic, dark gray mini dress with thin straps, perfectly accentuating her stunning figure. Her bangs fall over part of her eyes, which are a rich, coffee-colored brown that both comfort and excite.

"Hi," I say. I'm confused as to why she's talking to me. I'm sure any single guy would want to talk to her, and I suppose against all wishes in the world, I *am* a single guy—

"Want to get some air?" she says, putting down her drink. "It can be a little too much in here."

My first thought is that this is a trap—I can't say why. I glance up at the balcony and see Thanh and Art looking for me. They look worried. "Sure, air sounds great," I say, walking out with her.

The line of people trying to get in is still somehow replenishing, but we turn down the other side of the building where it's quiet. She finally stops, leaning against the brick exterior with an exhale. "Do you have a smoke?"

"Nah, sorry," I say, leaning a few feet away from her and struggling to keep my eyes open. Cigarettes aren't my thing, but if I were ever going to inhale a poison stick, it would be tonight. The burning just might feel good.

"That's fine," she says, looking into my eyes as her body shivers slightly. Her gaze is so beautiful that it's painful. "You look really sad."

"I am," I respond, not feeling the need to think or filter myself.

"I get that," she says, and we both let the silence hang between us. She shivers again and I hand her my jacket. She looks at it for a moment without reaching.

"Take it," I say.

She glances at me again, then quickly wraps it over her shoulders. "I'm sorry."

"It's fine."

She fidgets with her handbag for a moment. "Do you want to go to my place? We could have a drink and fool around a bit? Or just chat?"

I struggle to make sense of the offer. Having someone to hold and talk to is probably what I need, but there's a pitying look in her warm, coffee-colored eyes that I can't shake.

"I'm sorry. I think I'm just going to go."

"Oh. Okay." She sounds genuinely disappointed. She uses the toe of her glittering heels to shift a pebble absently across the pavement. "I'm not good at making people feel better."

"I'm just in a weird place. You're really kind for trying. For everything. Good luck...with everything."

I walk away from her as quickly as I can.

"Wait!" she shouts. She's taken my jacket off, shivering again with it stretched out toward me.

"Just keep it," I say, not wanting to stop. I wave awkwardly and skulk down the sidewalk. I don't know where I'm going, but I manage to find the same ugly, fluorescent liquor store we passed on the way in. I buy three more vodka nips from the clerk. I finish one of them before I leave the store and then head to the train station.

CHAPTER 12

"Tickets!" the attendant repeats.

"Shit, sorry," I say, rummaging for my phone.

The agitated train attendant is in a black polo and slacks, standing over me. I'm just another asshole who doesn't have his ticket ready. I quickly purchase one on the phone app, then he scans it and walks off. Somehow this always catches me off guard, even when I'm sober.

I look out of the window, head pressed dizzily against the cool glass. I have one more vodka nip left. I watch the towns and cities drift by...billboards for cannabis stores, chicken sandwiches, strip malls, and apartment complexes.

Next stop.

The city disperses into dilapidated neighborhoods. The miniscule backyards are cluttered with broken toys, old tools, and scrap piles. I remember one of the apartments we lived in had a backyard like these. We shared it with a family of nine, and their toys were cast about the fenced-in pen like a junkyard. My dad said he would get a bike for me one day, and I could park it next to our neighbor's bikes. Wouldn't that be nice, Cleo? I nodded.

Next stop.

Run-down factory buildings and salvage yards with crushed postal trucks flicker by. It goes on for miles, but in every gloomy backdrop is the same rusted barbed wire fencing, warped two-by-fours, and ripped cement bags, as if poverty compared notes. I try to tell myself that I'm not doomed to be back here—that I'll finish my degree, get a job, keep my apartment, and patch things up with Kelsie.

I stand early because I don't want to pass out and miss my stop; my body feels like it could shut down at any moment, and I need my eyes to stay open just a little longer. I clutch a seat handle to balance myself. A few people skirt by me, and I mutter an apology as coherently as I can.

An older woman glances at me and clutches her bag closer to herself. Her reaction doesn't bother me...because I finally see it.

The picturesque lake looms in the distance, a sheen of moonlight reflecting against the ice. I see it every day on the way to Rockwell, but I haven't visited it since that fateful day. Tonight is my chance to get it all back. Kelsie didn't know what it was when she threw it in the lake; she didn't know what she held in the palm of her hands. But I can show her. I can get it back and find the right words to say. I feel so thankful to my friends for taking me out tonight, so happy to be drunk, and so moved by the kindness of cigarette girl. But none of them are what I need. They can't fix this mess.

The train halts to a stop. I lurch forward again, this time using my momentum to usher past the attendant. "Thank you," I mutter. I finish my remaining vodka and step into the freezing cold. My jacket would have been nice to have, but I'm glad cigarette girl has it. This should be quick, anyway.

CHAPTER 13

I stumble through the dark forest. I don't know where the path is, but I can guess at the general direction of the lake. I crash through the brush—crack dead branches, trip on fallen logs. I'm sure thorns and twigs are whipping my face, but the world is cold and numb and drunk enough for me to be wonderfully, blissfully unaware of anything aside from the task at hand.

I find the biggest rock I can lift, stomping around it with my shoes to pry it loose from the frozen earth. The exertion is good; keeps me warm. I heave the rock around, finally leaving the wooded area for the beachy edge of the frozen lake. I step onto the ice confidently, waddling in short strides back and forth. Now...to remember where it happened. I know the foliage was ablaze over Kelsie's hair, her beautiful eyes full of life. We were near a small stream, or maybe a bed of rocks or something. And maybe a bush with some small berries on it? I made a joke about eating them. I don't remember if Kelsie laughed or not—

I lose my footing, slamming my hip into the hard ice. A few inches in front of me, the rock crashes down, leaving a large, cratered crack in the ice...but it holds. I shimmy back to my feet, relieved and quite confident that I'll feel that hip tomorrow morning. I pick the rock up again and painfully shimmy closer to the shore. A small, quiet part of me knows how stupid this is (all of it, from concept to execution), but the potency of love and loss—of a piece of myself being suddenly, violently taken from me—makes this foolishness a necessity. My psyche is a burning building, and in some twisted way I know this is what I need to put it out.

Wait...up there! Is that a short, round bush like the one that had berries? The rock's getting heavier, but I hobble faster, more recklessly. My arms are straining, veining under the weight. It occurs to me now that I could have found a closer boulder. Fuck it. This rock is special to me, too, somehow; special like the geode it will help to uncover. I close my eyes. I picture the day—handing her the geode, where she was, the arc that it took, the plunk that it made as it hit the water before sinking. The evocation of the sunny afternoon forms a precise calculation in my mind. We were here...which means the rock soared...there!

I don't see the geode under the ice, and I don't expect to; it must be covered by mud and sand after years of being under there. I take the boulder and lift it above my chest...above my head...and smash it down. Like my slip before, it leaves a giant circular web of white cracking, but no hole. I bend down, slipping a bit, and then pick up the boulder with every ounce of strength that I possess. I focus directly on the white circular web, raise the rock over my head, and send it crashing down into it. It smashes the ice and a loud splash of water spouts up.

I get to my knees in front of the hole and roll up my sleeve. I'll just reach my hand in and pull out any stones about that size. It'll be freezing cold, I know, but it doesn't matter. I am a graverobber, alone and spotlighted by the watchful moon, exhuming this relic. A cold wind whips my face, reminding me that this is real. I stick my hand in...

I expected the feeling to be cold. Cold like the air, like popsicles, like every other cold I have ever experienced. It is not. It is an immediate, immense pain in my hand, a screaming aching to its very core. The parts of my body that are not submerged dissociate from those under the ice. I hardly have enough sensation to feel the rocks against my hand—they feel as solid as a breeze against my numb skin—but I manage to grip them and pull them out. I drop them on the surface of the ice and go back in, knowing my time is limited. I reach further and further up the arm; I need to get everything. This is it, I know it is! The water is up to my bicep, almost to my shoulder. I reach...so close...

The ice cracks again, followed by an immediate shattering.

My chest and face jolt in, submerging into the water along with every stupid rock that I had pulled out. All is lost. I realize—only now, only seconds too late—just how meaningless all of this was. My chest collapses in. Pain ravages me and my brain is shutting down. I splay my arms out and find solid ice to try and push myself up. Somehow the ice holds without caving in around the edges, and the appendages that I have lift me out until I'm above the surface again. The wind isn't just cold—it's death against my wet skin. I howl in agony, flinging my sopping shirt off me like it's on fire. My skull is breaking. I try to rub myself warm, but my motor functioning is...

"HEY!"

I hear a shout nearby, but my mind has gone far, far away from wherever they are.

"WHAT ARE YOU DOING?"

What? What are they saying? I feel something heavy draped over me. A shadow lurks above me as I shiver so violently, so uncontrollably. My eyes glance up and I stare in horror. It's...oh god, it's her! She...

I am dying.

CHAPTER 14

She's guiding me up a wooded path, rubbing my shaking body into warmth as she supports my weight. She gave me her coat, too, even though she looks freezing herself. I'm able to stumble forward through the mossy trees, but my limbs shiver and twitch uncontrollably. My mind feels infinitely clearer than it did only a few minutes before; the shock of cold and flooding adrenaline have left me in a frenzied, live-or-die reality. I see each detail of the forest vividly—every rock, the texture of the bark, shadows under the moonlight—as my thoughts race. Why is she here? Where are we going?

She leads me to a small three-decker apartment with a warm porch light on. She reaches into the coat draped over me and fumbles for the keys in its pocket, unlocking the door and ushering me into a tiny but neat space.

"Alright," she breathes, quickly grabbing another coat on a rack near the door, draping it over herself with a shiver. "I'll get the shower going hot and you can stay in and warm yourself up. I have some extra clothes you can borrow, and then once we've settled down we can talk, okay?"

I nod my head twitchily—my body shaking to an almost convulsive state. She steps into a small closet that I realize is actually a bathroom. She turns on a shower, places some clothes and a towel on the ground, then leaves so that I can enter.

I step into the warm water and almost cry. The pain from the initial plunge into the lake is outdone by the sudden ache and burn of the shower singeing my skin. Slowly, in time, it begins to feel good. I breathe. I comb my fingers through my hair and let the warmth wash over me, seeping into my core, thawing me. I realize that this is probably the first healthy thing I've done for my poor, abused body in over a week.

I start to recover from the cold and am struck with a horrifying sense of shame. What have I done? How could I be so pathetic? Drinking that much, leaving Art and Thanh, the fucking ice...I should be dead. Instead, she somehow found me. Her, of all people. She had no reason to take me in; it was dangerous for her to go out there with me at all, especially in my state. I don't know how long I've been showering for, but my body is so starved for heat that I could stay in here for hours, boiling myself alive. I have to face her, though. To thank her and get out of her hair as quickly as possible.

I turn the rusting faucet off and see the tiny bathroom billowing in steam. On the floor is a pair of thick wool socks, gray sweatpants, and a navy-blue Rockwell University hoodie. I gratefully pull them on, already getting cold again. And then I step out. She's wearing fuzzy red pajamas and a thick gray sweater. She's curled on a crooked futon with a book in her hand and a steaming cup of tea beside her. The streak of scarlet hair cascades down to her shoulders.

"I don't know how to thank you...how to explain myself," I mutter. "I don't even know your name." I'm still standing by the bathroom door, steam flooding out behind me.

"I'm Eva," she says, her mouth a shy smile. "And you don't have to thank me; I'm just glad you're okay. You were a bit...off when I first found you."

"I'm so sorry," I say, struggling to meet her eyes. "My dissertation has been beyond stressful, I haven't slept in almost a week, my girlfriend of seven years...just broke up with me. My friends took me out to cheer me up and I had way too much. I got overwhelmed and—god, saying it out loud sounds so lame. Again, I'm really sorry. I'll just leave..."

I go to the bathroom to collect my freezing pants, making sure I still have everything in the pockets. I avoid eye contact at all costs, skirting around a side table and toward the front door.

"How did you get here?" Eva asks.

"The train..." I say. Crap.

"Well, it's after midnight. The next train isn't going to run until the morning. I don't have a car at the moment, so you might have to wait here until an Uber comes. At this hour it might be a little while."

"I've already imposed so much, I really couldn't—"

"Listen," Eva interrupts, "as someone who feels ill at the thought of being an imposition to anyone, I completely understand how you feel. That said, given your previous judgement in braving the elements, I'm not sure I feel comfortable with you running out without transportation. So I think the plan, with your consent, is to sit you down, sober you up, chat a bit, and then see you out safely when your ride arrives. You can wear my sweatpants home, add them to your laundry, and give them back to me clean. How does all of this sound?"

I rummage for my phone. It's cold and the faux leather case is a crumbly, chalky texture from the water, but it's miraculously still functioning. I quickly order myself a ride while blathering. "If you're willing to let me...I mean, I'm just so sorry..."

"Do you apologize this much when you're sober?" Eva asks, a playful smile on her face.

"Probably, but I also usually don't fuck things up this bad. It's a strange feeling—it's like I'm a bystander watching this guy sabotage himself, but I don't really know how to stop him."

"Can I ask...on the ice, were you trying to...you know...?"

"Kill myself? Oh no. What I was doing was far more pathetic and illogical."

Eva giggles, which catches me off guard. It was a risky thing to say, given the circumstances, and Kelsie never liked humor like that. "Well, if you have any stories you would like to share—whether dark or illogical—I would gladly listen. If it's embarrassing enough, I might even be tempted to share one myself. But first!" she says, getting up and disappearing into her bedroom. She returns with a throw blanket that she throws at me. "I assume you're still cold even after the shower. I'll grab you cheese and crackers, too, is that okay? And I can put the kettle on and make you some warm tea."

"Are you always such a good host for complete strangers?" I ask.

"I just like for people to feel comfortable!" she defends, pacing around her tiny kitchen, pulling food and plates and mugs out of scratched white cabinets. "And anyway, you certainly need food and water. Between you and me, you still look like a mess."

I look down at my lobster-red hands and aching body, feeling my stomach warring within itself after all the drinking I've done recently. "No offense taken. Just please don't make a fuss; you've already done far more than I deserve."

"It's nothing, really," she says.

In a few minutes, Eva has laid out an entire charcuterie board, a glass of water, and a mug of steaming, honeyed tea on the coffee table.

"You're insane," I say, gaping at the spread.

"Most people just say, 'thank you.' And which one of us dove head-first into an icy lake? With no coat, I might add."

"All fair points, I concede. Thank you for the hospitality and care."

"You're most welcome," Eva says, settling herself back under a blanket with her own mug of tea. "And now, chatting time. First question: What's your name?"

I laugh, forgetting it hadn't come up yet. "Cleo Thompson."

"I like that name."

"I've grown attached. Okay, my turn: What do you do at Rockwell? I'm a PhD student, but I've seen you around the library a few times."

"I'm an assistant professor in the psychology department. This is my first year teaching here. If you want my full bio you can add me on LinkedIn, but I primarily research and lecture on neurology. Next question: What were you doing on the ice?"

"This is my first embarrassing story, mark that down in the record."

Eva scribbles in an invisible notebook, then waits expectantly.

"Basically, about a year and a half ago I gave my ex—shit, it feels weird calling her 'ex.' Anyway...we were walking by the lake, and I found a geode and gave it to her because I thought it was special. She must not have thought the same because she threw it in the water. So, all this time later, I had convinced myself in a drunken, tired, sad stupor that I could find the geode again and give it to her as a kind of token of affection. I don't know..."

"That's really sad," Eva says. "And not in a pathetic way, just to clarify—it's kind of tragic. Relationships are hard and processing them can feel impossible until enough time passes. And not to condone your recklessness in any way, but what you did is also beautiful. Both giving it to her originally and going back to get it after all this time."

"I'm not able to give myself praise for any of tonight's festivities."

"Understood. Are you still interested in getting the geode back?"

I laugh, rubbing my eyes in exhaustion. "I don't know what I want. I definitely...there's a part of me that thinks it would be nice to have it." I intend to continue speaking, but there's a tightening in my throat that holds me back.

"Well, we could go searching for it if you'd like. When you're sober," Eva quickly clarifies, "and it's not one in the morning."

"That would be really nice, actually. I could probably use the help, considering I have zero survival skills and a bad sense of direction. Would you really want to help, though?"

Eva smiles. "Of course! I told you, I think it's sweet. I've read enough romance novels to feel undoubtedly qualified to assist in such a gesture."

"What type of romance novels? Like charming YA fiction, or the ones with men in ripped white shirts on the cover?"

She laughs at the question. "All of the above, include the boddice-rippers. The beautiful thing about creative works is that not all of it needs to be high art. I consume plenty of that, too, but reading something that's saturated in silly tropes and broken plotlines can be just as pleasurable, even more so at times. Not every journey needs to be an unforgettable trip to Venice or a painstaking attempt at Everest; sometimes it's nice to walk around the block on a sunny day."

I smile at the metaphor. "I'll have to remember that. Okay, my turn again: Why were you at the ice tonight?"

She shrugs. "I like walking, especially before bed. Usually they're relaxing and uneventful, but tonight I saw the shadow of someone on the ice, and two minutes later a gargled scream."

"And you ran toward it? You're either a superhero or your judgement is as bad as mine."

"The first explanation would be preferable, if it's all the same to you."

"I don't even remember screaming. God, I was so out of it."

"You did quite a bit of shouting and flailing. At one point you stared at me in horror and called me a 'harbinger of loss,' which freaked me out quite a bit. I thought I had a calming presence..."

"You certainly do," I say, laughing. "If that's the worst thing my drunken, twisted brain said—and I desperately hope that it is—then I'm okay with that."

"That's all good and well, but why did you call me a harbinger of loss?"

I hesitate for a moment. "Okay, if I had to guess, I think my psyche chose to use that word because I first saw you the day that Kelsie and I broke up. Then, I saw you the next day after no sleep, and my subconscious must have associated you with the whole thing. I'm not saying it's your fault, but an apology would be nice."

"You're right," she says, trying to keep a straight face. "I'm sorry that I am the bringer of misery upon you and humanity. I'll try to work on that."

At some point throughout the ease of conservation, the alert on my phone tells me that my driver is one minute away.

"Alright, you've recovered enough for us to part ways," Eva says, standing up. "Please text me when you get home so I know that you haven't been tempted by another soft patch of ice. Here's my phone number."

I punch it into my phone, the odd sensation coming across me of getting a woman's number. *And* after a night of clubbing. I can already picture Thanh and Art cheering me on, not understanding the strange and fully platonic situation. The headlights from my ride flicker through the curtains, inciting a sense of loss that I wasn't expecting to feel. There's an awkward moment when Eva pauses in front of me, struggling to know how to address a near-stranger at two in the morning.

"G'nite," I say, heading for the front door. "And thank you again for everything. Seriously."

She smiles, unlocking the door and letting me out. "Goodnight, Cleo!"

CHAPTER 15

The remaining day passes in a haze of sleep deprivation and delirium. Did any of that really happen? I go through the motions of an unproductive day in the library, my body jostling limply on the train ride home. When I finally get to my apartment, I stuff my face with enough peanut butter crackers to challenge my breathing, brush my teeth, and pass out in bed by 6:00 PM.

I sleep for fourteen consecutive hours. When I wake up, the sun is shining on my face through the edge of the curtain. I get out of bed easily, prepping my coffee with a slight smile as I await a fresh cup. I dig through my closet to find a nice pair of khaki pants and one of my favorite sweaters.

Oh shit. Do I feel...well? Good god, there's a bounce in my step!

I look around at the mess of my apartment, suddenly inspired to straighten it out for the first time in months. I get through the dishes in the sink, do a load of laundry, scrub away at the bathroom, and vacuum and mop the floors. I also stash any remaining liquor I have deep in the freezer, out of sight behind stacks of food. I'm not done drinking forever, but a few weeks hiatus will do me some good. At least until I can start using it for the fun kind of debauchery rather than the sad or scary kind. Finally, and with strange feelings of guilt and trepidation, I fill a trash bag with all the things that remind me of Kelsie, including the stupid walrus.

The place looks bare, and maybe even a little sad. A clean slate isn't necessarily a bad thing, though. I check the time; I still have about fifteen minutes before I need to head to the train station. I pull out my laptop and aimlessly browse Etsy to see if I can find wall art that might give my life a little color. I tab a few bookmarks for later and end up ordering two cheap album art posters: The Rolling Stones' *Let It Bleed,* and Andy Warhol's famous banana on The Velvet Underground album.

On my walk to the library I realize that it's Wednesday, which means I'm supposed to meet Mildred from the conservation office this morning! It won't be relevant to my dissertation at all, but surrounding myself with so many historical texts could spark some much-needed inspiration. I climb the marble steps, wave hello to the front desk librarian, and walk down into the Stacks. I stand outside the nondescript conservation office ten minutes early, which seems necessary for an appointment with a no-nonsense woman like Mildred.

I glance through my phone, smiling at a text from Eva. Our conversation started yesterday when I thanked her again and told her that I would return her clothes, freshly cleaned, as soon as I could. Her response was perfect.

9:17 AM Diving in a frozen lake again does not count as "washing" unless you scrubbed yourself in detergent first.

9:18 AM Speaking of which, when is operation geode?

We set plans for this Sunday. I was convinced we would stop chatting after making plans, but Eva's been so easy to talk with. She's turned me on to a few great music artists too, including one called Grimes. Her sound is unique, batshit wild, and unlike anything I've ever heard. I love my own music, but most of the bands I listen to are either geriatric or dead, which leaves little opportunity for new album releases—

A noise startles me back to the library. Not from the hallway, but from within the conservation office. A metallic groaning sound and a click. I look down at my phone and see the time just turn to 9:00 AM. Within seconds, the door unlocks and opens, revealing Mildred. She's wearing a black turtleneck sweater and a thick, gray skirt down to her shins.

"Hello, Cleo. I appreciate your punctuality. Please, come in."

My name sounds strange coming from her; I honestly can't remember sharing it when we first met. "Hi Mildred. Thank you again for inviting me here…"

As I walk into the doorway, I'm immediately enchanted by the smell of old pages and cracked leather. It's a bigger space than I expected as well; there are four rows of heavy wooden shelves that run far back into the room. Along the back wall is a speckled gray table and the same gray cart that I saw her wheeling last week, this time with a tarp bunched on the shelf beneath it. Near the right wall is a polished oak desk with a bright lamp and several instruments on it.

"I won't touch anything," I say, both to Mildred and as a reminder to myself. I walk forward, crouching to glimpse the torn bindings, the stained pages, and the handwritten scripts.

"Every book is unique," Mildred's stiff voice says, "as is its history. Therefore, every one of them faces a different challenge and approach for restoring its condition. For example, the process for making paper evolved near the year 1840. It surprises many to know that books bound prior to 1840 are often in better condition than those bound after. Do you know why this is, Cleo?"

"Did they change the amount of acidity in the paper? I know that can degrade pages and make them hard."

"That is exactly right," Mildred says, clearly pleased. Book doctor has got to be a lonely profession. "And do you know the greatest cause of harm to historical texts?"

I frown for a moment, considering. I feel like I'm in class getting cold-called. "The main natural factors are issues like insects, humidity, and water damage. But the biggest destructive force has always been human error; apathy and carelessness in the storage, handling, and preservation of historical texts."

"Yes! Yes exactly!" Mildred says, her features animating to an unexpected degree. She sounds eager—almost desperate—as if waiting for someone to know that answer for decades. "Come here! To my desk, Cleo," she says, and I walk over to the oak surface. "Book conservators have used the same equipment for hundreds of years: bone folders, needles, rulers, knives." She showcases each tool for me, her hand remarkably steady. "We have hundreds of techniques to preserve historical texts—filling holes in pages with Japanese paper pulp, freezing active mold to prevent it from spreading, adjusting the lighting on displayed texts to reduce ultraviolet radiation damage—and every decision we make can have a dramatic impact on the lifespan of a text. We wield the power to either contribute to or combat the apathy and carelessness that you spoke of, and it is a severe responsibility for anyone who values knowledge as much as us."

As she says this, her bony, blue-veined fingers stroke the tools on her desk, and I notice that she isn't wearing a wedding ring. She looks at the books in this conservation library as her prized possessions, her legacy. When I glance up, I see Mildred studying my features...reading me like one of her historical texts.

"Would you like to see what I am working on presently?

"Of course!" I say. "I wouldn't be in the way?"

"Not at all." She leans toward an open book on the side of her desk. "This work was likely damaged in a fire of some sort—despicable carelessness. Do you see the soot on this page? If I gently rub these eraser shavings over them...just like this...the shavings will absorb the soot away from the text. Watch closely." Her thin fingers press them with gentlest touch, and I watch as the shavings gradually tint from white to gray. She takes out a small brush and gently sweeps the gray shavings into the trash bin below.

"That's so cool!"

"It is, isn't it?" she encourages. As she sprinkles additional white shavings on the text, Mildred freezes suddenly. Her eyes glance somewhere behind me. I turn and see nothing there—just the speckled gray table by the cart. "The full process will take much longer, and a great deal of focus."

She says this with a finality that surprises me. She was eagerly quizzing me just a second ago, and now I'm being dismissed? "I'm sorry if I'm intruding...I appreciate everything you've shown me."

"It has been wonderful to hear your enthusiasm for the craft. I may be able to invite you back here for more in-depth observations, or perhaps to perform some of your own text repairs? Would that interest you?" Mildred says all of this while walking toward me, slowly backing me up to the door.

"That would be fantastic," I say, not quite understanding what's happening.

"Excellent. It has been great speaking with you, Cleo. You've shown outstanding promise. I will be in touch." She quickly closes the door behind me and clicks the lock into place.

I stand there, blinking. What did she mean by "showing promise?"

CHAPTER 16

I'm standing outside of her door. I hesitate as I reach my hand out...and knock.

She opens it almost instantly, and I smile with her folded clothes outstretched.

"Excellent service!" Eva says, smiling and letting me in. She's wearing black yoga pants and a dark green sweater with the sleeves rolled up. She has her hair in a ponytail and seems intimidatingly motivated. "Are you ready to get crafty?"

"Uhh, crafty how? My drawing skills never developed past the stick-figure era." I walk into the tiny beige apartment, taking off my shoes and sitting myself on the gray futon. I should probably be more polite about seeing myself in, but almost dying here has really depreciated my decorum.

"Well, we need to get the geode out of the freezing water," Eva begins, "so I'm envisioning that we create some sort of rig to extract it."

"Okay, I like it. How would we go about making a rig?"

"I have a few ideas, but would love to hear your first impressions."

I laugh. "Well, this is my first time generating a rig and my mind is immediately going to magnets. I can't say I know exactly how magnets work, though."

"Love the idea," Eva says, rushing off to her closet and burrowing for something. "I can't say that I own any extra strength magnets, but..." She reappears with her arms full of odd items—several metal hangers, a vacuum hose, a kitchen strainer, duct tape, and a paint-stained bucket—that she drops on the floor in front of me. "We'll see what we can do!"

"You're prepared for everything, aren't you?"

"You have no idea. Any music recommendations?"

"Nope, surprise me," I say, joining her on the floor.

"No pressure," she says, furiously scrolling through her Spotify app.

I pick at the items one at a time, laughing at the mental image of building a makeshift Mars rover with the oddities in Eva's closet. This is going to be harder than I thought.

Horns blare from her phone. She grabs a glass cup and sticks her phone in to reverberate the music.

"Aren't you a professor?" I ask. "I love the janky set up, but I'm surprised you don't have some fancy surround-sound speaker." I glance around the apartment and see the warped floor, marked-up walls, and ancient heating system that I hadn't noticed last time.

"I told you it was my first year! I'm not one for luxury anyway...if my cup has the capability of containing liquid and amplifying my music, it's all the more impressive. Anyhow, no distractions. This band is called The Go! Team and they're great; they sound like a middle-school music class tied up their teacher and went crazy with some kazoos."

"That is the coolest description I've ever heard. What's the album art like? I'm looking for inspiration for decorating my apartment."

"Their art is great!" Eva says, handing me her phone.

We spend the next hour in a hilarity of duct-taping her stuff to other stuff. We had very different visions of rig prototypes, but the common ground between the two is that they're massive disasters. Eva attaches a long broom handle to her vacuum to extend its reach. She feels a wave of accomplishment after standing at one side of her apartment and sucking a tennis ball against the hose...until she remembers that there are no outlets by the lake.

"So, how's your first year as a professor going?" I ask, helping her dismantle Rig 1.0.

"The teaching part is fantastic," Eva says, ripping tape remnants from the broom. "Lecturing and lesson planning are very rewarding, although I'm sure they'll lose their luster after thirty years. The research aspect is harder. My CV always needs new manuscripts added to it or I'll have no shot at tenure someday."

"Publish or perish," I say, echoing the common mantra of academia. "Is your research stalling?"

Eva considers for a moment. "Not exactly...it's just that I struggle with the broader system of academic grants. Funders don't award serious grants to junior faculty without a senior researcher backing them, and senior faculty often take credit for work that they've merely stamped their name onto. They also don't award large grants to ideas that are not guaranteed to produce results, which incentivizes neurology research to stay status quo instead of innovating. With so many researchers all pursuing the same ideas, it becomes cutthroat and political as to who ultimately receives funding. The researchers with the most publications and the best grant writing abilities are often not the best scientists; they're just well-connected and superb at spinning their applications. Then they underachieve and overstate what they've done."

I continue to nod my head, overwhelmed by the response.

"As a research assistant," she continues, "I was asked by multiple senior faculty members to shave results or alter graphs in shady ways. If you want to keep your job or get a recommendation for one in the future, you have to do it. That's what they threatened me with, at least." She glances at me, her expression softening slightly. "I'm sorry if I sound jaded...I don't mean to scare you off."

"I wouldn't say you seem jaded. It's just...I love research and academia. I've only worked for Professor Lewis before, and he *is* an ass, but he's not that level of manipulative. I know there are issues with this field like there are with every other, but it is tough to hear the dark underbelly of the basket I've been putting all my eggs into."

"It's not all gloomy," Eva says, reaching for her tea. I've noticed that she has this cute habit of wrapping both hands around her mug and lowering her face down next to it, maximizing the heat that one single cup can give her. "I'm in it for the same reasons you are. When I took my first psychology course in high school, I fell in love. School stopped feeling like work, and I felt blessed to explore the endless frontier of the human brain. My research focuses on using blood biomarkers to screen for and monitor diseases, and I can genuinely say that I still get excited every morning thinking about it.

I smile at the familiar sentiment. "So, is it worth it?"

She sighs, smiling too. "It is. It would just be beautiful if there were a world where people could do the things they love without having to take on the baggage of everything else. Learning and research without all the bureaucracy and politics. Much like the engineering feats unfolding in front of us," she says, presenting me with her current project: an old snow shovel that has several cooking pans taped around it.

"Has science gone too far?" I ask.

"The world will quake at my ingenuity!" she says, getting up to throw away some of the mess we've created.

I stand to help her, ears pricking from her phone speaker. "Wait, what song is this?"

"It's 'Sail' by Mareux," Eva says. "I haven't looked into a lot of their discography; I just heard this song at Ralph's and loved it."

"What's Ralph's?"

"It's the best bar in the world, right here in Brookline. It has unbeatable prices, amazing art, superior music...terrible food, but good enough if you need to sober up. I'd love to take you sometime."

"I'm in! Any chance we could wait a few weeks, though? After...the other night, I'm taking a bit of a break from drinking."

"Very sensible, I fully support you. I'm grading finals for the next few weeks, anyway, so just let me know when you're ready."

"Perfect. We'll celebrate the end of finals and me pulling my life together!"

"And a successful rig!"

The reminder brings us back to focus. I'm scared of breaking her vacuum, so I go lower tech. I tape a curtain rod to the kitchen strainer and practice scooping a tennis ball. Eva tries a few scoops as well.

Legitimate excitement builds as we both successfully capture the ball...until the strainer snaps off. I'm worried Eva will be upset, but she bursts into laughter instead.

"Oh, we're doomed!" she says.

"We are. It's okay, though; we can just wait a few months until the water isn't so ridiculously deadly." Maybe in a few months, the geode won't matter anyway.

After cleaning up our mess, Eva and I decide to bundle up and go for a walk outside. "To scope out the rigging location," Eva explains. "We're still very hard at work." She opens the door, and the two of us are bathed in a bright sunshine that fights off the frigid wind. We walk down the wooded trail toward the lake. Crows caw, crinkling leaves blow, and we chat endlessly as our mittened hands sway in time with one another. I feel the slightest, surprising urge to close the distance between them.

CHAPTER 17

"**Y**ou have no right to privacy around us!" Art shouts in Pizza Planet. "Now spill!"

"Nothing happened!" I whine, looking around for Thanh to protect me. He had a rough week, so Art ordered him crispy buffalo tenders on the side. I'm doing my best to be a good friend, but if he doesn't get back from the bathroom soon the chicken will be gone.

"If you don't start talking, I'll tell Pizza Mysterio that it's your birthday so they all come out clapping." Art glares at me from across the sticky table, never breaking eye contact as he drips a slice of pizza in his mouth. Never before has broccoli alfredo pizza been so intimidating.

"You psycho!" I say, grabbing myself a slice. "Okay, the detailed version is that I was feeling hot and claustrophobic in there, and she asked me if I wanted some air. She went out for a smoke and we just chatted. I thought about going home with her, but I was just burnt out."

"I get that, you're my sensitive little boy. Did you smoke with her?"

I screw up my face, thinking. God, that whole night is a blur now, and everything that happened at the club is by far the least important. "I can't remember. I don't think so? Why does it matter?"

"It matters for the atmosphere! The ambience! Are you this tragic character leaning against a brick wall, passing a butt back and forth with the noir damsel? Were there strained, sexual glances between the two of you? Was it raining dramatically?"

"You were there that night! It wasn't raining, just cold as hell."

Art raises his hands in defense. "A brief cloud could have passed by..."

"It didn't. We might have leaned against a brick wall before I left."

"Did you go home after?"

"I..." For some reason I hesitate to bring up Eva. Art and Thanh get so excited about this kind of thing, and for some reason Eva's presence in my life just feels so...fragile. Our meeting was the smallest wisp of smoke catching on dry tinder, and anything more than the gentlest breath could blow it out entirely. We aren't together (and I can't say that I would want to be, even if the stars aligned) but having her in my life has sparked some new hope in me that I haven't felt in a long time.

"Hecking Cleo arrives and my chicken disappears," Thanh says, accusations flying as soon as he returns.

"I left you some! There's still six pieces in there."

"Dude, you left me, like, the runt pieces. The pieces that get teased at school for being tiny and weird looking." He holds up a charred, bent mess as evidence.

"I'll buy you more, don't worry," I say, already pulling out my wallet.

"Cool," he says. "By the way, how'd your night go with that girl?"

"Precisely what I was getting at!" Art says. "So did you go home after you two 'just chatted?'"

Ahhh, what to divulge? I take too long in deliberating and they both smirk across the table.

"Has Cleo always been such a sneak?" Thanh asks.

"No, he hasn't," Art says. "This is as new to him as it is to us. We're on the precipice of a great discovery."

"Alright," I sigh, "just try not to interrupt. It's a long story." They're my best friends; if I can't tell them, then I have no one. They both patiently sit through the tale, and only interrupt when Art swears loudly after I mention going under the ice.

"Jesus, dude, I'm so sorry," Thanh says. "I wouldn't have let you go out if I knew you were in that tough of shape."

"Clubbing was a stupid idea," Art agrees, shaking his head.

I wave them both off. "You guys care, that's all that matters. You care enough to meet me at a train station, support me, and distract me from my problems when I need it. You also care enough to listen now. I'm just...I guess I'm just confused about things with Eva."

Art gets up from the table and hugs me. It's warm and comforting, and I only laugh and shove him off when twenty seconds pass without him showing signs of stopping.

"Don't bother being confused about Eva, dude," Thanh says. "Labels are always messy, and everything that happened with Kel only makes it harder. If spending time with Eva makes you happy, just follow that feeling and see where it takes you. And if it all blows up in your face," he says, shrugging his shoulders, "then we'll be here for you all over again. Easy."

I do my best to stifle tears in this dumpy pizza place. Instead of emotions, I opt for offering something more tangible. "Well Thanh, you've earned yourself a double order of tenders."

"Nailed it!" he shouts.

Art laughs and elbows him. "That wasn't a solo pep-talk, babe; I'm sharing those."

CHAPTER 18

Another unproductive day.

Now that finals are finished, the library closes at 5:00 PM which spares me the temptation of staying here all night. I pack my things, hoist on an old coat that I found buried at the bottom of my closet, and leave the study room. The Stacks are a ghost town this time of year. There's no noise other than the hum and pinging of the old heating system, and even that is muffled by the thick green carpeting and towers of books.

In the lobby I see Eva and another woman at the circulation desk, both pleading with the librarian on duty.

"Please, we didn't know the hours were revised for winter break. The printer in the faculty room is broken."

"I'm sorry," the librarian says, glancing at her wristwatch. "We close in one minute, and it sounds like your documents will take quite a long time to print. You're welcome to come back first thing in the morning."

"Thank you," Eva says, sighing and turning to leave. She sees me and waves, her gloomy expression dissipating slightly. "Hey, Cleo! Are you leaving, too?"

"Sure am," I say.

She joins me, and gestures to the woman beside her. "This is Dorothy. She's in the Psych department with me."

"Nice to meet you," I say, shaking hands with her.

"Pleasure's mine! Call me Dot!" Dot is a heavyset woman with dark skin, a dazzling smile, and the energy of someone in a musical. Art would be obsessed with her style; she has thick-rimmed purple glasses and incredibly long nails embedded with gemstones.

I lean closer to the two of them. "I overheard you at the desk. How badly do you need to print?"

"We're pretty desperate," Eva admits. "We're leading a department meeting first thing tomorrow morning, and the department chair is a bit of a dinosaur. Everything needs to be hard copy. I could probably find a UPS store and just pay to print, if you know any?"

"I might have a way for you to do it here, if you're interested in a little adventure?"

"I could be persuaded," Eva says, smiling.

"I've got to go, dear," Dot says, enveloping Eva in a hug. "Text me tonight if you get the goods printed—there's an iced coffee in it for you if you dooooo!" Dot walks off, heels clacking against the library steps.

Eva lowers her head next to mine. "What do you have in mind?"

I glance back at the librarian who's clearing up her desk. "Follow me. Quickly." We rapidly descend the same staircase as Dot, but instead of going out of the main exit I guide Eva down a narrow stairwell off the side. It leads us to a fire-escape that turns back into the Stacks.

"Why are you two getting iced coffees in the winter, by the way?" I whisper.

"Because we're New England trash," Eva responds, keeping up. "Where are we going?"

I stop halfway down the stairs, listening to make sure no one is around. "A few years ago, I found a hiding spot that the librarians don't check before closing. When they take their final rounds, we can stay quiet there until they leave. Then the library is ours. I know you're a professor and don't want to get into trouble, so if you aren't interested, feel free to back out now. I've done it a few times before without a hitch, so just thought I should offer."

Eva pauses for a moment, looking at me. Her hazel eyes are alight. "Lead the way."

We arrive at the Stacks, taking cover between the shelves until we get to my usual study room. I quickly hustle to the back wall.

"They won't check in here?" Eva says, slightly out of breath.

"Not all of it," I respond. I skirt behind one of the wingback chairs, revealing a metal grate in the wall that has a small crawlspace inside. From the front of the chairs, you can't see the crawlspace at all; it just looks like an empty study room. "Last chance to back out," I say, opening the grate for her.

"And you'll be in the other one?" she asks.

"The whole time. We'll crawl out when we see the lights go out throughout the library."

She hesitates for a moment. I walk to the other side, curl in, and shut the grate behind me. She peeks between the slats and smirks. "You're completely insane. Why am I about to do this?"

"Because life is dull enough as it is. Why deprive ourselves of cool experiences when we aren't hurting anyone?"

"Says the one who swam in the icy lake." I'll never live that down. She curls into the other crawlspace and shuts the grate behind her. We both stare through the slats, looking for signs of the librarian and grinning at each other. The few times I did this by myself I was either stressed or bored while waiting. Tonight, Eva and I have each other, giggling like kids sneaking out at a sleepover—

A nearby door—maybe the study room next to this—suddenly slams shut. Muffled boots stomp closer, closer. The door to our study room clicks open. More footsteps only a few paces from us. We could both get in trouble for being here after hours, why did we—

The lights shut off. We're in total darkness aside from a few blinking smoke detectors. The remaining two study room doors open and close, and the sound of footsteps slowly fades into silence.

"Oh my goddd," Eva whispers. "I can *not* believe that worked! And I can't believe you did that yourself! I was always too much of a goody-goody in school to try something like this."

I reminisce back to my theatre closet days with Aisha. "I...had a few moments like this before. Nothing too serious, though."

"Ahh, so this is how you charm all the ladies," she says, egging me on. "The daring scholar type. Is that on your dating profile?"

As soon as she says it, I hear the regret in her voice. "Oh, I'm so sorry. I didn't mean..."

Not long ago that might have sent me into a spiral about Kelsie, but I'm too busy having fun to care. "It's totally fine," I say, laughing. "I've actually never done dating apps before—never had to—but I'll probably give it a try sometime soon. You can help me make my profile, if you're up for it." The two of us open our grates, stepping back into the dark study room.

"Very happy to provide my feminine insights. We'll have to discuss at another time, because this is WILD!" Eva takes her phone out and shines the flashlight toward the Stacks. "And we don't have to worry about cameras?"

"For the most part, no. There's only a few and they're primarily on the main level. We can plan our route to avoid them. I'm not convinced that they even work, or that the footage is ever reviewed unless there's an incident...but better to be safe."

"Agreed. Lead the way, and let me know if there are any laser beams we need to dodge."

"Will do," I say, walking into the Stacks.

It's as great as I remembered. The already quiet library is a cemetery at night. Eerie rows of towering tombstones house tomes hundreds of years older than us. The shallow phone light can't reach the end of the library; it merely fades into the distant maze of shelves in the darkness. We creep forward slowly, both savoring and fearing the spectral form of this familiar place.

"Head to the printers?" I ask.

"No," she breathes. "Can we explore a bit first?"

What a woman.

CHAPTER 19

Our reverence for this hallowed space is lost as soon as we find the book cart.

"You're going to topple over!" Eva says, giggling in front of one of the shelves.

"Not if you help stabilize me! Grab the handles at the end." I sit on the lip of the cart and drop my weight into the center. My feet dangle in front of me, brown shoes limp in the air. "Push me?"

"I have library arms; you aren't moving an inch."

"I only weigh 170 pounds!" I say.

"I don't think you understand library arms. I sit. I read. I go home. At no point in the day am I doing anything close to lifting weights."

"Fine," I say, squeezing myself out. "You hop in. I don't workout either, but I'll see what I can do. I won't even ask how much you weigh."

She fits herself easily in the cart. "Ready. Let's start nice and slow, just in case—" her voice raises as I get momentum going, the two of us flying between the aisles of books. "There's no way you can turn this thing without tipping me!"

"I don't have any qualms about tipping you," I say breathlessly, enjoying the rush of wind. I finally slow her down as we approach the back wall.

Eva wiggles herself off the cart, standing unsteadily. "No more rides. Have you ever looked behind the circulation desk?"

"No, never."

"Fantastic. Lead the way!"

I take us between the shelves, toward the back staircase where I'm certain there aren't any cameras. On the way, we pass by another familiar door. I pull the handle...locked, as expected.

"Where does this lead to?" Eva asks.

"The conservation office," I say, still staring at the door.

76

"I didn't even know we had a conservation office. Hey, what are you doing?"

I pull out my trusty childhood library card and start wedging it near the locking mechanism. "I've only been in here once before and it was amazing. The conservation lady that runs it, Mildred, is kind of intense—very protective of her books, and she was weirdly studying me until she chased me out all of a sudden. I just want a chance to look in here without her breathing down my neck. There's some really cool stuff!"

"I believe you, but is it a smart idea to break into the office of an intense, meticulous person like that? How do you know she doesn't—"

"A-ha!" I feel the card slide in and the door glides open. We shine the phone light inside, seeing the shelves, books, and instruments exactly where they were when Mildred let me in. Something about her absence from the dark office makes this place even creepier. "It's all sorts of old books," I whisper, continuing past the shelves to the oak desk in the back. "Some of them have got to be incredible to see. I don't want to touch anything in case one of them disintegrates or something, but there was at least one open on her desk before—"

"You said she was really protective of these books?" Eva says, walking toward the back wall. "Then why is that old wooden text on the floor, and all bent? There's no way that's good for the bindings." She shines her light on an old text that's several feet underneath the gray-speckled table, resting on top of a massive vent and splayed on its bending pages.

"Wow, you're right. It must have fallen off that cart or something."

"How could it fall off a cart and go that far underneath a table? And without Mildred noticing?"

I don't have an answer. It looks like someone haphazardly threw it on the vent and it landed like this. I get on my hands and knees and crawl under, picking up the fragile bindings. It's a pothi format: the pages are made of yellowing palm leaves bound together by a string and covered by wooden planks.

"Holy shit, this is ancient Sanskrit! What is this doing in the Rockwell library? And what is it doing on the floor like that?!"

"How old is it?" Eva asks.

"Very. Probably close to a thousand years old."

"Oh my god. What are you doing with it?"

"Just looking," I say, cradling the unprotected pages and putting it on an open section of Mildred's desk. I stare at it in complete awe. I've never seen a Sanskrit text like this in person: the handwritten script, the beautiful illustrations, the—

The two of us turn back suddenly, hearing a faint but distinct ringing sound from the back wall. There's nothing there, aside from the vent underneath the gray-speckled table.

"This place creeps me out, Cleo."

I exhale. I didn't realize I'd been holding my breath for so long. "Me too. Finding this text is incredibly strange, and it might even be relevant to my dissertation. I've never heard of this title before, but its binding style dates it shortly after the period that I'm looking into. Would...would it stress you out if I took it?"

Eva glances at me. "Just bring it home with you?"

"I'll bring it back as soon as I'm done!" I rush to say. "And we can leave separately if you'd prefer; I don't want any of this associated with you."

"You're an adult. You don't need my permission to do anything."

I nod, hurriedly unzipping my backpack. I take off my coat and gently wrap it around the text before placing it in. I hold the bag in my arms, not risking it slung over my shoulder.

"Okay, let's go," I say. We exit, quietly pulling the door shut and tugging at the handle to confirm it's locked again. "Printer first, then a quick detour to the circulation desk."

We sneak upstairs, and Eva singlehandedly kills an entire redwood forest with the amount of printing she does. We discover nothing scandalous in the circulation desk besides crotchet hooks and yarn.

Kathy, you rascal.

CHAPTER 20

I don't dare set my backpack down on the beet red pleather seats; what I'm holding is precious cargo. I look around at my fellow train-goers: a tired mother who lets her toddler watch cartoon truck videos on her phone, an undergrad bobbing her head to whatever's playing through her massive headphones, an old woman reading a romance novel, two drunk guys on their way to a Celtics game. Each is as inattentive as always, yet still a paranoia creeps into me that somehow, someone will know that I broke into the office and took this previous historical text.

I continually revise my plan of action. How do I extract as much information as possible and return it without being discovered? Should I wait until tomorrow to do anything? My mind is reeling and I'm dead tired.

I need to relax. Take my mind off things. I pull out my phone and check my email—just fidgeting for something to do. Art would make fun of me; I only have about eight apps on my phone to occupy my time, and I have the suspicion that he wouldn't count the compass and calculator apps as recreational. I think back to what Eva said about dating apps, laughing to myself as I download Hinge on my phone. It can't hurt just to swipe around.

I quickly make a profile, adding some of the few photos I have of myself. I answer the prompts in a stream of consciousness, hurrying to finish the stupid thing:

I'm weirdly attracted to...women who can spend inordinate amounts of time in libraries.

I won't shut up about...how Sanskrit has 100 synonyms for elephant.

Most spontaneous thing I've done...broken into a zoo at night. My punishment was realizing that the animals were asleep, so all the enclosures were empty. I was 14.

My profile won't win any awards, but finally the app lets me in so I can start swiping. Wow, people are gorgeous. I swipe right on essentially everyone, knowing that I have no shot and that I'll probably panic if they do swipe me back. It's fun to see how similar the photos and prompts are. Is watching *The Office* and liking puppies really a personality trait? And why is putting pineapple on pizza such a heated controversy? Studying modern dating tropes should have been my dissertation, this is fascinating! I glance around the train, wondering if any of these poor souls are on Hinge, and whether their profiles present the versions of them that I'm witnessing tonight...

It's her. On my screen is a stunning photo of Eva. She's wearing a navy-blue dress with a low neckline, standing next to some of her friends at an outdoor wedding. She doesn't have the scarlet streak in her hair in this photo...I wonder if she only got that recently? Everyone in the photo is happy, but she is beyond radiant. Her next photo shows her presenting at a conference, wearing a blazer and confidently standing in front of a podium. Twenty-nine years old. Assistant Professor at Rockwell University. Drinks casually. The next photo is of her and what looks like her family. I see her parents standing behind her, and maybe her younger sister?

I start to panic. This feels like a weird invasion of privacy. Most importantly, do I swipe on her? I don't want to reject her, but if I swipe right things will definitely be awkward. Can she see that I'm hovering over her profile like this? Fuck, why don't I consult Art with decisions like this!? Without thinking, I close the app before swiping in either direction. There's no way my seven-year relationship can be forgotten and healed in a month's time, but more and more I find myself thinking of Eva, hoping she'll text me or that she'll be in the library. No, it's just that she's been such a great friend for the past few weeks...

I almost miss my train stop.

I get off the platform and quickly walk back to my apartment through the dark, frigid night. I rummage through my pockets to find my keys, then quickly let myself in and place my bag on the kitchen table. I stare down at it, considering. I should just leave it for tomorrow. I'll get a good night's sleep and then have a clear head to tackle everything in the morning. The possibilities of what could be in there whizz through my head like a slot machine. Is fate giving me a cure-all fix for my dissertation? Could a book like this really just fall into my lap by chance?

Fuck it. I brew a pot of horrible instant coffee. I find Saran wrap and mummify my table, making it pristine and stain-free for the delicate tome. I rummage under the bathroom sink cabinet and find a pair of nitrile gloves—a relic from the early COVID pandemic days—and put them on. I scoop my hands into my bag like I'm delivering a baby, gazing down in wonder at the ancient text. I pull out my laptop, charger, Sanskrit translation reference, and red headphones (blasting Sex Pistols, for maximal focus). My supplies form a crown around the text, spaced well apart to avoid anything bumping into it. I keep my coffee safely on the floor, in the unlikely event of a spill.

I start by taking pictures. Not glamour shots, but a systematic documentation of every page, front and back. I use my gloved fingers to delicately flip the palm leaf pages and lay them flat on the table. I'm not trying to read or decipher anything just yet. I'll bring the book back to school first thing tomorrow, and then use the photos to translate the script so that I can take my time with it. While I have the physical text in my possession, I want to examine it for any material information it can provide within the object itself: stains, textures, dates, and other abnormalities.

Its pothi format is the same as the other ancient Sanskrit texts I've seen. Its appearance, when fully opened, resembles an open venetian blind. The string used to bind this text looks modern, though; someone must have repaired this within the last twenty to thirty years. If it was recently well-repaired, then why was it left abandoned and horribly stored in the conservation office?

I pour myself another cup of coffee.

The palm leaves are brittle to the touch. You can still see the veiny, squiggly lines of the initial palm plant running vertically across the thin pages. There's some smudging and a few tears and holes that might have been from insect damage. Still, it is all remarkably legible. It is sixty-three pages long, with five lines of Sanskrit text vertically on each page, stretching about sixteen inches wide. The number 252 is inscribed on it, which is likely a date based on the calendar year under the Nepalese king Mānadeva's rule. By the modern calendar, the date of this text...would be at around 830 CE.

Holy shit.

I push my chair back, rubbing my eyes deep enough to pop them back into my head. It is 1:00 AM. My mind is buzzing from so much information, a growing list of questions, and caffeinated exhaustion. I can try to do more digging with the photos tomorrow, but for now the original is thoroughly catalogued. I put the text in an old Amazon package with bubble wrap, which will make it much easier and safer to carry tomorrow. I sigh, taking off my latex gloves and flinging them in the trash.

I collapse in bed, dreaming that Harrison Ford needs me to discover an ancient Sanskrit treasure with him. It's stressful.

CHAPTER 21

I wake to my alarm at 5:30 AM and take the first train back to school. The fervor from last night is somewhat dulled by sleep deprivation, but I'll still be on edge until this book is back where I found it. I walk briskly across the hard, frosted lawn to the emergency exit of the library. While the front façade of the building beckons students with an impressive marble staircase and columns, the side exit is a flat, dull parking lot for library staff to take smoke breaks. Which is an important detail to know, because...

"Morning, Kathy!" I say, delicately hoisting my backpack over my shoulders.

Kathy is standing next to the propped emergency exit door, exhaling her cigarette. She glances at me and smirks. "Can't wait until we open?"

"I swear I have a decent excuse this time! Last night I left a book in the study room, but I need it for Professor Lewis first thing."

She looks at me shrewdly for a moment, tapping her ashes. "And the rules and hours of operation for the library don't apply to you? Is that it?"

"Correct!"

Kathy bursts into laughter. "One of these days you'll find somewhere else to go," she says, opening the door for me.

"What a sad day that will be. By the way, how'd your grandson like that Pokémon game I recommended?"

"Mason is in love with it!" she says, her facing lighting up like it does every time I ask about him. "He keeps trying to teach me all of their names and abilities, which was delightful until I learned how many there are!"

"Back in my day there were only 151 Pokémon. God knows how many they have now."

"*Only* 151," she mocks.

I laugh on my way down the stairs and into the Stacks. I dig my old library card out of my wallet, hovering just before the conservation office door to listen for signs of life. Nothing. I pop the lock...and immediately sense that the office has changed.

The gray cart that we saw in the back was empty late last night, but now it's filled with something—likely books—and covered over with a gray tarp. Mildred was here between 7:00 PM last night and 6:00 AM today? I glance around the small office, half expecting her to emerge behind me. I'm desperately curious to look under the tarp, but at this point I'm scared to disturb anything else. I unwrap the Sanskrit text and return it exactly where I found it, splayed on top of the large white vent underneath the back table. It physically pains me to leave it in such condition, but I run out before I can agonize too much. The door clicks shut, and I pull a book out of my bag to complete my alibi. I sprint back through the Stacks and out of the emergency exit.

"You're the best, Kathy!" I say, waving the book.

She smiles at the flattery. "Stay warm!"

The next few weeks pass in a blur of productivity and discovery. I haven't felt like this since Professor Lewis first had me translate his early Sanskrit version of the *Charaka Samhita*. Every day I sink into my favorite study room, spread out my supplies, and work. I begin by putting photos of the Sanskrit text side-by-side with a Word document so I can type out the original text. For any characters that are smudged or unclear, I add parenthetical notes indicating all the characters it could potentially be. Once the whole thing is typed out in Sanskrit, I slowly work toward translating it. I don't know what will be in this text or whether it will be relevant, but the act of having it has been healing in and of itself.

So has having a study buddy. After teasing me for being in the library so much, Eva started joining me occasionally to work on lesson planning.

"So kind of you to leave room for me," she says today, entering and finding the study table (made for four people) fully occupied by my belongings.

I smile, scooping papers, books, and pens toward me to shrink my orbit. "Two seconds in and you're already distracting me. I should never have invited you to my nest."

"Too late for that now," she says, unpacking her own bag. "Any progress?"

"Lots. I've managed to create a translation I'm relatively comfortable with."

"Of the whole text?"

"The whole thing. Luckily and unluckily, it's pretty short. There are a lot of illustrations and a long introduction that take up space, too. The work is essentially a how-to guide for farming in early India."

"Oh, interesting. Is any of it useful for you?"

"It's not directly relevant, but maybe. Medicine back then wasn't pills in a lab—it was all plants, which makes agriculture important. The text provides information on crop rotation and other simple, historically known farming techniques. It seems that the intention of it was to pass down information from more experienced farmers, because local officials noticed that younger generations were sucking at farming and their families were starving. We've seen similar texts in history before; the Roman agronomist, Cato the Elder, wrote *De Agri Cultura* back in the day. But if you look here, there's something that mentions healing herbs specifically."

"In times of great famine—when animals have perished and their dung is not plentiful for improving the soil—certain crops may be used to nourish the land in their place. Beans and vetch are primary in this. Others have been attempted, however, and must be done with great caution. At times they have been highly effective, but there are many tales of young men

poisoning their land and their people. When growing healing plants, all available nourishment should be provided to maintain their supply."

I glance at her puzzled face. "The concept of green manuring, or fertilizing soil with plants, is nothing new. The last few lines are interesting, though. Obviously mixing the soil with toxic stuff can poison the ground and the plants, but what if farmers got desperate and used something that *positively* impacted the growth of the plant? Not just something that made Brahmi plants grow faster, but possibly more potent as well. Obviously it's a long shot, but current dementia research has focused on the Brahmi plant as a monolith, assuming that they're all the same. What if the missing ingredient was a special variant of the plant, cultivated by fertilizing the soil in a particular way?"

Eva nods, considering. "And how does this fit in with the *Enlightened Rituals* text that you've mentioned? Are they two separate tracks for you to follow, both separately impacting Brahmi's impact in healing?"

I smile. I know Eva and I have spent a lot of time together recently, but it's infinitely touching to see how invested she is in my work. She's already referencing key texts and critically thinking about the big picture. I feel awful for the thought, but I know that Kelsie could never do the same even after seven years together.

"Exactly," I say. "I'm not convinced this will lead to anything significant, and the *Enlightened Rituals* text is infinitely longer based on the references that mention it, so I'm sure there would be more there. But this is something I have in my hands; it's concrete and gives me a new angle to approach. Not that I have high hopes about sharing anything with Professor Lewis. He'll just tell me I'm not doing enough and then talk about the newest book he's writing."

"Have I told you how I used to deal with my old PhD advisor?" Eva asks.

"I think so, yeah," I say, laughing. "Her name was Professor Cohen, right? You used to bully her into being a fully functioning human being?"

"I did not bully her! I just focused her entire life. Every week I gave Professor Cohen an updated timeline of my project and a list of things I needed from her. Whenever she would start on a long-winded ramble about her pharmaceutical career thirty years ago, I would shift the color-coded timeline closer to her and say, 'Great point! That reminds me of another question I had...'"

"You're not going to turn into one of these unhinged tenured professors one day, are you?"

"Oh, I plan to!" Eva says eagerly. "I haven't decided what weird niche I want to embrace, but I'll make sure it's a fun one. Perhaps I could be a practicing wiccan, and students could bribe me for professional references with spell books? Or I could stop using email and only respond to questions via wax-sealed letters? I need something to keep my lectures interesting."

"What are you working on now?"

"A double-lecture on proteins. Fascinating stuff," she says, self-deprecatingly. "It's not a complex topic, but it is extremely hard to cover in a way that's engaging for students. Unfortunately, 'What's your favorite protein isoforms?' isn't a great ice-breaker."

"I'm a big p-tau217 man myself, but I know that's controversial."

Eva stares at me in confusion. "How do you know about specific phosphorylated tau proteins?"

"I looked into blood biomarkers after you mentioned your research the other day," I say, now slightly embarrassed by my joke.

"Yes, but you even differentiated the tau phosphorylation site; that's not some cursory glance."

"Sorry, I just fell into a research wormhole. I was interested, and then kept finding more and more information until...it was two in the morning." God, why do I have to be so weird? I probably seem like a stalker, obsessing over her work like this.

Eva's confusion turns into laughter, and I wait a few seconds before joining her in relief. "You don't have to apologize, Cleo! I'm so flattered. Also genuinely curious what caught your interest; maybe I can structure my lesson based on what drew you in."

"Happy to help!"

Eva shifts her chair closer to me so I can review her slide deck.

Afternoon rolls into evening, but we hardly notice as we hole ourselves up in the study room. Occasionally when Eva smiles, I'm reminded of her beautiful Hinge photo from the outdoor wedding. I try to ignore that, simply enjoying the pleasure of having her here with me. We're friends and intellectual partners, and for now that's enough. Together, we can conquer every obstacle in our path: my advisor meeting, her class lectures, and, most fearsome of all, what to meal prep for the week.

CHAPTER 22

"Cleo, my boy! Just the person I was hoping to see. Please, have a seat." Professor Lewis is beaming at me behind his polished cherry desk, his framed awards a garland around him.

"Great to see you, Professor," I say, giving him a jovial handshake. Lewis loves a firm handshake, especially when they're slightly less firm than his own.

"How goes our research? Important updates, I hope?"

I open up my laptop, already poised to show photos of the Sanskrit text. "Actually, yes," I say, turning the screen toward him. I tell Professor Lewis everything I've learned, in detail, redacting only where I found the text in the first place.

"This is quite interesting," he says, rolling up the sleeves of his dress shirt. "Your hypothesis about green manuring could be an excellent opportunity to broaden your search and find some additional materials. We could look for more detailed agricultural instruction, reports on local crop yield, and accounts from healers."

"Yes, that's exactly what I was thinking. I've done some preliminary searches and I'm running into more dead ends; I'm honestly shocked that this sort text was written down in the first place, let alone preserved. I'll obviously keep looking for more, though."

He smiles at me, spreading his arms wide as if gesturing to an audience. "Of course you will, Cleo. You've always been so dedicated, so *tenacious* with this work. It is the main reason why I took you on as my advisee for your doctoral program, and why I chose to fund you, above all others, to lead the research for this grant. But despite this tenacity, the most consistent reports that I'm hearing are 'dead ends.' I trust I don't need to reiterate to you how important this work is?" He's still smiling—his body posture still calculated and relaxed—but the edge to his tone is new to me.

"Of course not," I say. "Any translation and analysis work has gone incredibly smoothly, and I've kept close track of every physical and digital search that I've completed—thousands of attempts. The only roadblock that has slowed me down is the literal existence of the texts that we're looking for..."

"Absolutely," Professor Lewis replies, his tone dripping with patience and understanding. "You've been very communicative and professional about the entire process—the quintessential researcher in all regards, and no one could say otherwise. But the reality of this grant opportunity is that producing results is essential for continued funding. Gone are those precious years of my career when I could be a pure academic, thinking only of my scholarly pursuits. On my shoulders now, I bear the weight of the entire Ancient Studies department. Academia is unquenchably competitive, and for Rockwell to simply maintain the status quo would be for us to fall behind. Ancient Studies departments do *not* receive massive government and pharmaceutical support like this; our grant is simply unprecedented. All we can count on is that we have the funding now and must strike while the iron is hot. If we really work at this, we will make leaps and bounds under my leadership to transform a dusty old field into the trademark of this institution! And Rockwell into the leading authority of Ancient Studies *globally*. Imagine, Cleo!"

His eyes are blazing in a way I've never seen. I have plenty of experience massaging his irritating, avant-garde ego, and I thought that was the depth of what was happening. With each prattling justification that Professor Lewis provides, however, I'm reminded of Eva's harsh description of academia. My stomach feels hollow at the naïve notions I had about becoming a professor in this place, just because I liked learning and enjoyed studying history. My dad spent his life searching for some pie-in-the-sky fantasy to get us rich and happy; how the fuck am I still falling into these traps?

"That sounds wonderful, Professor," I manage to say. "I've always known this is a unique opportunity, and I won't let it go to waste. I...I'll turn over every stone I can think of."

Another smile across the desk. "I'm certain that you will, Cleo. But please ensure that you turn over every stone that *exists*, not just those that come to mind. We mustn't rely on your creativity to sustain tens of millions of dollars for this university. Your course work has been exemplary, and your final dissertation may eventually be acceptable. Unfortunately, since you have not provided significant results thus far, I am unable to offer funding for your PhD stipend after this semester. With grant deadlines looming and so many capable young minds at the university, it would be a dishonor to your peers not to give them the opportunity of finding that which, to-date, you have been unable. And should future employers ask for my recommendation of you, I wouldn't feel it appropriate to omit the critical fact—should it prove consistent—that you have struggled to produce meaningful outcomes here. Of course, I am steadfast in my confidence that you will be able to disprove this with your efforts in the coming months. I want you to search as if the very security of your PhD candidacy depends on it."

My throat goes completely dry. "Understood, sir."

"Wonderful!" he says, standing up and clapping me paternally on the back. "So glad we had time for this little chat; it's always a struggle to squeeze in more meetings, particularly at the start of a semester. It never ends." He chuckles to himself, walking me to the door. I'm left standing in the musty corridor of the Ancient Studies department, wondering if that fever dream of a threat actually happened.

CHAPTER 23

The day of reckoning has come. Eva is taking me to Ralph's Bar. I mentioned that Art and Thanh also hadn't been before, and Eva gladly invited them and her friend Dot to join the pilgrimage. It's an odd group for sure, but they're all social and weird enough to thoroughly enjoy themselves.

It's a cold Friday night and the city is alive with angry commuters and college students going out. The five of us shuffle along the sidewalk in our hats and coats, sometimes chatting with the group and occasionally breaking into different pairings. Dot develops a healthy fear of Thanh's angst (made visually apparent by his black and white My Chemical Romance sweatshirt), but Eva just giggles at their banter. While the others are busy, I grab Art and pull him back a few paces. I quickly recap my Hinge debacle and how I freaked out when I came across Eva's profile.

Art rubs his eyes, nearly at a loss for words. "You know, I really do blame myself. I should never have let you near the internet unsupervised."

"I agree! Tell me how I fix this."

He shrugs. "There's nothing to fix. If you didn't swipe in either direction, she won't be notified of anything. But some part of you *did* want to match with her...?"

"Fuck, I don't know," I moan.

"I do," Art says. He smiles a shit-eating grin at me, then shoves me forward so that I stumble up close to Eva. "Love you lots!" I hear Art call from behind.

Eva glances back at him. "What a charming guy!"

I laugh. "He's too charming for his own good."

With every step we go farther off the beaten path. Pizza places, flower shops, and busy crowds slowly fade to auto repair garages, barbed wire fences, and unpaved roads. I glance at Eva after another surprising right-hand turn. "I'm positive," she says, rolling her eyes and pointing ahead.

Far off the road, there's a blinking, half-lit neon sign reading "Ralph's." The parking lot is a massive dirt field with cars parked at crooked angles. There's a bouncer by the front entrance, but he doesn't ID us or acknowledge our existence; he's chatting with his friend about a wrestling match he saw with his brother the other day. We swing open the front door and see a crammed train car diner lined with stools on one side and a sizzling grill on the other. A song by The Misfits is blaring on the speakers, which feels fitting; the clientele here is more varied than I've ever seen. Dusty construction workers in faded sweatshirts line bar stools beside goths in full black trench coats, chains, and spiked hair.

A bartender who is in the process of burning a burger turns to us, clearly unharried. He has gauges in his ears and a t-shirt with a uterus on it that reads "Don't Tread on Me." He raises an eyebrow at us. "Well?"

"One pitcher of Genesee," Eva says, opening her bag and sliding a few bills to him.

"Seven dollars for a full pitcher?!" Thanh says.

"Told you this place was special," Eva says, grabbing the drinks and leading us to the back of the dining car.

We pass through a cramped hallway—squeezing by another bouncer who also doesn't ID us—and enter a large, chaotic seating area. Every square inch of the walls is covered in art: band posters, pin-up girls from the 1950s, abstract paintings, graffiti, taxidermy, and punny signs. We grab a circular booth in the back next to a ratty pool table, and Eva pours out drinks for us.

"Cheers!" Art says, clinking plastic with everyone. "To cool places and cooler people."

"Cheers!" The five of us echo.

We spend the next few hours in a scattered harmony together. Art talks with Dot about her nail techniques ("You do this shit yourself? Girl, reveal your secrets!"). Thanh and Eva chat about a neurology documentary he recently watched that was related to her PhD dissertation. An older couple with matching white ponytails invites Eva and me to play pool doubles against them. They're kind enough to show us all the places where the table is warped, which provides us with the perfect excuse for our horrendous playing. Art sneaks in with a group of goths at the jukebox to see if they can play "Fat Bottomed Girls" by Queen; they already have it queued, and they spend half an hour talking to him about what concerts they've been to recently. Dot and Thanh have a heart-to-heart about being single but feeling like they don't have the bandwidth in their personal lives to date. We all take turns getting pitchers for the group.

Ralph's is jam-packed now, with the eclectic crowd swelling and laughing. Eva and I find two stools at the end of the bar, and we have to lean closer together to hear one another over the noise.

"Are the walls inspiring any new decorations for your apartment?" Eva asks, glancing around the room.

"Definitely. Thanh says he can give me some old posters, too, which should help."

"That's really sweet. Your friends are great, by the way."

"I can't say I deserve them," I admit. "I'm glad this all worked out, though—they've been begging to meet you every time you come up, and Art can be disturbingly persistent."

"Ooh, and do I come up often?" she asks, eyebrows raised.

"Yeah," I say, meeting her gaze. "I've known these guys for seven years, but other than them I don't have many people that I'm close with. Especially after the rough patch I went through, it's been incredible to have so much added to my life." I gesture at the room, the people, the atmosphere. "You've brought all of it."

"I can't say it's all been selfless," Eva says.

"The ice—"

"—The ice was one moment of poor judgement, on both of our parts," she finishes, "but I've spent so much time with you after that first night because I've enjoyed every minute. You're smart, driven, and spontaneous in a way that I know is good for me. I've always waited for moments of excitement to come knocking at my door, but they've rarely materialized, and I've been left to live more quietly than I'd hoped for myself. I have met thousands of people in school, networking events, parties, and professional settings, but I choose to prune them out if they don't enrich me."

"And if they do enrich you?"

Eva smiles, leaning closer. "I hold on tight. I give them everything I have, because I know they will give it all back, and more."

I trace my fingers gently across her knee. Eva glances down, then shifts herself closer to me until our legs are woven together.

"Is this too soon for you?" she asks.

"No," I say, with a strange certainty. I lean closer, my right hand sliding up to her thigh. For a moment we simply look at one another, inches apart, while our eyes lay bare every feeling that has gone unspoken and unrecognized. The noise and lights from this dingy bar envelop us, creating a hollow in the world with space only for two. Our lips hover closer to each other...a mere breath away...until they finally join. Our mouths twist and meld together in euphoria. Her hand grasps my face, pulling me closer as if making up for every second it had been denied. My hand slides further up her thigh, desperate for—

We remember where we are and both slowly pull away, smiling giddily as we look into each other's eyes. A middle-aged woman with frizzy gray hair and a Grateful Dead shirt raises a hand up to Eva.

"Up top, sister! Go get some!" Eva laughs and high fives the woman, who walks off muttering, "Now I gotta go find *my* man. Pete! Pete, get your ass over here!"

"I take it you've never met that woman in your life?"

Eva shakes her head. "Ralph's is a beautiful place," she says.

I reach for her hand, and she clasps it as naturally as if we had never been apart. "It certainly is."

CHAPTER 24

We thought about hiding "us," but ultimately decided the optics of that could make things even worse. Eva and I looked at the university handbook and apparently students (even undergrads, shockingly) are allowed to date professors, so long as they aren't enrolled in their courses. In many circumstances this archaic rule might feel morally icky, but here I am benefitting from it.

We've walked past the circulation desk several times over the past few days, and the librarians are...obsessed.

"Ooh, if it isn't my two favorite study birds!"

"Very subtle, Kathy," I say as she openly gapes at us.

"I haven't said a word! Just don't be up there too late, I'll start to get nervous you—"

"Thank you, Kathy!" I interrupt, hurrying away before her comments can get more descriptive.

"I don't feel bad about snooping through their desk anymore," Eva mutters to me.

My usual study room is too cramped for both of us, so we've been legally coming up to the larger conference room upstairs. Out of habit, I pull out my childhood library card. Eva rolls her eyes and uses her employee key card to scan into the room.

"So you just sneak anywhere you want to? Do you have a full lockpicking kit in there, too?"

I flop my heavy backpack on the table. "No, just my little card trick. At one point I was passable with a bobby pin, but the harder locks always gave me trouble. Gave it up in my youth."

"I think that's probably for the best," she says, setting up her laptop and a stack of quizzes across from me.

The spacious room is surrounded by large potted plants, two full walls of whiteboards, and a wide, arched window that overlooks the Rockwell campus. It's a dreary and gray winter's day, and the world is bracing for more snow to come tonight. It's the perfect day to be holed up researching. The sleeves on Eva's sweater are already rolled up, her mind deftly focused on her screen. I smile, turning on my headphones to David Bowie's *Hunky Dory* album.

I spend hours falling through Google wormholes—searching for historical examples of Indian green manuring, growing techniques, healing practices, and herb preparations. Three and a half years ago, many of these topics were exciting and groundbreaking for me. At this point, however, I've become intimately familiar with almost every academic article and primary source on the subject. I broaden my search and click on anything I can get my hands on—slides from a University of Glasgow presentation fifteen years ago, a scanned table of contents page from an unknown 1957 text, a flyer encouraging people to sell "ayurveda supplements"—all while tracking the sites in my reference log.

Additionally, I explore an article that Eva (neuroscience expert that she is) sent me last week. It assesses two indigenous groups in the Bolivian Amazon that have the lowest known percentage of dementia in older adults worldwide—about eleven times lower than the United States. I dig into these cultures and others to draw comparisons, but unfortunately it leads nowhere; researchers concluded that it is their active lifestyles of fishing, hunting, and farming well into old age that give these cultures extremely low rates of heart disease and diabetes, which are both risk factors for dementia. Older adults in ancient India typically enjoyed sedentary and peaceful lives, while their children took care of things for them.

The article sparks a new idea, though: searching for other isolated cultures to see if they have aging and lifestyle attributes that modern researchers haven't investigated. The scope is beyond broad, but what else can I do? No stone left unturned. Search as if the security of my PhD candidacy depends on it. I need—

"Cleo?" Eva says.

I blink my eyes a few times, realizing that the sun has set outside. Flashbacks of me ignoring Kelsie in just the same way flood back to me. "Eva, I'm so sorry..."

"You don't have to apologize," she says, "just checking in to see how you're doing. You haven't had anything to eat or drink in the last four hours, and it seems like you're swirling a bit."

I glance down at my laptop screen, confirming the time in the bottom-right corner. "I'm trying everything I can think of. I *need* to find some answers, or Professor Lewis is going to—"

"I know. But maybe we take a step back, refuel ourselves, and think of a more efficient way of handling this."

I lower my laptop and rub my dry eyes. Now that she's mentioned it, I do feel pretty terrible. I dig out a bag of emergency granola, reaching for larger and larger handfuls as each one reminds my body of how starved it is. I nearly finish my water, taking massive gulps until some is dripping down my chin. Eva laughs at me, and eventually I join her. "I can be a little intense sometimes."

"I'm noticing," she says. "My only request is that you channel some of that intensity into chewing; it's been a long time since I was trained in the Heimlich maneuver, and you're currently decimating that granola."

"That's an achievable goal," I say, laughing and slowing down.

Eva shuts her laptop too, rubbing her shoulders after a long afternoon of work. "I'm assuming you didn't make a lot of progress today?"

I shake my head. "I'm completely tapped."

"Did you look at the article I sent you last week?"

"Nothing relevant, unfortunately. It might have inspired a few new ideas, but I'm not hopeful."

Eva sighs, lost in contemplation.

"What is it?"

"I can't believe I'm about to suggest this," she says, shaking her head. "Where was the last place you searched that gave you a shred of new material?"

I pause. "You want to sneak back into the conservation office?"

She shrugs. "Ideally we would ask Mildred, but from everything you told me she seems hard to get to know and won't let you look through anything willingly. Last time we happened to find a rare Indian text sprawled on the ground, so it's not unreasonable that something else might be in those shelves. I don't think we should make a habit of going, but if we inventory everything in one sitting—taking out anything relevant, cataloguing them at home, and then returning them all—we would never have to risk going back. It would eliminate the conservation office as a source."

I know that Eva's right; I'm honestly just surprised that she would be willing to so this much for my dissertation. "Will you be my lookout again?"

"Will you buy me coffee in the morning?" she retorts with a smile.

To date, Eva's only weakness seems to be caffeine dependance.

CHAPTER 25

W e walk past the circulation desk, waving goodnight to Kathy. "You two have any fun plans tonight?" she asks.

"Sort of," I say, willing my cheeks to blush slightly. "There's a sushi place near my apartment that we were thinking of trying."

Kathy beams at us. "That sounds delightful! Let me know all about the restaurant tomorrow, I want full details! Off you go!"

"Can we actually go to a sushi place afterward?" Eva whispers, quickly following me down the side stairwell.

"I'd be happy to fulfill our alibi; I don't want the reputation of a sushi tease."

"My thoughts exactly," Eva says. The two of us hurry through the Stacks and into the study room. "I want your vent this time," she says, walking behind the wingback chairs. "Yours seemed a lot more spacious than mine."

"It is," I sigh, cramming myself into the one across from her. My knees are jammed against the metal walls, but I manage to close the vent behind me. After a few minutes, like clockwork, the thudding boots arrive and turn off the library lights before fading away.

The two of us step out, grabbing each other's hands as we walk through the dark shelves. "I'll never get sick of this," Eva says, gazing at the empty, spectral library. It is completely quiet in here, peaceful like a still, moonlit lake.

"Me neither," I say, squeezing her hand a little tighter. When we arrive at the nondescript door of the conservation room, I pull out my old library card and start jimmying. After a few seconds, the door clicks open.

"Will you have time to review them all?" Eva whispers, glancing at all the shelves inside.

"I think so," I mutter. I start the cataloguing process at the front-right shelf and work my way backward. The problem with most old texts is that they don't have titles on their covers or spines, so I have to take them out individually and review the content inside. I can rule them out fairly quickly by language, year, and subject, but speed will ultimately be the biggest challenge; I have to go through them quickly so we can get the hell out of here, but still be delicate with these already fragile texts. Then again, Mildred left one bent on the fucking floor, so does it really matter? Deep breaths, book-nerd. Keep going.

"Find anything?" Eva whispers, glancing out into the hallway occasionally.

"Nothing yet," I say, about a third of the way through the shelves. "This was a great idea, but my topic is so niche that I can't expect to find anything else. We were probably just lucky the first time." I say this and mean it, but with every irrelevant French or nineteenth century book I open, a fresh disappointment hits.

"Well, at least we can cross this off," Eva says. "If it amounts to nothing, we'll think of something else."

I reshelve another book, smiling at her use of "we." Halfway through the final shelf I feel the recurring dead end come crashing down. "Yeah...nothing."

Eva abandons her post and walks over to me, putting a hand on my back. "Sorry, Cleo."

I close the last book and take one final glance around the room. "It's fine. I just...I don't understand why the only useful text in here would be found on a floor vent. How the hell does that make sense?"

"It doesn't," Eva says. "Not at all, actually." There's a strange tone in her voice. She moves toward the corner where we originally found the book, looking underneath the gray-speckled table against the wall. "It doesn't seem like Mildred keeps books over here, and even if she did, how would a text fall off and land on a vent that's this deep underneath the table? And without her hearing it? That's no accident."

"What are you suggesting?" I ask. I get on my hands and knees, crawling under the table to look more closely at the white vent.

"Weird...there's a light glowing here. It's not bright, but it's not pitch-black like it should be."

"It might be a boiler room below the library?" Eva suggests.

"The boiler room is on the opposite end of the Stacks," I say. "The janitor let me see it one time." Eva glares at me and I smirk. "I can be awfully charming when I want to be."

When Eva and I stand up, she uses the gray-speckled table for balance and feels it wobble in the middle. Glancing curiously, she lifts underneath and a section of the table flips up, hinging like a bar counter. But there's nothing behind it—just a blank wall. The opening is perfectly centered with the floor vent underneath, and the gap is about as wide as the book cart beside us.

"Why would the table hinge open up to reveal the vent?" I ask. "Maintenance?"

"They would just move the table..." Eva says, almost shaken. Her fingers trace against the vent, examining a small latch on it. "And there isn't dust on this at all. When have you seen anything in this old library that isn't dusty? Especially a vent in the basement."

I swallow. "Maybe...Mildred cleans a lot?"

"There's dust on the bookshelves."

I look back, confirming that she's right. Why would Mildred...?

Eva reaches for the latch and pulls. We both stare as the lip of the metal slides inward and the vent hinges down. Eva slowly lowers the vent until it makes a clicking sound. The angled vent creates a ramp down to a narrow stone tunnel with a faint, fiery glow.

"Cleo," Eva breathes, standing and stepping away from the hidden passageway.

"I won't go in very far," I say, walking forward and standing tentatively on the vent to make sure it can hold my weight. It's surprisingly sturdy and doesn't make a sound.

"What are you doing?!" she hisses, grabbing me by the coat and pulling me back. "We have no idea what's down there."

"I have one guess," I say. "I need to quickly check, and then we can get the hell out."

"Sneaking into an office is one thing, but this? And what am I supposed to do, just stand here?"

"You're welcome to come with," I say, "but I'm sure it's safer here, and I would definitely appreciate a lookout."

She's lost for words. I don't want to upset Eva, but whatever is down here has to be the answer that I'm looking for. My ticket to fixing my grant work. I...I can just feel it. I kiss Eva quickly, then turn and duck my head into the tunnel.

"Be careful!" she whispers behind me.

I crouch forward a few steps, but once my shoes reach the stone floor I can fully stand. The tunnel is about seven feet tall and three feet wide, with smooth, perfectly mortared stone bricks along the walls. It's very old; the architecture reminds me of an eleventh century church that I saw during my study abroad trip to Rome. After about a hundred feet of straight tunnel, I arrive at a spiraling ramp that leads downward. It has no railing, and I peer over its edge—shockingly far down—and see...

Holy shit.

I see another library. It in no way resembles the Rockwell University library that we came from. Instead, it's row upon row of rustic wooden shelves cascading down a seemingly endless room, illuminated by candle-lit chandeliers. Faintly, I hear a cluster of echoing, dissonant voices, much like those heard in Gregorian chants.

It's too much. I look behind me in a panic, seeing no one in the dark tunnel—no one on the ramp below me, either. Dizzy and disoriented, I sneak back through the tunnel as quickly as I can. I make it to the vent and peer up to see Eva's panicked face in the conservation room. I step up the vent, head bowed, and pull the latch back up until it clicks back into place on the floor.

"What happened?!" Eva asks.

I don't respond. I lower the desk flap back down so it's exactly the way we had left it. All of the books on the shelf are back in place. I scan the room for anything off—anything that might look amiss.

"Cleo," she says, grabbing my arm. "What was down there?"

I look into her eyes, desperate for answers. "It's...it's absolutely incredible, Eva."

CHAPTER 26

E va and I spend the next day discussing what we found. After reviewing every detail for the hundredth time, we decide to assemble a great council. We summon the best and brightest minds of our generation—Art, Thanh, and Dot—to Arlo's Pizza Planet. We pick our usual sticky table, but have to add a few more chairs at each end to make room for our growing numbers. We remove our puffy winter coats, kick our boots free of snow, and bask our chilled faces in the heat of the pizza oven. When the group finally settles, we tell them everything.

The intensity of revealing a secret underground library is severely undercut by the arrival of Pizza Mysterio. "You ladies n' gents need a pie before we close shop? My rig's all loaded n' ready for takeoff."

"You guys are open for another three hours," Thanh says. "We'll have one cheese, one sausage and pepper, and one chicken bacon ranch. Also, an order of buffalo tenders."

"Onion rings too, please!" Dot adds."

Mr. Mysterio scribbles our order and saunters away.

Dot's eyes follow him all the way to the kitchen. "I think I'm in love with that man. Do we know his story? Is he single?"

Art laughs and begins explaining the Mysterio lore.

"Sorry, can we focus on the secret occult library again?" Thanh says irritably.

I shrug. "Well, we don't know that it's occult necessarily..."

Thanh lunges his phone at me, showing a series of Reddit posts about secret societies in the modern world. "You said there was a massive, gothic library underneath the school revealed only by a trapdoor in the floor. I've read enough to know what cults are. There are probably religious fanatics with robes down there!"

We all look at Thanh skeptically; Art and I have heard plenty of rants like this, although there's certainly more evidence this time.

"What do you think your options are?" Art says.

"Well..."

Eva cuts in first. "Cleo is debating whether or not we should go in there and look for the *Enlightened Rituals* text that his dissertation has been missing. He thinks—and I agree, on this point at least—that we found the shorter Indian text under the table because it had fallen off the book cart that's used to transport texts in and out of there. That's why the vent has to be so wide and probably why there's a ramp leading down."

I can't refute what she says. I know (seriously, I do) how ludicrous it would be to go down, but every time I tell myself it's too dangerous, I remember my last meeting with Professor Lewis. Everything I have and hope for—my stipend to pay for rent and groceries, getting my PhD, job prospects after graduating—all depend on these results. I don't have many other options; how many employers are looking for a twenty-seven-year-old with a bachelor's degree in Ancient Studies? Professor Lewis wants no stone left unturned, and this discovery is a fucking boulder.

Beyond work and academic justifications, I can't pretend there isn't a nagging curiosity to be down there again. Since I first saw the library, I haven't been able to stop thinking about it. Imagine uncovering the equivalent of the Library of Alexandria! There could be anything down there if historic treasures are spilling onto the floor like crumbs. How much regret would I have if I didn't at least see a glimpse?

"So," Art says, watching my face as he folds his hands over the table, "it seems like the debate is over. Dear Cleo, are you planning to go back in there to look for this book?"

"It's like he's trying to get me to start smoking again," Thanh says, running his hands through his hair. "How the duck are we even going to pull this off?"

I glance at Thanh. "How are *we*...?"

"Have you ever seen spy movies?!" Thanh shouts. "You need backup, you need people keeping watch, you need gadgets..."

"Thanh just wants an excuse to use the walkie-talkies he got for Christmas," Art adds.

"You are *quite* the individual," Dot says.

"Of course I want to use them—I won't pretend otherwise—but we also can't leave Cleo alone to explore some creepy library dungeon."

"Agreed," Art says.

A flash of hesitancy hits me. Going on my own seems worth the risk, but I can't imagine letting my friends get involved in this. "I won't let you—"

Art holds up his hand to silence me. "We don't want you to go down there at all, but if you insist on it, then we insist on helping." He glances at Eva. "Are you going down with him?"

She nods. We hadn't discussed that either. "You said you saw dozens of shelves down there? And you just barely stepped in; there could easily be more. I'm familiar enough with your work to be able to do a cursory review of texts and have you confirm their relevance. That would allow us to look twice as quickly and hurry out. Also, as a bibliophile, it is a difficult opportunity to pass up. I would never do it alone, but with the gentlest push I could be tempted to have the opportunity of a lifetime."

"Alright," Dot says, "so I suppose that leaves me to get cozy with the walkie-talkie twins? You owe me coffee for a week, dear, and you know that's a fair shake!"

"Done," Eva says, smiling.

"And what exactly is the plan?" Art asks.

The group turns to me, which for some reason catches me by surprise. "It might be hard to describe without seeing the space..."

Eva pulls a pen out of her bag and reaches for a napkin, quickly sketching the library hallways and major entrances to the Stacks. "Accurate?" she asks, sliding it toward me.

"Yes..." I say, studying it. "The only thing I'll add is that here"—I grab her pen and add a small box—"is a utility closet that might come in handy for hiding." I point to the diagram, describing where everyone can keep watch in the Rockwell library and where Eva and I will be in the conservation office. "The vent that we'll be going down is in this back corner. We'll sneak through the tunnel, down the spiral staircase that I saw, and then start looking."

"When are we doing this?" Dot asks, lowering her voice. "And how soon can we get the walkie-talkies ready?"

"The walkie-talkies are always ready," Thanh replies, rolling his eyes.

"We go down tomorrow, then?" I propose. "It's always quietest on Friday nights during winter break."

The suddenness silences the group...but they all agree.

CHAPTER 27

Eva and I slink up the dark stairwell, opening the side door of the library to the cold winter air.

"Shit!" Thanh whispers on the other side, clutching his chest. "I thought someone caught us before we even made it in."

I wave them in and they follow, one by one. Without asking them to, the group decided to wear all black. Thanh has black jeans and the same My Chemical Romance sweatshirt he wore to Ralph's. Art, always hitting the fashion memo, is wearing black leggings, a turtleneck sweater, matching scarf, and a black beret. Dot is in a black trench coat with six-inch heels. I look down at her shoe choice dubiously.

"I can work wonders in these, don't you fret!"

Eva laughs as she guides the group into the Stacks.

"You two have been hanging out in the dark library quite a bit, ehh?" Art asks.

"Not the time," I respond.

"Disagree," Dot says, clearly more interested in our relationship than the secret library.

"Cleo, do you want to show them the office vent first, so they know where we are?" Eva asks.

I nod, jamming the door with my old library card.

"We are so cooked if we get caught," Thanh mutters, glancing around the conservation office. "We don't even go here anymore..."

Eva walks to the back table, flipping up the hinge and crouching down to the vent. She pauses to listen and then pulls the latch. The vent swings down and clicks into place.

"You two are insane," Thanh says, gaping at the tunnel. "Like...like this is Illuminati stuff!"

I take a deep breath, ignoring the momentary panic. "I'll take you to your posts and we'll get going." We step out of the office, and I guide Dot to the utility closet. Unfortunately, it's locked and won't budge.

"I'm certainly not hiding around sewage mops for an hour anyway," Dot says. "I'll just stand in the middle of the hallway by the door."

"What will you do if someone comes in?"

She smiles, and then immediately transforms. "Thank God you're here!! I left my bag in here and the librarians they...they just *left*! The lights went out, and I thought the alarms would go off, and my cell phone isn't working! Oh, you're a godsend!" Her backstory is so effortless that I almost believe it myself. "Think I could give that pizza gentleman a run for his money?"

"No contest," Art says laughing

I turn to Thanh. "Are you staying by the bathroom?"

"I am. My plan is simple: if someone enters the building, I hide in the bathroom stall. If they come in the bathroom, I'll be keeled over and make them think I'm having some kind of medical emergency. They won't question who I am or why I'm here after hours; I'll just be comatose and they'll call an ambulance. Then I'll try to find a way to escape the ambulance. If I can't, you're on the hook for the bill."

"So kind of you to include me in your plan," I say. "It should work, though, if it comes to that."

Thanh nods, slapping my shoulder. "Be safe, man."

Art comes with me and Eva to the conservation room. "You should be able to hide behind the shelves," I say. "And if you need, you can slink into the tunnel as well. Just remember that you have to listen mostly at the tunnel; the others have the library covered."

"You don't have to worry about us," he says seriously. "I know Thanh is panicked about sneaking into the school, but you're the ones going into somewhere unknown and likely dangerous." Art has always been able to read people, and I have the feeling he knows I'm not dreading this as much as I should. "Just get in and get out, love," he says, hugging me.

"I will," I say.

"Come here, you," Art says to Eva, hugging her as well. "You're too good for him; don't go dying as soon as Cleo dates a woman we actually like."

"Rude!" I say.

Art doesn't bother responding; he quickly peers out of the conservation office and signals for us to get a move on.

Eva and I look at each another once more before crouching and descending into the vent. We step into the stone tunnel with a faint echo, the walls reverberating our every movement. We slowly step forward, past the comforting light of our friends' flashlights and into the looming darkness.

"It's like we're in a tomb," Eva whispers, grazing her fingertips against the stone walls. As we go further, the darkness gradually transitions to the warm, flickering glow of torchlight. We finally arrive at the spiraling ramp leading down. "Oh my god..." Eva says, her eyes widening as she looks over the edge and into the library.

We make the long descent down.

CHAPTER 28

It's everything I glimpsed above, but now that we're actually standing in the library it takes my breath away. For a moment we forget to be on guard. Eva and I stare at the massive marble columns that connect to groin vault ceilings. Circular iron chandeliers hoist dozens of candles, bathing us and the library in a warm, shadowy glow. The room is a straight hallway with seemingly endless rows of shelves on each side.

Eva pauses, craning her head to the side. "Do you...hear that?"

I do; she's referencing the same eerie, monotone chant that I heard when I first entered. I had no idea what it was then and even less now.

We creep forward, our shoes tapping quietly against large, multicolored limestone tiles that are laid in labyrinth patterns. I turn into one of the rows, tracing my fingers against the handcrafted walnut wood shelving. Filling them are rows upon rows of ancient texts. Their spines are cracked and primarily leather-bound, all blank and begging to be opened.

"We should split up," Eva says, forcing herself to be practical. "Not far—I don't want us to be out of eyeline of one another—but I take the shelves to the left of the main aisle, and you take the right?" I nod absently. "Sanskrit, Cleo," she says, glancing over my shoulder to the small book in my hand with the prominent name "CAIVS IVLIVS CAESAR," as in Julius Caesar. I want to devour it, to read through every book in here, but we don't have the time.

"Right," I say, closing and returning this perfect piece of history. "We should be able to scan through the shelves quickly; a beautiful library like this has got to be organized in some way. Find the theme of the shelf you're on, rule it out, then we'll advance up one row at a time."

We rifle through each row like a petty home burglary. I take a few books out randomly, confirming that they're all Latin and Greek texts describing classical history. "Next?" I whisper across the aisle. I get a thumbs up, and we both advance to the next set of shelves. Still ancient history, but now it is in some form of Japanese well beyond me. We breeze along, and as we move forward the texts become centuries younger.

Eva eventually finds a few Sanskrit texts that are from the thirteenth century, which slows downs our progress quite a bit. While I skim their content, Eva breaks her own rule and ventures one or two rows beyond me to speed up the process. I go through dozens of them until I eventually finish the row. All the books I scan are about battles, legislation, and trade routes. I glance up at the vaulted ceilings again, shocked at the sheer size of this library; it must be at least as long as a football field.

I put the book away and hustle over to Eva, struggling to find her among the shelves. She's crouched down about five rows up, clearly making good pace.

"No luck?" she whispers.

"Not really, but listen. I think this whole room...might just be the history section."

Her brows furrow for a moment. "You mean there's *more* rooms like this one, for different subjects?"

I pull her out into the aisle and point toward the wall we're closing in on. Above the shelves, we can see the top of large archways. "If those are doors, then yes. It's possible this is just a history library, but there could be sections on religion, biology, or medicine that would be more likely to have the *Enlightened Rituals* text."

She takes a deep breath. "Should we still quickly scan through the rest of this library and confirm it's all history? I'm hesitant to go into other rooms if we don't have to; there could be people in there, creaking doors...who knows."

I nod in agreement. We systematically continue forward, although we move much faster as we see more texts published near modernity. After reaching one of the last rows (all history, based on the languages I can understand), I hear Eva suddenly gasp. I turn quickly, expecting to see someone attacking her. She's only holding a book, however, but with a mixture of horror and intrigue on her face. She turns the modern, twentieth century German handwriting to me. It's a collection of letters signed by Heinrich Himmler...the highest-ranking official in the Nazi army.

"I think there's a lot more over here," Eva says, pointing uncomfortably at the shelf in front of her. "All in German."

I glance down at them, flipping through a few covers and wondering how all of this could be in a library beneath Rockwell. We're clearly past anything relevant to us, though, and in front of us lies the doorway. "Are you ready to move on?"

"If it can be carefully opened, and there are no signs of anyone."

The front wall is adorned in gothic arches with three abutting doors, all perfectly centered.

"How do we choose which door to go through?" Eva asks, listening at each of them for signs of life.

"I'm rusty on my architectural history, but they should all go to the same room. Gothic architecture used three doors next to each other to represent the Father, Son, and Holy Ghost."

She considers for a moment. "How likely is it that we're about to walk into the religion section, then?"

I don't answer. My palms are already damp with sweat. I grab the large iron ring—ornately twisted and surrounded by metal moons—and pull back as slowly as I can. The door gratefully swings in silence, which reminds me that this place must be well-maintained if the hinges are greased. Even if Mildred is involved, this is all far too much for her to care for on her own.

The next room is even more shocking than the previous one. What is this place?

CHAPTER 29

Yes...this is the religion section. Again, our eyes are drawn immediately upward—looming above is a vaulted ceiling with beautiful frescoes. I recognize a perfect remaking of *The Creation of Adam* by Michelangelo, but there is far more than Christianity represented here. Beside God and Adam is Zeus being crowned on his throne, Hindi gods and goddesses found at Sneh Ram Ladia Haveli, and references to Celtic druids and Satanism that I'm unfamiliar with. The room is a massive dome with double rows of bookshelves down the center and an aisle down the middle. Along the perimeter are lavish worship spaces for various religions, each with altars, statues, and precious gems.

Eva and I continue working through the shelves systematically, creeping across the black and white checkered limestone. I pick up the first book and see Latin, ready to put it down until I see a word I recognize: daemonium, or "demon." Shadows of gruesome faces flicker in the torchlit paintings and statues around me, and I quickly look over my shoulder to confirm we're alone.

In the next aisle I find a text in English, likely nineteenth century, that discusses the cannibalism of the ancient Aztecs. I expect it to be a history of their rituals, but, in time, I recognize it to be a research log:

> *"Like the many great warriors before me, I have captured my sacrifice to Huitzilopochtli. For the past week I have fed him maize, as was wont for the great civilization. Throughout his screams I comfort him by explaining the importance of what he is doing—how droughts that plague the American colonies come because we have not paid homage to the divine. Our harvests shall be bountiful, now, all due to his great sacrifice. I have sewn a deer pelt over his body, and on the feast day of Huitzilopochtli, will carve into his flesh to—"*

I slam the book shut, disgusted and horrified. I clear my throat to get Eva's attention. "Find anything?"

She shakes her head. "Some condemning letters from the papacy in the eleventh century, but nothing relevant."

Still poring through the texts, I rack my brain for any reference to *Enlightened Rituals*. There are such blurred lines between medicine and religion in the ancient world, so determining whether we're even looking in the right room is a challenge. There would be more on the Brahmi herb and how to prepare it in a medical library (if such a library exists), but the healers who would have written about them were spiritual leaders. I check my phone—no service, but it's 9:58 PM which means we've been down here for about twenty-five minutes. I'm sure Thanh is losing his shit, but I know we're getting closer.

Eva and I make it halfway through the room, where we find a line of study desks hidden among a gap in bookshelves. They are purely utilitarian: rectangular slabs of walnut wood and plain chairs with seat cushions. One of the desks catches my eye—not because it is different, but because there are books and notes still on it. I peer down at a thick leather-bound copy of the Qur'an with illuminated pages. Next to it are scrolls of notes written with quill and inkwell, still wet. They're written in English, and scribbled in normal, messy handwriting that you'd find from any university student. For some reason, this surprises me more than anything else that I've seen down here—it's an informal, human connection in an otherwise daunting temple of learning. I imagine myself writing those notes, hunched over a candle instead of the fluorescent lighting in my study room.

"Over here!" Eva whispers. She's holding a short, wide book that I quickly recognize as Sanskrit. The strips on the inside are palm leaves—exactly the pothi format of the first text I had found on the vent—but this looks to have been bound together by a leather cover within the last hundred years, rather than having its original wood cover. "There are more," Eva says, pulling out several others.

"Be careful," I warn. "Don't take out too many at once; I want to make sure we can put everything back exactly where we found them."

I sit down at the nearby desk, cosplaying as a student in this library for a few hurried moments. It pains me to sift through these as if they were dog-eared cowboy westerns, but that's all I can manage. At the very least, my years of schooling have enabled me to produce passable work at an unrelenting pace. Prayer book, creation story, philosophical dialogue—no, no, no.

"What can I do to be helpful?" Eva asks, glancing over her shoulder.

I shift the book I'm looking at over to her. "This text is potentially relevant. Rather than us diving into it now, could you take pictures of the pages and I'll review it in detail when we're out of here?"

She takes the book—not before I can lean forward for a kiss—and sits at the desk next to mine. The two of us, individually academic weapons, become unstoppably productive. We hardly talk. By the time I finish a new text, she's putting away the previous one I gave her. After establishing a satisfying workflow—a flow that I've chased on every train ride as a child and in every study room at Rockwell—I do one final scan of the bookshelf before checking the time.

"It's 11:02," I say, suddenly nervous. "We shouldn't have stayed down here so long. C'mon, let's go."

Eva puts away her last book and grabs my hand. We quickly walk down the center aisle, glancing at the temples, shrines, and frescoes one final time as our shoes click against the checkered flagstones. "Imagine being able to stay down here without rushing," she says, glancing at me with a smile. The flames flicker against her cheek, shimmering in her hazel eyes.

"I know," I say. "All of this still feels like some sort of fever dream."

We have about a hundred feet before we reach the three arches to the history room, and the two of us relish in the blissful feeling of awe and satisfaction...until it crumbles in an instant.

The doors creak open.

CHAPTER 30

M y first thought is that Thanh was absolutely correct about cultists: a figure walks through the door in a gray robe, with a hood drawn over him.

Eva and I both duck into the nearest row of shelves, hands still clasped. The bookshelves are solid, so we can't see who is there without completely sticking out. But we listen. The door clangs shut behind the person and a single pair of soft leather soles pad across the center aisle in our direction. Eva tugs me away, guiding us to the outside edge of the shelf near the altars. The door opens again, and a female voice calls out in an authoritative address.

"Acolyte Benjamin," she says, and the leather padding stops.

"Yes, Instructor Fauna," the man replies. He sounds much younger and slightly nervous.

"The elders will be pleased to hear that you are taking your new responsibilities so seriously. However, you were elected to watch over the men's dormitories this evening, as you are well aware. Need I ask why you have left your post?" The woman, also padding along in a similar leather sound, walks purposefully toward him.

"I..." he begins, "I apologize, Instructor. I know how the halls can echo, but I swore I heard footsteps in this direction. I wanted to quickly investigate before returning to the dormitories." I can feel the shakiness in his voice...and the death grip of Eva's hand squeezing into mine.

"In the future, you are to report this to the instructor on watch, without abandoning your designated guard. Now, let us quickly sweep the religion wing and be off, shall we? I'll take the perimeter."

I turn to see Eva slipping off her sneakers and waving at me to do the same. We both sprint down the left perimeter of the room, shoes clutched in hand. We turn around the ring of the dome—just out of eyesight of the woman—and hear her chatting to the man as he walks down the middle.

"How have you and your cohort found the new position? I can remember during my first night of guard duty, I..."

My desperate curiosity is overcome only by fear of being discovered. As they chatter on, the two of us sprint to a door at the far back-left of the room. To our left, kneeling at a golden altar, we see a blindfolded young woman in a white gown that's soaked in blood. She's carving a knife through the body of a crow, smearing her bloodied hands into patterns on the altar. She's muttering to herself, body shaking slightly as if she's in some form of trance. How long has she been in here?! Did she not hear us...or did she not care? My eyes struggle to leave her as we arrive at the door. It's hard to stop abruptly with my socks against the marble, but I prop myself against the stone archway—chest heaving, begging for an audible exhale that I can't allow—and silently pull the iron knocker back. Eva and I shuffle through, then guide the door slowly shut from the other side.

I turn to see a stately room with a large bronze statue of a man who looks uncannily like Sigmund Freud.

The psychology section.

"Do you think they'll check in here too?" Eva asks, looking at the space.

It is drastically different from the grandiosity of the other two libraries. It's designed in a sixteenth century English Tudor style, with white-washed plaster ceilings and exposed wooden beams steeped in a tall gable-pointed ceiling. The floors are distressed brick and covered in warm animal skin rugs. Rather than one large space, the room is laid out like a series of private home libraries. The small gathering nooks are furnished with leather armchairs, loveseats, and wide oak desks in each section. It's as if they are all imitating the intimacy of a therapist's office.

"I don't know," I mutter, glancing into each of the nooks. "Let's find a good place to hide for a few minutes, and if we don't hear them, we go back through the religion and history sections to get out."

"Okay," she says, grabbing my hand again. I take the briefest moment to appreciate the ease with which Eva and I connect. We pad across the room quietly until a sound behind us—possibly in the religion room, but that robed figure was right about sound echoing in this place—startles us behind one of the shelves. We lean back against the books, waiting.

"I can't imagine how horrific some of these psychology texts are," Eva whispers.

"Would it be any worse than the other subjects?"

"I suppose not. But honestly, the *known* history of psychology is shockingly recent and unethical—using orphaned children as test subjects, 'curing' homosexuality with electroshock therapy, developing faulty tests to support eugenics. I don't want to imagine the experiments we don't know about..."

Our eyes widen at the sound of the religion door opening. Eva and I shuffle away quickly, not wanting to get trapped. We find a door in the back that's already propped open, and step through without looking. We're greeted by a massive courtyard filled with about sixty rows of polished wooden tables—a dining hall.

We move to the right, weaving between the tables toward a small, non-descript door in the corner. Each wooden table is marked from years, decades, possibly centuries of wear, and is lined with matching Queen Anne style chairs and candelabra centerpieces. Enormous French Empire crystal chandeliers hang from the ceiling. The dining hall is entirely devoid of people and cleared of plates, cutlery, and food, yet traces of humanity are still evidenced throughout: chairs pushed in crookedly in haste, a few rolls of parchment strewn about, a nub of gray bread fallen between the chairs and left unseen. As we zig-zag past the tables, the faint sounds of the chanting are growing louder. We're getting closer to it.

More echoing voices emerge behind us. We hear padded footsteps—always footsteps, will we ever outrun them?!—when we finally reach the door. Again, we're forced to sneak through and pray they haven't heard us. This small service door clicks louder than the others, but we step through.

We emerge into a disorienting maze of hallways. To our left is an opening with a stone octagonal room in the center. Each of its eight walls have two massive doors that are a rich royal blue with elaborate golden symbols. From within those doors, the volume of the chanting is its loudest—as if that is the very heartbeat of this cryptic palace. I can't be certain, but each hallway seems to be a wheel spoke that goes out from the octagonal center. I try to keep this mental image in mind, if we're ever going to find our way out.

Eva's eyes, like mine, look absolutely lost. We're faced with the imminent need to decide which way to go, with potential life-threatening consequences should we get it wrong.

"Straight?" I suggest.

She bolts for a small door across from us, throwing it open.

It's a laundry room. Clotheslines stretch across the space, and a massive iron cauldron of soapy water is soaking dozens of robes, kitchen towels, and aprons. To our right are numbered rows of clothing cubbies that are largely empty, each one labeled: Eighty-Four, Eighty-Five, Eighty-Six. Beside these shelves are racks of leather slippers, all uniformly made but fairly worn-out.

The noises outside grow louder. More doors open and close—voices calling to one another in alarm.

"Hide," I say, grabbing Eva's arm to bring her behind the wash basin. She resists for a moment, only to grab two sets of tan robes and slippers from the cubbies. "You sure that's a good idea?" I ask.

"We've been running around like maniacs for the last ten minutes," she says, thrusting the robes in my hand. She rapidly undresses herself while crouching low. "I would love to not get caught, but if we do, I'd much prefer it to be as students who are supposed to be down here rather than outsiders. It could at least buy us some time."

I slowly undress myself, watching as Eva fully strips off her sweater, tank top, and black lace bra.

"I would also have preferred you to see me naked for the first time under more luxurious circumstances," she adds, thrusting the tan robe over herself, "but given the circumstances, we don't have time for propriety. HURRY UP!" she hisses, batting at me to stop glancing. "Everything off," she adds, discreetly slipping off her black underwear underneath the robe. She wedges her modern clothes in a deep corner beneath the iron wash basin. "If they're writing with quills by candlelight, these people aren't going to have Hanes socks and Victoria's Secret bra straps sticking out."

I follow as quickly as I can, slipping the robe over my bare chest and stripping off my pants and boxers. I tuck my things beside Eva's belongings, then try to wrestle a leather slipper over my foot—

The door opens. We're still momentarily hidden behind the wash basin, but if they check behind here, we'll be found immediately...

Eva pulls me onto her. She's lying flat on the ground, hood up, and begins desperately kissing and groping me. For a moment I forget where we are, who we're afraid of, and the imminent danger that we're most certainly in. We've kissed a few times before, but this is an intensity I wasn't prepared for. Her tongue twists into mine, her lips are soft and wet, her hand grips me as if I were a life raft keeping her afloat in a stormy ocean—

"Scholars, at attention!"

We freeze. The shout came from behind us, and for one brief moment we stare at the fear etched on each other's face. We stand up, flattening our robes and drawing the hoods far over our heads. We bow down like children standing in front of the school principal...waiting to hear our sentence.

CHAPTER 31

Three robed figures stand in front of us. The first is the woman from before, referred to Instructor Fauna. She is wearing a navy-blue robe, made of a finer material than our coarse tan ones. Beneath her hood, she has a short bob of gray hair with severe eyes. There are two men in gray robes behind her, both closer to my age. The first one is the shy Acolyte Benjamin, who up close has thick, sheepish brown curls and a hooked nose. The second, clearly far from shy, is sniggering as quietly as he can (not very) at the notion of catching us kissing.

"Silence, Acolyte Thomas," Fauna says.

Thomas stifles his laughter but can't manage to take the glint out of his eyes. He is very thin with prominent cheekbones and a rough crew cut. All three of them, I notice, are almost translucently pale—as if they haven't seen the sun in years.

"Scholar Ninety-Four, Scholar Ninety-Seven," Fauna announces, looking down at the two of us. I notice now that both of our numbers are sewn onto the arms of our robes. "Our registry indicates that the two of you were in the infirmary with the stomach flu, from which several of your other new cohort are suffering. Is it safe to presume that the two of you have made a full recovery?"

We both nod, heads lowered.

"How delightful to see," she responds, arching her eyebrows. "I know you must be weary after illness, but considering you missed some of the orientation activities, it would be prudent for me to provide an expedited tour for you now. Come," she says, stalking down the hallway, her navy robes billowing behind her.

Eva and I glance at each other nervously, but Thomas shoves us forward with a laugh. We are shepherded through the maze of hallways until Fauna stops, fingers clasped in waiting.

"Please," she says, waving her bony hand into a room.

Eva and I step in pace with one another, cautiously entering. All we see is a small inner chamber with two large, thick iron doors. Each has two locks and is completely solid, except for a small, grated iron window in the top-center—

The door behind us slams. Thomas—grinning like a child that's just discovered fire—and his colleague Benjamin flank the door behind us, slipping short night sticks out of the sleeves of their robes. Fauna breezes by us, pulling out an old keyring and unlocking one of the large iron doors. It screeches open before us, revealing a medieval jail and interrogation cell: wrist, ankle, and neck manacles are bolted to stone walls that are caked in dried blood. Along the side walls are racks of rusty metal hooks, barbs, and spiked clubs that are being dripped on by some unknown cave condensation.

"As you both know, The Sanctum was founded nearly three hundred years ago as a haven for free thought—for us to learn without persecution or hinderance from the narrow-minded populace. We are able to continue this important tradition due to the order that we maintain here. Acolytes Benjamin and Thomas can attest to the fact that I do not offer warnings frequently, and certainly never more than once. Each of you will become acquainted with these cells, and our eager disciplinary staff, should you decide to sneak off again. Do we understand each other?"

"Yes, Instructor Fauna," we both say.

"Excellent," Fauna responds. "And to be certain that you two don't lose your way again, your superiors here will escort you to your *separate* male and female dormitories." She nods to the two of them.

"Follow me, Ninety-Four," Thomas barks. I glance down to confirm that's me, and follow him with one final side-glance to Eva.

"This way, Scholar Ninety-Seven," Benjamin says with a sputtering attempt at authority.

I'm still shaking as I follow Thomas down the hallway. How close are we to being discovered as outsiders? We were almost tortured even as students who are supposed to be here! And now we're being split up...

Thomas, for what it's worth, seems completely unfazed by the threat of torture. "Dude, props to you man! Don't sweat getting caught like that on your first week, everyone finds ways to sneak off. Just have to be smart about it."

"Yeah, I'll know better next time," I say, attempting to execute my most convincing bro voice. "We both saw each other in the infirmary and she gave me *the* look. You know what I mean."

"Maaan, are you serious? Hold on, I gotta hear this. We'll take a detour; just say we heard something and I took you along with me."

I spend the next five minutes being personally guided through the library while I invent, in real-time, a tale of unencumbered sexual lust that is juicy enough to keep my guide excited, but also vague enough to maintain the illusion that I know who I am and what this place is. Once I have him, I take a stab at weaseling some more information.

"I really was sick before, though. I swear it was like being in a fever dream, seeing this place my first night. Any chance you could fill me in on the orientation stuff?"

Thomas rolls his eyes. "Dude, I hear ya. I swear my first week I thought I was on ayahuasca or some shit. So you got the acceptance letter, obviously. What university did you come from?"

I panic for a moment before answering "Rockwell." I know I should remove all ties from my actual identity, but if he asks me any follow up questions, I'd be clueless for any other school.

"Cool, I have a few buddies from there. So your new cohort here has like seventy-something people in it. Each one of the Ivy and Little Ivy league schools has one faculty rep who's secretly affiliated with us, and they each nominate a few to be considered. I only know the name of the guy who nominated me at Princeton because my dad's good friends with him—I sure as hell didn't get in from academics, ha!—but lots of people make it in based on, like, scholarly interests, discretion, and disconnect from outer society. They aren't taking goody-goodies or people with normal families who would miss them.

"I won't bore you with the program details—that's why you chose to be here. For the day-to-day, everyone has chores they've got to do to keep this place running. Just check the list in the dorms and you'll figure it out. If you stick around long enough to be an acolyte, you're not stuck cooking and cleaning and doing people's nasty laundry anymore—you can do guard duty and mentorship. Other than that, the food's shit and there's less drugs than there should be, but we do our best to manage a good time. I'd deny ever saying it, but lemme know if you need anything special. The shrooms they have down here have been growing and perfected for, like, centuries. Out of this world. If I had any background in botany, I'd have swapped projects in a heartbeat. On the side I also make a little moonshine, but that'll really cost ya."

Thomas hears the squeal of a door, and is seemingly startled back to his responsibilities. "I should probably get you back to the dorm. Fauna is perfectly willing to lock me up if I screw off too much. Thanks for the scoop on you and Ninety-Seven, by the way. I'll let everyone know you two got a thing."

"Appreciate it, man. I'm sure you have plenty of stories from down here, too," I add, nudging him.

This last remark massages his ego just enough for him to keep walking with me. "There's this one freak redhead girl that I'm with now. She's really into medieval torture, and she has, like, the *biggest* tits and you can totally see how huge they are, even through the ratty robes..."

As Thomas regales me, he guides me into what I take to be the political science library. It's extraordinary, just like every other area I've seen, and is designed to be an identical remaking of the main reading room in the Library of Congress. A ring of inner wooden desks surrounds a gargantuan statue of George Washington on horseback, with bookshelves circling the entire golden marble room.

I'm desperate to see more and weasel as much information as I can from Thomas, but I'm worried about pushing too far. I'm definitely on his good side right now and I want to keep it that way. After quickly passing through the political science library, we return to the center hallway and arrive at the door of the men's dormitory.

"Alright, head on in, newbie. Try not to wake the place up."

"Thanks, Thomas. Take it easy."

I creak the dormitory door open uneasily, and the hall torchlight spills into the pitch-black room. The dorm almost resembles a military bunkhouse; oak bunk beds are stacked in rows close to each other on the left and right of the room, going far back lengthwise. There are small, numbered signs on the bunks, presumably indicating the assigned scholar. Utilitarian hooks are attached to each one, where people are hanging their robes, bags, and leather slippers. I tip toe into the darkness, passing by dozens of sleeping bodies and a cacophony of snores. I eventually find my number on the top bunk of an empty bed. I climb the wooden slats as quietly as possible, then flop down on the hard mattress.

My breathing gradually joins the frequency of the room, and for the first time tonight things slow down. I have time think. We are deep in a hidden underground academy with no cell service. We know the way out. It is somewhat guarded, but we don't know how well. I have a rapport with one of the guards. For now, they do not realize that we aren't who we say we are; the scholars that are "us" are still in the infirmary, which is our ticking clock. As soon as they get healthy, or someone with authority goes in there and notices that there are two Ninety-Fours and Ninety-Sevens, it's all over. Eva and I need to lay low in our dorms until we can reconvene in the morning.

My brain continues to ask the question "why?" Why go through the cloak and dagger of creating this entire institution? Yes, we saw some gruesome books and things down here, but you can find gruesome things in a Spencer's gift shop at every mall in America. What else is down here that would require such secrecy? My first thought goes to the chanting in the center of the Sanctum. There's no way for me to tell what's in there, and despite all the eagerness in the world, I know it's best for me to stay away. Just get in and get out.

My head whirls with every tome, every work of art, every detail that I've glimpsed. We came down here with a purpose, and that purpose has been overshadowed by a world too overwhelming and dangerous to comprehend. Somehow, as time drifts ahead, my thoughts fuzz and fade into a dream-filled sleep, of a world similar to the one I've found myself in.

CHAPTER 32

A shrill clanging pierces the air.

I bolt upright in terror—almost slamming my head against the ceiling—and see a gray-robed man ringing a bell. The entire room groans and shuffles out of bed. The man ringing it doesn't look too pleased himself; he had to be up earlier than everyone else for the honor of blaring that thing in his own ear.

I have plenty of experience joining a new school during the middle of the year. As a kid, I learned to observe patterns of behavior in my peers, studying their rhythms so that I didn't stick out too much or make any egregious social faux pas. Many of the scholars sluggishly pull their robes on, draw their hoods up, and ready themselves for a day of work.

"My back is still fucked from these mattresses; I don't know how I'm the only one complaining..."

"I'm stuck in the laundry room again?!" one says, glancing at a white slip of paper on the wall.

"Kitchens ain't much better, dude," another says, and the other rolls his eyes.

I hear the faint flush of a toilet toward the back of the room, and several young men chatting while they brush their teeth.

I climb down the ladder of my bed, hoping to avoid my bunkmate. I head directly to the paper on the wall, correctly guessing that this is the chores list that Thomas referenced. I scan down until I find "Ninety-Four: Kitchens – Morning." I see that another nearby scholar, Eighty-Nine, is also listed as "Kitchens – Morning" and decide to follow him toward the public bathroom.

A group is lined up at the wall of sinks and bathroom stalls. Surprisingly, this is the least antiquated section of the Sanctum so far. Sure, the sinks and the toilets look old, but they all function exactly how I'm used to. I marvel, for the first time in my life, at the fact that all modern plumbing is somehow done without electricity.

"Anyone else doing kitchens this morning?" I ask nonchalantly, washing my face in the sink.

"Yes, I am," Eighty-Nine says, with a slight South Asian accent. He's about my age with dark chestnut skin, thick eyebrows, and a tired but kind face. "Supposed to be very difficult, from what I have heard. I haven't done it yet myself."

"Me neither," I say. "I actually just got out of the infirmary last night, so this is my first time doing chores. Do we just head there now?"

"Oh no," Eighty-Nine says. "For morning shifts we go to breakfast first, and then go to our assignment at the bell. Here, come find me after breakfast and we'll walk there together."

"Awesome, thanks!"

I take my time in the bathroom before returning to my bunk. The others aren't ready to leave yet, so I stall for time by making my bed and examining the bunk hooks assigned to me. I find a satchel with my number on it and bring it up to my bed. Even a brief perusal of Ninety-Four's work is a good idea, in case someone asks me about it. There are several scrolls of paper with handwritten notes on them. When I unravel them, I find what looks like a preliminary outline to guide his research. He certainly seems...focused.

Procedure for inciting political insurrections:

- *Map out long-held, suppressed regional grievances (e.g. hatred of a race/religion) – ideally with historical incidents of violence to call upon as rallying cry*
- *Create propaganda to fuel grievances*
- *Support local, well-known, charismatic face to lead insurrection (historically more successful with war heroes? Find examples, esp. after Revolutionary and Civil Wars)*
- *Organizing the movement around leader*

- *Arming the movement — look into transport/hiding strategies*
- *Targeting attacks to high-impact, symbolic infrastructure (e.g. places of worship, historical/government buildings)*

Broader Questions

- *How to maintain momentum after initial spark?*
- *How to monetize these efforts from interested parties?*
- *Plant own insurrection groups, or support and reorganize existing groups?*
- *How to stamp out internal quarreling/idealistic differences?*

My initial reaction is shock and disgust—imagine spending your academic life studying and perfecting how to commit acts of terror. How could this, of all topics in the world, be your primary interest? As I continue reading, however, I'm struck by an odd sense of familiarity. His methodologies through the early research stages are incredibly similar to my own. Even his messy, slanted handwriting isn't very different from mine. I feel a sort of disembodied dissonance within myself; who or what is Ninety-Four? Some nameless, faceless researcher...and here I am sleeping in Ninety-Four's bed, wearing his robes, poring over his notes. There's some part of me that's tempted to continue writing underneath the existing words...just to see if the penmanship is distinguishable at all.

I put the scrolls back quickly, almost ashamedly, and shoulder the satchel like some of the other scholars. A group of them are leaving for breakfast and I hurry alongside them.

"I heard there's a *major* rift with the science and humanities students," one of them mutters. "That's why my bunkmate won't even talk to me. They probably have state of the art labs and are doing all sorts of wild experiments—like building nuclear weapons a thousand feet from where we're pressing our noses to Lee Harvey Oswald diary pages." The others laugh, but all I can fixate on are the secrets hidden in this place. I didn't even think to look up Lee Harvey Oswald!

"Probably a lot more job mobility with nukes, too," one student says, hustling through the hallway to keep up. "My father came here with a science background and went straight to the Pentagon after. Some of his friends went to Area 51 and the Svalbard Seed Vault too."

"Who cares about job mobility?" one greasy-haired boy says. "My eyes are on the Vatican Archives, and I'll gladly spend a lifetime there. They have more than enough to keep me busy. And hello, ladies!" he calls out, turning the corner to see a group of the female students in tan robes making their way to the dining hall as well. He practically has to shout over the growing volume of the chanting, which noticeably induces discomfort among some of my peers. The newbies aren't quite used to it, apparently.

We meet up with the women, and I scan their robes for any signs of Eva's Ninety-Seven patch. I start to worry when a blonde woman wraps an arm around me like we're old friends.

"Ohhh, so you're the Ninety-Four I've heard about! Word gets around here, what with all of these echoes." She smirks, looking me up and down. "Your girlfriend didn't even wait for you to have breakfast—awfully stuck-up, if you ask me. I'd be more than happy to eat with you if—"

The dining hall is fully illuminated with every candelabra lit, and the place is bustling like any other school cafeteria. Among the crowd, I spot Eva walking by with two trays. I make a beeline for her, shouting back, "Let's get food another time!" to the blonde girl behind me.

I tap Eva on the shoulder. "It's me. Thanks for...breakfast," I say, grabbing one of the thin metal trays in her hands. Everything on my tray is either white, gray, or black. There are cauliflower-like vegetables on the side, a hard hunk of bread with very little rise, and a few black disks that look to be ground into some form of sausage patty substitute.

She sees the grimace under my hood and smiles. The two of us wordlessly find an empty table in the far corner of the dining hall.

A long, silent look passes between us. An ocean of emotion hits me—a desperate fear, a thrill of discovery, and a deep relief that Eva is alive and well. I think of all the things I want to say to her and all of the things I can't.

I clear my throat. "How did you sleep last night, honey?"

Eva laughs—a beautiful, warming sound in this dark place. "I suppose well, given the circumstances."

"And your dining experience? You've hardly touched your mystery disks," I say, prodding cautiously at the sausage on my tray. The two of us watch in horror as it crumbles like a charred cookie.

"We should try to eat," Eva says. "I know we're planning to be down here for as little as possible, but we need energy when we can get it. Given the circumstances," she says, grimacing as she chews on the rubbery root vegetable.

"You make it look so effortless," I say, eating some of my char crumbles with the same enthusiasm.

"Learn anything interesting from our classmates...Ninety-Four?" she asks.

I tell her everything—the chore schedule (which she also figured out), the acceptance process, the student hierarchy, and anything else I can remember. I end by describing how I'm on good terms with Thomas, one of the night guards.

Eva nods, leaning forward. "So I assume that's our ticket out? Keep a low profile today, follow the herd, and beg him to look the other way in the history room while we 'get romantic?' When we disappear, he'll just think we snuck back to our dorms."

"That's what I was thinking. I'll grab Thomas before I leave breakfast. I'm sure he'll be eager to help if I tell him what it's for; the guy seems starved for sex stories. They must be puritans down here or something."

Eva raises her eyebrows. "You sure about that, Ninety-Four?" By the teasing way that her tongue pauses on the edge of her teeth, I get the feeling that she's enjoying a bit of roleplay as anonymous, star-crossed occult lovers.

"Tell me, then, Ninety-Seven. What have you learned?"

"Oh, you know women," she says, using her fork to toy with her unidentifiable food.

"Not as well as I'd like to. Please, go on."

"Well, women have engaged in whisper networks for millennia. It's been a long-standing survival tool for us to share information and learn about threats, without letting others know what we know. So, once you engage with the pattern of chatter, you can learn quite a bit."

I bite my lip as I almost say her real name. "Ninety-Seven...?"

"Fine," she begins, smirking and leaning forward until our hoods are practically touching. "This is essentially an unpaid PhD program. The first two years are considered the scholar years, where everyone renounces their names, their egos—in principle, at least—along with everything and everyone they knew on the outside. Without an identity, they believe they free the self from the societal judgements that hinder progress and intellectualism. Scholars are considered vessels for learning. None of them are required to produce a thing, although almost everyone ends up generating a tremendous amount simply from intellectual curiosity. There are no boundaries for their topics and no regulations on their work. They make requests for materials, and the instructors somehow always acquire what they need. In their third and final year, the tan-robed scholars rank up to the gray-robed acolytes. They are allowed to take names, although almost all take a pseudonym, learning to prefer the anonymity that their numbers offered them before. The acolytes serve as peer advisors to scholars, get roles with higher responsibility, and work on transitioning to a future in the outside world after the program ends.

"There are a few instructors for each subject, but not many. They oversee discipline, but their primary work is to continue their own research and do one-on-one tutoring for students. The elders are the final ranking above instructors, and they serve for life. There are nine of them, one for each subject, and when one dies they select among the instructors for their replacement. Apparently, they're hardly ever seen. There are rumors that they have their own project—one singular, cross-disciplinary aim among the nine of them—that they spend their time pursuing. But, of course, none of the scholars or acolytes can confirm it."

I glance up at the room of robed scholars, chatting to one another like students in any other dining hall at any other school. "This place is insane," I say, rubbing my red-rimmed eyes.

"We're leaving first thing tonight," Eva says. "Just talk to your friend about getting the history section empty, and we'll be out before anyone can notice. If we get desperate, we could also just run for it—it's not like they have guards at the exit ramp. We were able to walk right in last night."

"Maybe we could just run..." I say, glancing nervously at the crowd. If almost everyone is here, the history section is likely quiet. "I'm just worried about being seen at all. We don't want anyone to chase us, but we also don't know what kind of alerting system they have with the outside world. What if they push a button and there's security waiting on the other side of the tunnel? We know this place is affiliated with Rockwell University, and I swear some kid mentioned working at the Pentagon on our way here. Who knows what other high-profile organizations this is connected with?"

A bell rings, and the scholars and acolytes in the dining hall slowly rise and begin shuffling out.

"Shit," Eva mutters. "Okay, let's just follow the day's schedule. You have chores in the morning and then study in the afternoon, and my schedule is reversed. Somewhere in there, try to talk with Thomas. At dinner we'll reconvene."

"That makes sense," I say, seeing the worry on her face. "I'm so sorry for getting us into this. I didn't mean for—"

"We both made the decision, Cleo. Get your book and get us out safely. That's all that matters."

I nod. "Right. Eva, I..." My words trail off. I was on the verge of telling Eva...that I love her. I can't tell if it was just a habit (Kelsie and I used to say it routinely), if the danger that we're in suddenly sparked the emotion, or if there's some deeper part of me that knows more than I'm willing to admit.

Eva reads the confusion (and possibly more) on my face, and leans forward to kiss me. "We'll be together again soon. In case things go wrong, where are you working this morning?"

"I'm in the kitchens. What about you this afternoon?"

"The nursery," Eva says, pointedly.

"Wait, like plants? Or...infants?"

CHAPTER 33

S tudents scatter from the dining hall, all advancing to their morning chores or independent study. I find Eighty-Nine and about a dozen others slowly making their way toward a service door in the back. I idle behind them, listening to the others chat and watching to see if they're aware of some procedural steps that I'm not. As we all squeeze inside, I again find myself surprised by the Sanctum.

It is a large industrial kitchen, but not at all like the modern ones I've worked in. Rather than stainless steel, everything is wood, cast-iron, and clay. A large basin has pans soaking in it, with several scrubbing brushes, mops, and straw brooms leaning nearby. To the side, an open larder is lined with shelves of earthenware pots, each labeled with a slanted script. An entire shelf is reserved for various kinds of mushrooms, while another, unfortunately, is filled with something far more loathsome: black ants, crickets, cockroaches, and worm paste. Objectively, I know cultures have survived and thrived on bug protein for tens of thousands of years. There's nothing wrong with it...but picturing all of them crawling inside that pot makes my breakfast sit even worse. The resourcefulness is remarkable, though, even if it is a bit vile; the Sanctum has managed to remain undetected for centuries because of this self-sufficiency.

While many of us glance around the space (clearly I'm not the only new scholar here), a short, sharp-cheeked woman storms toward us. She has raven-black hair and the only white robes I've seen. Her sleeves are rolled up to reveal muscular, amateurishly tattooed forearms, and her hood is lowered to make room for her puffy white cap covered in years of food stains. She glances at us and clicks her tongue sharply.

"Alvays zee new ones," she spits, a thick Eastern European accent jabbing at us. "Alvays zee new ones to fuck up my beautiful kitchen. My name is Anika. You vant to cook?" Eighty-Nine and a few others tentatively nod, while I stay dutifully still. "Too bad! You vill ruin everything. Older students cook, you lot clean, you scrub, you make zees place spotless and stay out of our godforsaken way! Zees is no daycare, it is *my* kitchen!" She reaches for the brooms and mops, thrusting them into our quivering hands. She hands me a heavy-bristled brush and a bucket with soapy water, then points to a door in the far corner. "Zee assholes keep tracking in dirt. Scrub zee floors until you vant to leek it! When you feenish, scrub other floor!"

I move to my station and become the most invisible scrubber. Again and again I grind the hard bristles into the stone floor—my forearms burn after only fifteen minutes, and I periodically dab the sweat off my forehead with my robe's sleeves. Other scholars and occasional acolytes walk by me, measuring out spices from clay jars or replacing utensils. No one says a word to me or to each other. I had worried that I might get teased for having such a shitty Cinderella job, but it seems that Anika has created such an overwhelming culture of fear that no one dares act out, knowing all too well that they are one slip up from scrubbing floors, or perhaps worse.

After thirty minutes, I lean back to admire my handiwork; I still don't want to lick them, but the gray tile and grout are nearly spotless. As I lift up my bucket, I hear clanking metal, scraping boots, and laughter on the other side of a flimsy wooden door. The door is kicked open with a groan, and I watch helplessly as dirt-stained acolytes wearing yellow flashlight helmets barge in. They drag in large, messy bags that look like laundry sacks. The smell, however, suggests otherwise.

"Were you guys picking mushrooms?" I ask, sabotaging my goal of being invisible.

"Mushrooms, bug traps, and more," one of the acolytes says. She has tan skin smudged with mud, large almond eyes, and straight black hair that peeks through her helmet. "Everything we harvest is down in the caves," she says, pointing back where her group of five came from. "It's a whole network of tunnels down there, but we mostly stick to the areas where things grow or rodents can be trapped."

"Except on special occasions," a boy with dusty brown hair says, winking. The others laugh, and I smile politely.

"Like holidays?"

More sniggering from the group. "Of sorts. Always a nook and cranny for people to stash and trade a few things, a quiet hole for self-expression, or a private space for couples to reconnect."

"Sometimes a lot more than couples," another acolyte says from the back, eliciting a few knowing looks from the group.

"I think the battery on this thing is dead," one of them says, whacking a flickering light on his helmet. With one final thump against the palm of his hand, the light dies completely. "Is someone putting in an order?"

"Talk to Anika," the girl in the front says. "She's ordering a few spices, too."

"You could use the battery in mine," the dusty-haired boy offers. "It's newer, so should have plenty of juice left."

"Then you won't have a flashlight, dumbass," the dead-helmet acolyte replies. The two of them walk into the kitchen with their sacks of goods, bickering the whole way. The others gradually follow.

"Sorry about the mess," the girl says, looking pityingly at the dirt clods and crawling ants that the others left behind. My poor, beautiful floor.

"No worries," I say, suddenly overcome by curiosity. "Anyway, if I wanted to have something ordered, how would I do that?"

"You probably couldn't; orders typically only come from instructors, and even they are pretty selective with what they ask for. There's a kind of arrangement where deliveries get brought in."

"Where do they come in from? The Rockwell University library upstairs?"

The girl points back to the caves. "The only forbidden tunnel down there is the delivery entrance; some say it's forty miles long and exits out into some historical state forest on the border of New Hampshire. When supplies do eventually come, a dented pick-up truck drives all the way through, and we have to unload it at the end. The man in the driver's seat wears a mask and never says a word."

"That's wild," I say, picturing the scene.

"There's far wilder here, I can promise that. Anyway, good luck newbie," the girl says, leaving.

I wave to her, then go back to my work. My arms are already aching again, but I continue scrubbing hard, my mind elsewhere.

CHAPTER 34

I again find myself trailing a sea of scholars, the tide now leading us to a midday snack in the dining hall. The front tables display a buffet of crispy beige wafers with a thick schmear of light orange paste. Students snack on them while milling about, chatting with one another about the pangs of chores and the excitement of their work.

"You aaaalways do this," I hear one woman, Seventy-One, say to two others.

"It's an important question!" her friend defends. He makes eye contact with me and eagerly pulls me into the conversation. "Maybe you can help us sort this out, Ninety-Four. If you were to import slaves into the U.S. right now, where would you want them from?"

I pause, trying to casually consider the staggering question.

"Seventy-Eight here always talks about his grandfather's connections with the North Korean government," the scholar continues, "and I know they have such a strong leadership presence there and the highest *percentage* of slaves, but I think you'd be a fool not to get them from India, or at least China! Still a very docile people, but their existing slavery infrastructure is massive, and they create the most slaves in sheer numbers by an incredible margin."

"You can't buy the level of discipline and brokenness that exists in North Korea anywhere else," Seventy-Eight retorts, exasperated by his friend. "There's too much individual spirit in India and China—not much, obviously, but still more than you want—and you'd spend a fortune in the long-term from lost production, uprisings, and suicides. Casting a wider net with India is short-term, idealistic thinking." The two of them, having made their cases and knowing they won't sway each other, turn to their audience to await our verdict.

"You know I'm still team India," Seventy-One says, filing her nail on the edge of one of the tables. "It's an endless supply chain."

They all glance at me.

"It depends," I say, stalling. "What would we be using the slaves for?"

The three of them laugh at the naïve question. "What wouldn't we use them for?" Seventy-Eight says. "The whole global economy runs on slavery and has for most of human civilization. The greatest human achievements have come free or barely paid workforces: the Pyramids of Giza, the Great Wall of China, Chichén Itzá...and those are just international! The White House, U.S. Capitol Building, and Wall Street were all made by enslaved workers, too. Today people complain about how much back-to-school shopping costs, and that's already tremendously discounted by some child in Vietnam stitching backpacks for pennies a day. Just imagine the riots we'd have on our hands if you had to pay sixty dollars for every t-shirt because it was made 'ethically.'"

The three of them giggle again and I do my best to join. Obviously I've read about enslaved people throughout history, but there's always been distance—both physical and temporal—that divorces me from its emotional weight. That might be part of the comfort of history, if I'm being honest: the knowledge without the responsibility. Historical texts have always hidden the experiences and plights of enslaved people, but I hadn't considered how they also remove the emotion and intent from those who do the enslaving. I hadn't expected it to sound so...cavalier. To discuss the destruction and suffering of human lives over lunch-time biscuits.

"Sorry guys...I think my vote is for North Korea," I say, and I'm met with two playful boos. "I've studied the history of India for a long time, and there have been too many peasant revolts and overthrown rulers. I'm sure your grandfather knows best, anyway."

"I've heard the North Koreans have a bunch of deformities from generations of bad conditions there," Seventy-One adds. "There's no way they would be as versatile as a Chinese worker."

"Ugh, we need to talk to someone from biology," Seventy-Eight adds, craning his neck to find one. "Some of them are working on eugenics projects; they would know genetic characteristics across countries better than anyone."

Thankfully, I'm able to slip away while they look. I move toward the tray of wafers, hoping that if my mouth is stuffed then no one will be able to talk to me. I grab a stack of them and start nibbling off to the side. To my utter disbelief, it tastes...pretty good. Whatever is in the paste has a kind of zesty spice to it, and the wafers are hard and plain, but delightfully salty. I finish them far too quickly, and head back the table to grab more.

"Not bad, ehh?" one of the scholars to my right says, snacking on his own. He's incredibly tall and lean, with a delicate, skeletal look to him. Scholar Ninety-One. I have the feeling that he could eat a thousand of these and not gain a pound.

"Not bad at all," I say. "I was in the infirmary for the first few days, so this is my first time trying the standard fare. Today's breakfast made me nervous."

He snorts with laughter, and the people around him do, too. I quickly recognize one of them as Acolyte Benjamin, the shy one with curly hair that escorted Eva to her dorm.

"You get used to it," Benjamin says. "How was your first day, by the way?"

"Decent so far," I say. "Kitchen work wasn't thrilling, but I'm excited to start diving my project."

"It's why we're all here," Benjamin says, smiling. He seems far more relaxed and in his element than he had been on guard-duty. "There's nothing like getting lost in your own world. What's your topic?"

"Best practices for inciting political insurrection," I recite.

"Ugh, that's so cool!" Ninety-One says. "My topic is great—creating models to predict the likelihood of class civil war in the

U.S. after job automation—but every time I hear someone else's I get serious FOMO. There's just never enough time."

"Trust me, enjoy every second while you have it," Benjamin advises, glancing at the dining hall fondly. "I'm in my final year here, and I'm already getting sentimental."

I nod, knowing the feeling well.

"Anyway, if we can ever get you out of the library," Benjamin continues, "tonight a few of us are going to the dorm to play-test a board game I've been developing. It's nothing special, but it always helps to have more minds around to help me polish the gameplay."

"Ben is always modest," Ninety-One chimes in, elbowing his older classmate. "He designs the coolest stuff; his mind is wasted on nuclear chemistry."

Benjamin smiles, some of earlier bashfulness returning.

"That sounds awesome, I'd love to!" I say. This might not be the cautiousness that I had planned, but a connection with another acolyte guard can't hurt.

A bell rings, alerting us that the second half of the day has begun. We head into the main hallway, walking by the octagonal epicenter of the Sanctum with blue and gold doors. As before, the echoing chants are loudest from inside there.

"Does anyone know..." I begin, but Benjamin shakes his head.

"We call it the Nexus. I've tried asking around, but no one has any answers. The few who do—maybe only the instructors and elders—won't tell."

I nod, disappointed but not surprised. Our groups disbands down our own hallways, but before I can wave goodbye, Ninety-One hands me two more cracker sandwiches to take with me.

"Don't let the instructors see," he says, scurrying off with five more palmed in his own hands.

I smile, snacking on them as I turn down the hallway to the political science library. I'm surprised to find that I'm already getting acquainted with the Sanctum; the men's dormitories are to my right, the women's are in the hallway next to this one, and the history library is to my left.

I open the heavy oak doors, still just as awestruck as I was when Thomas showed me last night. It isn't full, but there are at least two dozen students hunched over desks, milling about with parchment, and chatting in whispers by the bookshelves. I expect everyone to turn and look at me at once—to gape and scream "intruder!"—but I continue to walk, unharried and unmolested, across the beautiful library. I pass by the center statue of George Washington on horseback, tracing my finger around the smooth, cold marble basin on which it stands. It's incomprehensible that this place is real, and shares the same world as the junkheaps I pass on the train each day. More incredibly, I cannot believe that I can study here, even for one single afternoon.

I head to the circular back wall of bookshelves, walking lazily and occasionally pulling a book out to orient myself on the different sections. The shelves have a brief gap in them, leading to a stone stairwell that ascends to a second floor. I climb up, circumnavigating the hall and glancing over the marble railing to see a bird's-eye view of the statue in the center. After a few minutes of perusing, I find a section that has books on political uprisings in ancient India. I know that they probably won't be relevant to my dissertation—which is why we're here, I remind myself—but I should stay in this room for some time at least to corroborate Ninety-Four's topic focus. And who knows, multi-disciplinary research often sparks all sorts of novel ideas. I grab two thick leather texts and search for a place to work.

At one of the desks, I'm pleasantly surprised to see Thomas. He has seven rows of parchment splayed in front of him, and his eyes are fixed on one as he rapidly writes. He's focused and serious in a way that I hadn't expected from the meathead who relished in the sight of our punishment. I almost feel bad interrupting him, but nothing is more important.

"Hey Thomas," I say, approaching the side of his desk.

He looks up, startled for a moment. "What's up man?" he asks with a lowered voice, glancing around. I can't tell, but he almost seems embarrassed to be caught working.

"So I just saw Ninety-Seven and we were hoping to get a little extra privacy tonight in the history room. Any chance you could help us out, even if it's just for ten or fifteen minutes?"

"That desperate?" he says, slapping me familiarly. "Listen, I'm not on guard tonight, but I probably can tomorrow night. I assume you two can keep it together until then?"

I hesitate for a moment. "Is there anyone else on duty who you could put in a good word for us?"

"Would you relax, dude?" he says, dropping his quill in frustration. "I barely have the clout to pull this off without getting into deep shit, I'm not asking someone else. You'd owe me big time for tomorrow night anyway; you and your girl aren't my first priority."

Crap, not how I was hoping this would go. Struggling for words, I glance down at his parchment and notice the header: "Need to expand military size—where to find soldiers??" There are a few scribbled ideas below it, but the list looks light.

"I don't know if this is helpful," I say, nodding down at his paper, "but throughout history, countries have found tons of ways to increase soldier recruitment. Did you know in World War II, two-and-a-half million Indian soldiers fought for the British—making it the largest volunteer army in all of history—even though they hated them? All it took was a few carrots promised from the British, many of which weren't even given in the end: future self-governance, social mobility through military service, lowered food prices during a British-caused famine. They essentially created conditions necessary for India to rely on them, and then eased the yolk as a 'reward' for good behavior from the colonies."

I watch, in real-time, as Thomas' expression goes from annoyed to shocked. He quickly starts scribbling notes, barking "repeat that again, newbie!" as his quill struggles to keep up. "I was going to help you out anyway cuz I'm a decent guy, so don't think you can do my homework for me and expect a favor any time! I'll see you and your girl tomorrow night."

"Tomorrow is perfect," I say, not daring to close the door on any ticket out of here, even if it's a day late. "You're the best, seriously."

Thomas flushes with pride. "Just make sure you stretch beforehand, Ninety-Four. You two keep at this pace and you'll end up in the infirmary again."

I ham up a laugh for him as I leave, off to find my own workspace.

The other desks are all taken, but just in front of the bookshelves are several leather armchairs with small end tables next to them. I sit down in one, sinking more deeply and comfortably than I was expecting. There are no clocks ticking or classes ushering by noisily; it is simply quiet.

I dive into a Sanskrit text that discusses the Kaivarta rebellion and other agrarian conflicts between the eleventh and thirteenth centuries. It explores several important factors that shaped history: armies being sent by the government to seize lands for a village...Buddhist practitioners, called Mahasiddhas, inspiring peasants to revolt...rulers bribing unsupportive commonfolk with land and wealth to fight for their causes...

The thrill of information spreads like wildfire. Every cause leads to ten new effects—to countless implications on the regions, rulers, and culture. For years, looking for new sources for my dissertation has meant traversing intellectual deserts with the desperate hope of finding an oasis to get me by a little longer. Down here, the floodgates are open; there's more to drink than I could in a lifetime, and all of it is accessible in a way that I've never experienced. This feeling is exactly why I wanted to be an academic in the first place...

Then again, what I'm reading has very little to do with Cleo Thompson's work on dementia. This text was meant for Ninety-Four's research, which I'm only here to pretend to do—

"So sorry to interrupt," someone says, standing above me. He has a tan robe, and all I can see beneath his hood is a red-flecked chinstrap beard poking out from a pale jaw. "Can you read Sanskrit?"

"I can," I say.

"That is so cool! I thought I was the only one who could down here. Isn't it such a rich language?"

"I was obsessed as soon as I was first introduced," I say, relieved that my visitor is here for a friendly cause. "It's precision of vocabulary is incredible; it often takes five English words to describe one in Sanskrit."

"I know! I've always said the field of linguistics overlooks it more than it should. Anyway, didn't mean to disturb. I'll leave you to it."

"No problem! By the way, do you know where I can get any extra parchment? I found a few passages that I was hoping to copy."

"Oh, here, you can have mine," he says, clumsily shuffling his notes and placing some blank parchment next to me. His hands are pale and splotched in black ink. "I always grab more than I need. There are stacks of the supplies just behind the main doors, if you need more of anything."

"That's perfect, thank you!"

"See you around!" the scholar says, turning to leave.

I'm still smiling to myself as I jot down a few farming passages.

CHAPTER 35

I'm thrilled to hear the dinner bell ring. No, not for the delightfully brown stew with unidentifiable lumps; I'm dying to hear about Eva's experience in the nursery. I wait at a table with both of our trays, watching as a group of tan-robed figures approach.

"Sorry lover-boy, we'll be borrowing Ninety-Seven for dinner," a woman in front says. "She was in the middle of some *fascinating* news about the two of you." The scholar gives off strong sorority girl vibes: a nasally valley-girl accent, wavy blonde hair, and perfectly manicured gray nails (are there black-market cosmetic supplies down here, too?). Behind her I see a serious-looking woman with pale skin and straight brunette hair. She looks oddly familiar...and then my throat tightens. When we first arrived, she was in the religion section performing a trance-like ritual, covered in blood. She doesn't break eye contact—not even to blink—as the group walks by me to leave. I slurp through my stew alone, occasionally waving to a scholar that I recognize.

After the meal ends, the Sanctum transitions to its evening free period. Some go to the library for additional study (tempting, I won't lie) while others linger in the dining hall. I remember Benjamin's invitation to try his board game and decide to head back to the dorms. Upon entering, I notice the odd sight of several women in the men's dorm. There are clusters of people lounging on the lower bunk beds, perched on storage trunks, and lazing on the ground together. Someone in a top bunk is tuning an old guitar by ear, playing scales and strumming chords at random. One woman bridge-shuffles a bent deck of cards, with several others waiting to be dealt hands. A few top bunks are filled with couples fooling around, while others house casual readers, one of whom somehow procured himself a copy of *The Hobbit*.

"Hey you!" someone says, placing a hand on my shoulder. I turn to see Eva's bright hazel eyes. "How did everything go today?"

I smile at the mere sight of her. "Good! Want to come up and chat?" I ask, nodding up to my bunk.

She leads the way, climbing up and laying across the coarse gray comforter. It's a tight space two, but I manage to sit cross-legged next to her.

"So, what did you learn?" she whispers.

I rest my hand on her knee, absently stroking the fabric of her robe. I tell her everything I can remember, primarily details about Ninety-Four's disturbing research topic, the mysterious delivery man, my conversation with Thomas, and the high caliber cracker sandwiches that are provided.

Then she reciprocates. "First and foremost, I confirmed that there are no rules against visiting other libraries outside of your project. It is a little abnormal so you might draw attention—the subjects can be very cliquey—but you can definitely search the biology and medicine library for *Enlightened Rituals* tomorrow. A good justification, if anyone asks, is that you're researching poisonous herbs that have been used against political figures during insurrections."

"That's good to know," I say. "And what about the nursery? What did you see in there?"

Eva grimaces for a moment. "Infants, as you can imagine. There's plenty to tell, but my first reaction is that it is strangely more progressive than any other academic or professional environment in the United States. I can't tell you how many stories I've heard from women who don't receive certain jobs, promotions, or opportunities because of their children, or simply because they're women and their employers expect that they'll get pregnant. Down here, it's very different. There are three current pairs of students who have children, but all of them are still fully enrolled and engaged in the Sanctum's program. The parents have sleeping quarters with their children, and while they go off to do their studies and chores, a rotation of scholars and acolytes go in and receive childcare training from one of the full-time staffers.

The parents came in occasionally to breastfeed, pump, or watch their children playing. It was beautiful to see.

"That said, there's a definite strangeness to the Sanctum's regard of intimacy. They were angry at us on the night we arrived because they have strict schedules that they adhere to, but they *do* encourage mingling. They organize rituals around it at times, providing spaces for couples as well as groups. All of it, I believe, is the same reason why worshippers of Catholicism or Orthodox Judaism have historically large families: 'be fruitful and multiply.' The people here are so loyal to the Sanctum as an institution, and if they have children together, that's another person who has joined their ranks. They have designated middle names that they give their children so that when they grow up and apply to jobs, they can use it as a sort of signal to any alumni. The boy I was assigned to today—who was adorable by the way; he had the most gorgeous blue eyes and was such a smiley baby—had the middle name Veritas, the Latin word for truth." Eva leans forward, now inches away from me. The fear in her eyes conveys more than her words ever could. "I cannot express how much bigger all of this is than we thought. The Sanctum is not just a fancy library or school; we've stumbled into a massive network of knowledge, power, and conspiracy, and we need to be extremely cautious while we're here."

I let out a long exhale, glancing around the room as if we are being hunted this very moment. No, everyone is fully enraptured in their own lives—still playing guitar, laughing, and talking. I imagine running out of here now, not knowing who would see us and spending the rest of our lives looking over our shoulders. I lean closer to Eva, almost lying on top of her in this crammed top-bunk.

"Should we go to the history section now and see if we can find an opening? Just bolt through the tunnel if the coast looks clear? We talked about waiting for Thomas, but the longer we spend here, the more likely it is that something goes wrong. The real Ninety-Four and Ninety-Seven could be out of the infirmary any minute."

Eva's eyes look up at the bare ceiling, searching for some inspiration. "I've been worried about that, too. It would be risky to leave if any of the guards spotted us again, particularly since we were already—"

"Ninety-Four! You up there? We're ready to start the game if you're still interested."

Eva and I peer over the bed, seeing the suddenly horrified face of Benjamin.

"Sorry...didn't mean to interrupt anything with you two..."

Eva glances at me sharply, her look saying, "Play the stupid game with the acolyte guard; we could use the help."

I start climbing down before Benjamin hurries away. "Hey! Yeah I'd love to play. Ninety-Seven and I were just catching up. If she wants to play too, is she welcome?"

"Of course!" Benjamin says.

He leads us to a group in the back of the dorm. They're seated on a blanket, adjusting a parchment game board that's weighed down with stones at the corners. There's an odd assortment of game pieces piled together on it: empty vials of ink, pebbles, coin-sized slices of a candlestick, quill feathers, and fabric squares cut from our robes. The board is organized by a series of neat, hand-drawn tiles that curve and zig-zag across the parchment, each of which is marked with a symbol.

"Okay," Benjamin says, adjusting a few pieces, "I know some of you play-tested the alpha version of this—"

"Yeah, and I wiped the floor with all of you," one scholar says.

A woman sitting next to him swats at his shoulder. "Only because the dice that we used weren't weighted right and you kept rolling sixes!"

"Yes, but *I* figured out how to roll the dice so that they would always come up a certain way. Strategy is still important, even in a rigged game..."

"Anyhow," Benjamin cuts in, clearly concerned about the bad press his game is already receiving, "the dice have been completely eliminated from the game, and the randomness is now based on card drawing which is far more reliable." He takes the first few cards off the pile, revealing symbols that coincide with different board tiles. "Your token will move to the nearest tile of the symbol you draw, and you will also receive the resources associated with the symbol. Feathers are wool, pebbles are ore, candles are wood—"

"So...you just made Settlers of Catan?" the guy asks, receiving another swat in the shoulder.

"There are *some* similarities," Ben defends, "but you can craft buildings to fortify yourself, and make weapons to sabotage the other players with the resources you get. Just stay with me for a second!"

After twenty minutes of everyone asking thousands of questions, the group starts to get into it. I've somehow ended up with the majority of feathers, which I thought would be useless until Benjamin explains that the other players need my feathers to build. The cutthroat negotiations ensue. Some of the scholars are overly competitive (the one who kept interrupting looks like he might pop a blood vessel), but Benjamin looks thrilled at the turnout for his passion project. Two hours later, we're on our second game and even more students are joining the sizable cheering section. I'm still at it, but Eva wanted to give someone else a turn to play. She's sitting behind me with her hand on my back, talking with Ninety about some of the skincare routines that the older acolytes discovered and passed down to the new generations.

At one point, someone pulls out a small tan sack with bits of mushrooms. "Anyone in for a ride?" he says, raising an eyebrow.

"So generous today," one woman says, helping herself to two small pieces. "Oh come on, none of the gentlemen are chivalrous enough to join me?"

Two guys quickly reach into the bag, only grabbing one mushroom each.

She glances across the board at me. "Nothing but composure from this one. Could I interest you in a little levity?" she asks, teasing the bag in front of my face. Some part of me wants to go for it even though it would be an indisputably awful idea. How wonderful would it be to feel uninhibited in such a beautiful place, surrounded by happy people?

"Very tempting, but I think we're having a lowkey night," I say, glancing back at Eva. She wraps her arms around my chest from behind, perhaps as a reward for my begrudging display of self-control. She leans forward and kisses my ear in front of the group. I feel a tingle in my skin from the sensation, my face happily reddening. While most of our existence down here is a sham, I am beyond grateful that this part is real.

I step away from the board game (I was hopelessly losing this round anyway) and lean back against one of the beds with Eva. We're nestled against each other, the two of us part of the crowd of onlookers but also tucked in our own little bubble. Those who indulged in their little late-night snack gradually become sillier. A few board game purists insist on finishing the game, despite being unable to recall the rules or whose turn it was. Others get handsy, kissing and caressing each other lazily with heightened sensations. And the woman that tried to tempt me with shrooms? Fully on her back, staring up at the ceiling with a plastered smile. Occasionally she giggles to herself from some great cosmic joke that's being told to her and her alone. Those of us who didn't partake laugh at the ones who did, and a stoic few are gradually relaxing into the evening and settling for bed. The atmospheric sounds of bed springs and teeth brushing blend in among the noise.

I love nights like this. Some will rise early and get a lot accomplished before breakfast, while others will explore the night to its very limits—breathing in the experience, relishing in life, pining about love and loss and dreams left wanted. There's no pressure to do or be anything you don't want...only a space where anything is allowed.

"Is it strange that a part of me will miss this?" I ask Eva, looking wistfully at the room of people I hardly know.

"No," she says after a moment's reflection. "We've seen and experienced some incredible things in the Sanctum. Just...don't forget why we're down here in the first place."

I nod. "There's still a chance we can find *Enlightened Rituals*. Even with the materials we've already found, I'll get better results for my dissertation. Professor Lewis won't have much to complain about."

Eva looks at me hesitantly. "That's great for the university requirements and your career...but remember that the ultimate goal of your work—the reason why the school received so much funding—is to find a cure for dementia. There are major, real-world implications to what you find that go well-beyond a grade in class. About sixty million people suffer from dementia, and the rates are only growing as life expectancy continues to increase."

I look at her questioningly. "How do you...?"

"My grandfather passed away from it last year."

A sinking feeling weighs down my chest. I struggle for the right words to say, but Eva waves me off before I can manage to find any.

"He was old, and he had an amazing life before the severe parts of the decline. For family reasons that I won't get into, I was left to shoulder a lot of the caregiving for him. It..." She pauses briefly, considering. "There is no good disease to die from—and I'm certain that I'm biased—but to me there is no worse ending to a life. It dragged on for years, with his constant confusion and shame because he would forget who his loved ones were, how to pay bills, how to bathe himself. He was an Army medic in World War II, a pediatrician for thirty-five years, and after he retired, he ran campaigns to get veterans and first responders the healthcare access that they were originally promised but was taken away from them. He cared about the world and gave everything that he had...only to have his life and independence stripped from him over the course of an agonizing decade. We did our best to keep him safe at home like he wanted, but every time I would drive away, I felt this nagging dread that it was just a matter of time. *Something* would happen as soon as I was gone because something always did. The pain, guilt, and fear that people with dementia and their loved ones feel is astronomical. Its effect on society—yes financially, but also emotionally and intellectually—is incalculable."

Eva speaks all of this with a kind of strained calmness. Time has passed and she has moved forward, but it's clear that this isn't something she's shared easily with others, possibly ever. This unseen, unknown weight has been with her at every conference, lecture, and date night that she's gone to.

"I'm so sorry, Eva. About you and your grandfather, and also about my project. I should have been more focused."

Eva's eyes look up, and I struggle to meet them. "I know all of this is an intellectual puzzle for you to solve more than anything else; that you're a smart and curious person who enjoys exercising those parts of yourself. But what I admire about you is that you're *choosing* to make your puzzle an important one. You could have studied any topic in the world—much like the scholars surrounding us—but you're dedicating your brainpower and work ethic to help the sixty million people like my grandfather and all of their loved ones. Maybe it wasn't a deliberate choice initially, but I think it's a very admirable one for you to keep. You're sifting through millennia of human thought and wisdom for the betterment of the world. What you're doing...it matters."

"But I'm not doing it for some grand purpose," I say, unwilling to accept the praise because I know I don't deserve it. In all the years of obsessing over my dissertation, the people living with dementia have hardly held a periphery thought in my mind. I didn't talk to them or the doctors and nurses who provide their care. I didn't picture them when I made daily progress or worry about them when I was stuck. Even before my dissertation I spent countless hours reading—learning about the Medieval monasticism on a Friday night, outlasting the librarians during finals week, studying an SAT prep book on the train ride to a new city—knowing in my heart that it was always selfish. These books were grounding and unchanging in a life where I couldn't remember half of the addresses I lived, or the name of my closest friend who offered to share her lunch on the bus. My own existence felt like it was slipping away, forgotten...

"Is anything real if it's not remembered?" I mutter to myself.

Eva looks at me strangely, unsure whether she should respond. I try to avert my eyes, but she cups her hand around the scruff of my beard and gently turns me toward her. "You don't have to fixate on the past for it to be real, because the universe remembers it all. The soldiers that my grandfather saved may have died later in life, but their children grew up with fathers because of him. They may never have heard his name, but his impact ripples throughout their lives and those that come after them. You may not be doing all of this for a 'grand purpose,' but what matters is the deliberation with which you continue to use your talents. If you were to choose how exactly you ripple the universe—how it remembered you, even if your memory fades from others—what impact would you like to have?"

I'm speechless for some time, knowing that I will probably spend a lifetime considering Eva's words. We sit in a challenging but comfortable silence together, certain only in the companionship of one another. I glance around the room, noticing how the others are ending their evening. The guitar has been put away, and a few distant snores reverberate from the back. Shrooms girl rolls over and slams her arm onto the board game, knocking all the pieces over. Benjamin quickly leans in to see if she's hurt, caring more about her well-being than his homemade game. She kisses him in appreciation, and his face quickly goes red.

"What I'm struggling to reconcile," Eva whispers, finally breaking our silence, "is the duality of everything down here. After seeing so many barbaric texts and evidence of cruelty, I assumed we would be surrounded by monsters. It's terrifying how ordinary and personally kind these people can be, yet still they contribute to so much wickedness. In some ways, I wonder how different we are from them."

CHAPTER 36

The morning bell shatters the silence of the men's dormitory. The room groans awake, slowly shuffling out of bed. It's abundantly clear who the sober ones were last night, many of them already up and brushing their teeth. I climb down my bunk and glance at the chore sheet: "Ninety-Four: Candle-Making – Afternoon."

Fascinating! The afternoon placement works perfectly for me, too; I can spend the morning in the biology and medicine library searching for *Enlightened Rituals*. Today, I worry less about following the herd, now that I have a better sense of the Sanctum's routines. I wash my face and head to breakfast early, the first few eager faces already in the dining hall with mugs of steaming black tea. I grab an identical tray to yesterday's breakfast, but today there are two large pills on it as well. I pick them up, trying to examine the sides for any markings or indications of what they might be.

"Every Sunday we get multivitamins," a woman next to me says, noticing my confusion. "So we don't get scurvy eating cave food."

I look at her uncertainly. She smiles and pops hers into her mouth, then walks away. I do believe her, but I stuff mine into the pocket of my robe regardless. No need to take any unnecessary risks. I find a table and wolf down my food as quickly as possible, eating everything in case I have to skip meals later today.

Eva walks in with a few other women by the time I'm finished. "Didn't want to wait for me?"

"I have a lot of research to do this morning. I'm heading to the biology library," I add, not daring to say more with the others around.

"Actually, I'll join you. I'm not very hungry this morning anyway."

"Thanks...Ninety-Seven."

"Oh, you two!" one of the women sneers as us. "I don't want to know what gross pet names you call each other when you're not in civilized company."

Eva shoves the girl playfully and follows me out of the dining hall.

"I think it's this way?" I say, pointing down one of the hallways I haven't entered before.

"I think so, too" Eva says, looking to get her bearings. "One of my new acquaintances is in biology, and she usually heads in this direction."

We arrive at the end of the hallway, staring down a massive arched double doorway. I take a deep breath, then pull it open. Stepping inside, we're greeted by an oddly dichotomous biology lab. To our right is antiquity—gorgeous mahogany shelves, rows of standing human skeletons in all sizes, and glass cases filled with old flasks, beakers, and vials of colored liquids. To our left, however, is an enormous modern laboratory. The walls, counters, and instruments are all either solid white or stainless steel. Most shockingly of all...it has electricity. It is blindingly bright compared to the flickering torchlight and cavernous hallways we've existed in for the last day. A white, fluorescent glow follows the room in strips, lining the drawers along the walls. Where did this modernity come from? How could they have installed so much...?

A vague memory comes to mind: I was annoyed last winter break because Rockwell closed their library due to "renovations." When it opened back up, nothing had perceptibly changed. Presumably large-scale projects need to be completed down here—renovations that require significant materials, infrastructure, and manpower. Some of it could come in through the tunnels, but would work crews really be willing to drive forty miles underground without getting suspicious? I imagine workmen being led to the vent in Mildred's office, confused but willing because they were promised great pay from a prestigious university. They nervously install everything they were asked to, and when they've finished, they look for the exit. They are slowly surrounded by an army of hooded students...and they never come out.

"A bit lost, aren't we?" a gray-robed acolyte shouts to Eva and me. One of his peers slides a pristine white drawer out from the wall, revealing a stiff, pale body. Oh god...this is a morgue. "Run home to your safe, dark little hole in history or whatever. We have actual work to do."

"The girl can stay!" one of the acolytes shouts, nudging his friend and laughing.

"We're just looking for a book for my project," I say, not at all intimidated by the weaselly students, but entirely so by the corpses in the walls. I want both of us away from these creeps as soon as possible.

"Upstairs," he says, rolling his eyes. "And make it fast."

Against the far wall, between the two generations of the biology labs, is a spiraling metal staircase. We climb it steadily, entering a plain, utilitarian library with rows upon rows of books.

"Let's get started," Eva says, clearly overwhelmed by the volume. After a few minutes of scanning the shelves, we've crossed off the sections for anatomy, disease, and surgery. We continue zig-zagging through the rows, almost out of breath from their endlessness. I quickly replace a book about genetics when I see Eva waving me over.

"Pharmacology and therapeutics section!" she whispers. "It'll be somewhere here."

"Oi!" We hear a shout from downstairs. "You two better wrap that shit up soon; we don't like you sniffing around up there!"

Eva glances at me, but I just shrug. "Nothing we can do now. Let's read as fast as we can."

There are no desks for me to use, so I grab piles of books off the shelf and stack them on the floor. Eva and I sit down beside them, legs tangling in the fabric of our robes. What we find...is beyond comprehension. Every civilization throughout history has had their own means of healing, whether practical, fantastical, effective, horrible, or nonsensical. All of them lie before us in this moment, and I can't help but read more than we have time for. Many of these methods are not only documented from their original century, but also replicated recently. There are accounts of bloodletting and leech experiments conducted in the 1990s. Records from a 1960s study tests the use of dead mouse paste as dental pain reliever, originally used in ancient Egypt. No idea is too silly, expensive, or unethical for the Sanctum to have reproduced. In the words of Professor Lewis, no stone left unturned.

My heartbeat skips when I see several books about historical Indian treatments. I—

"Your bodies are going to be the next ones in these drawers!" one of the acolytes shouts from below. There's no laughter in the voice.

"Are you close?" Eva whispers.

"I think so," I say, more desperately than I mean to.

"Okay, I'll go buy some time. Put everything back and come down as soon as you can."

"What are you going to...?"

She's already up, her robes billowing as she hurries down the staircase and out of sight. I can still hear her from down below, though.

"Hi guys!" she says in a voice far more bubbly than her own. "Sorry we're taking so long up there; Ninety-Four is a slow reader, and definitely doesn't have the biology background that you all have. What are you working on?"

"None of your business," the angry one says, although he sounds more flustered than before. "Just...go hurry up your boyfriend."

"Are you trying to provide blood flow to the cadaver's brain?" she asks. There's some murmur of assent. "It looks like you're focusing in on the external carotid arteries, but if you roll the cadaver on its side, you could also access the vertebral arteries that lead into the skull. If you haven't already, you may want to look into the transfusion rate as well; an aggressive rate for blood transfusions is 150 milliliters per hour, but obviously you have less safety risks to consider..."

I laugh to myself. Obviously I'm aware of how brilliant Eva is, but it's a delight to hear her in her element. I can't waste the opportunity she's giving me, though. I could spend years up here with this singular stack of books, but instead I flip through the first one as quickly as I can to scan for titles, dates, and table of content pages. It's definitely important—it is a written account from the 1800s that describes many of the historical and geographical origins of the herbs that were used in ayurveda rituals. I painfully set it aside and move on to the next. And the next. Torch flames flicker and blaze around me, and below I hear the clinking of tools alongside Eva and the acolytes' conversation. I place my fourth text down, reaching for the fifth—and set it down immediately.

No...

The tome underneath it is revealed. It's a short and long wood-covered pothi manuscript that I recognize without ever having seen it before. Texts referencing it have described the cover: the red and gold depictions of Dhanvantari, the Hindu god of health and medicine. He has four arms, each one carrying a different icon: medicinal herbs, a book of ayurveda, a conch, and a bowl of amrita—the elixir of immortality.

This...is the *Enlightened Rituals* text.

It's real, and it has somehow survived, disproving every academic and every ayurveda practitioner for a thousand years. I open the wooden covers, revealing the wide strips of dried palm leaves. There are some dark brown stains and a few frayed edges, but otherwise the condition is impeccable given its age.

I need time with this. My phone is with our old clothes, hopefully still hidden in the laundry room. If I can't take pictures of it...I'll just have to take it. For now, at least. I close the covers back over the book and tie it shut with the outer string. I stuff it into my arm sleeve, curling my hand around one end and keeping it pressed against my forearm. If I let my sleeve slink down, no one can see a thing.

I rapidly descend the spiral staircase. When I glance across the room for Eva, I find her...and a horrifying scene. There's a cadaver on the stainless-steel table with IV drips that are pumping a thick, black liquid into its arms and back. Eva is standing behind the acolytes, nervously watching as they open the corpse with sharp, prying instruments.

"All set, Ninety-Four?" she says, hustling across the floor to me.

"Turns out your girlfriend isn't just a pretty face," one of them says, looking genuinely impressed.

"Thanks," I say, not knowing what else to say to the back-handed sexism. Eva and I hurry to the door, desperate to get away from the creepiness. Just before we reach the handle it opens wide. Another acolyte barrels into the room, nearly out of breath with excitement.

"Did you hear?! Everyone's talking about it!"

Eva and I lower our heads and try to navigate around him.

"Heard what, fuckhead?" one of the biology students yells. "Spit it out!"

We pass by the acolyte and into the hallway.

"An outsider broke into the Sanctum!"

My eyes go wide, body freezing in horror. What do we do? Should we just run? Eva wordlessly tugs me forward and I slowly begin to move with her.

"Bugger off, newbies!" one of them shouts, but the eager acolyte grabs my arm.

"Surely you've heard it too? God, you all hole yourselves up too much."

"Well?" one of the others asks impatiently. "Did they catch whoever it was?"

My throat seizes. We need to get the hell out...

"Obviously they caught him," the acolyte replies, rolling his eyes.

An immediate relief comes over me. Whoever it was—

"The idiot stuck out like a sore thumb! He was wearing jeans and a My Chemical Romance sweatshirt, if you can believe it. I don't know how he found this place, but there's no way he'll find his way out. He's in a prison cell awaiting his sentence. If y'all are lucky, you'll have a new toy to play with soon."

The acolytes all smirk over their cadaver.

Thanh.

CHAPTER 37

After being threatened by Instructor Fauna on our first night, Eva and I know exactly where Thanh is held. We weave through a small crowd of people in the hallway, all of whom seem to have heard the news as well; every conversation we pass is buzzing with questions about "the outsider."

We arrive at the prisons, staring at the two solid iron doors in front of us. I hear a clinking of chains and a muffled groan from the one on the left. I'm sweating as I approach—knowing how horribly real our situation will be as soon as I lay eyes on him—but I slowly step forward to the barred window.

It's him. His arms and legs are manacled to the stone walls in a Y-shape, and he has a dirty gray rag stuffed in his mouth. His hair is matted in front of his face, and his forehead is scabbed with blood.

"Thanh!" I whisper.

He stirs as if from a nightmare. His eyes go wide and manic when he sees us, and I remember that we, like his captors, are wearing robes.

I briefly lower my hood to reveal myself and make a shushing gesture. "I am so sorry. Eva and I are in disguise down here—we got trapped and are working on getting out without being seen. We're planning our escape for tonight, and we'll..." I glance around, looking at the sturdy double-locks of his cell.

"We'll find a way to get you out," Eva finishes, with a confidence that I can't understand. "Do you know where they keep the keys?"

He mutters through the rags, desperately trying to articulate but succeeding only in gagging himself into a wheezing cough. Eventually, through sheer force of will, Thanh manages to wriggle the dirty cloth out of his mouth and onto his chin. "One of the people in a blue robe has it. They were surrounded by a group of others in gray robes."

I nod, knowing how difficult it will be to steal the key from an instructor. "How did they find you? And where are Art and Dot, are they safe?"

"They were when I left, but I've been gone for a long time already, and I don't know what they'll do if I don't come back either. I was safe until a guard blocked my exit, and then I had to come further inside. I hid for hours in some giant room with a George Washington statue, up on a second-floor balcony. A bell eventually rang, and a swarm of robed people came in. One girl screamed when she saw me and I tried to make a run for it, but I was surrounded by cloaks everywhere..."

All of this must have happened just after today's breakfast. I shake my head, thinking once again how my obsession is costing the ones I care about. If I had just laid low in the political science library where Ninety-Four is supposed to be, I would have found Thanh first. I could have hidden him until we escaped tonight. Instead, I was in the biology room...

"Footsteps are coming," Eva says, nudging me back to reality.

"We'll figure this out, Thanh," I whisper through the barred window. "We *will* get you out. Eva and I aren't leaving without you."

"I know," he says, a faint smile overtaking his beaten face. Somehow, after all this, he still trusts me.

Eva and I exit the prison just as a patrolling acolyte enters. He glares at us on our way out, but says nothing. We walk to the Nexus, leaning by its blue- and gold-ornamented doors so that our voices are drowned out by the cacophonous chants from within.

"Have any ideas?" she asks.

"Umm...a few, maybe," I say, glancing over my shoulder in paranoia. "Well, I guess only one idea is moderately decent. I *used* to be able to pick actual locks—not just sliding my library card through a door—with bobby pins and things. I have no idea what type of lock his cell door has and I haven't done it in years, but it's all I can think of."

"Okay," Eva says, nodding her head as if this were a viable plan. "Should we try to find the engineering library and see if they have tools? Maybe I can find a guidebook there to help you, in case the lock is something unusual?"

I shake my head, not in disagreement but in disbelief. "We would need to make a diversion in case the acolyte is patrolling. I won't be able to do this quickly."

"One thing at a time," she encourages me. "We'll figure this out."

"The guys in the biology lab were literally carving up cadavers when they were talking, and they seem certain he'll be killed. These psychos..." My voice falters for a moment, imagining Thanh's pale body sliding out of a drawer in the wall while sneering students carve into him—

"Hey," Eva says, reaching for my hand. "We have access to every library and all the materials in the Sanctum. They aren't expecting an internal breakout. However severe the situation is, we'll give everything we have to get him out. I'm certain Thanh would do the same for us."

"He would," I say, nodding. Everything Eva says makes sense, but it hasn't dissolved the growing pit in my stomach.

A loud bell clangs behind us; the doors from each of the libraries swing open, and the chatter of incoming students grows louder.

"The midday snack just started," Eva says.

"Not much of an appetite."

"I agree," she says, kissing me quickly on the cheek. "But that'll be a great diversion for us to use another library. Now, let's go save Thanh."

CHAPTER 38

I've been down every main corridor except for three; the only other remaining subjects that I've overheard are chemistry and computer science. Luckily, Eva knows the way.

"The engineering library is right next to the women's dorms," she says, half-running through the hallway. "We occasionally hear loud bangs from them late at night. God only knows what they're working on in there."

"We're about to find out," I say, coming to a stop in front of heavy double doors. I pull the handles with a groan, and they swing back to reveal the vast engineering library.

"It's...kind of a mess," Eva says, grimacing.

I couldn't agree more. I don't know what I was expecting...maybe some marvel of geometric architecture? Like the Museum of Modern Art mixed with Google headquarters? Instead, it's a simple, massive concrete warehouse. Every square inch of the space is cluttered with tools, workbenches, scrap materials, and scrolls with complex diagrams and instructions. There's scaffolding surrounding large machines, tanks of water with floating devices that blink and beep, and something that looks eerily like a homemade rocket held together with duct tape. The walls of this massive arena are blackboards, and every inch of them is chalked with complex math equations and symbols. Not a single decoration or aesthetic pleasure warms the space. And no bookshelves to be seen.

"I'll look for a guidebook while you search for tools," Eva says, walking toward a staircase in the back.

I move forward slowly, peering around the space while carefully stepping over electrical wire and sheets of plywood. I bump into a small bin labelled "bolts" that mostly has screws in it. I find a lump of a tan-robed scholar snoring on a workbench with his head next to a rotating saw. He has a plate piled with the potatoes that were served for dinner last night, and I pray for his soul that he hasn't been working since then. Next to his hand, I see parchment with scribbled notes and diagrams of bridges:

> *"Sound waves can form small bubbles that rapidly implode and release shock waves – these shock waves produce enormous heat energy which could destroy city infrastructure at the scale of bridges and skyscrapers."*

I shake my head, ignoring the implications so that I can stay focused. The first thing I grab is a small cord of rope near the scholar's workbench. In the terror of hearing about Thanh, I'd forgotten the fact that I've been palming the *Enlightened Rituals* text this whole time. I hike up my robe, tie the rope around me with just enough wiggle room for a book to fit, then slide *Enlightened Rituals* in between. The wooden cover scrapes my stomach, but the robe is baggy enough that it conceals the text entirely.

Next, I quietly rummage through bins and tool chests to find anything that could be used for lockpicking: a tiny knife, a thin screwdriver, a pin. Each bin has similar tools, but all with slight variations that make me question which version will be best for the prison locks. For now, I don't care; I shove it all into my deep robe pockets until they're overflowing. I'm about to go look for Eva—every second we spend here could lose us Thanh's freedom—when I find a small leather pouch at the bottom of my current bin. I open it...and am amazed to find an actual lockpicking kit! There are tension wrenches, dimple rakes—anything I could need! I remove most of the other tools in my pocket and shove the kit inside. Maybe we will figure this out.

I hurry to the staircase that Eva went down, ducking my head to clear the ceiling. Like the rest of the warehouse, there are no frills or decorations; the engineering library is a dusty cement floor with hundreds of industrial metal bookshelves. I make my way along the rows, peering for Eva among an array of confusing topics: hydraulics, geotechnical, aerospace. Where the hell would lockpicking be in any of this?

Eventually I spot her, sitting on the floor with dozens of books surrounding her.

"Any luck?" I ask.

"None whatsoever," she says. "I'm out of my depth on this one. Do you have everything?"

I show her the lockpicking kit. "Better than I could have hoped. If we can't find a resource book soon, I think we should just try it without. Do you think—"

"At attention, Ninety-Four and Ninety-Seven."

Eva and I flinch. Behind us stands an instructor in stiff navy-blue robes. He has a long, black-and-white grizzled beard, strangely shaped burn marks on his cheek, and a searing suspicion in his gray eyes.

"Why are you not in your own library sections, which are...?"

"Political science and psychology, Instructor," I say. "We slipped in here during break, but time got away from us. I have a question I wanted to research while the engineering students were away. I've heard...they do not always like outsiders in their space."

"Aye, we don't," he says, still glaring at us and the mess of books we've scattered on the floor. "And that means you also missed the elders' message about the ceremony this evening. Another reason why you should *not* be snooping around in here. What exactly is the research question that brings you so far from political science?"

I concocted my alibi on the way over. Two truths and a lie. "My project focuses on planting political insurrection in enemy nations. In my research I'd heard of a man, Tim Jenkin, who spread political rebellion during Apartheid South Africa when the government was banning texts. He went to prison for his actions, and he and a number of his cell partners escaped by crafting their own handmade keys. This feels like a necessary skillset that should be in the arsenal of those interested in changing their government, given the likelihood of incarceration. A revolutionary's bread-and-butter, in a sense. So, I wanted to learn how it could be done, and I thought the engineering department would be the best place to start my search. Unless you knew of a better place, Instructor."

His nostrils flare, clearly annoyed that I have a reasonable trail of evidence leading me here. I had read a biography about Tim Jenkin years ago, and it was the first thing that came to mind when I read Ninety-Four's notes. But is it too suspicious for me to mention lockpicking just as the Sanctum received a high-profile prisoner? I hold my breath, waiting for the grizzled instructor to issue our judgement.

"Check the security engineering section. That way," he adds, pointing to a few shelves in the back. "Make it quick. And *every* text you've taken must be returned exactly as you found them. Things will be most unfortunate for the two of you otherwise." I have the sense that he offers more leeway to the disorganized engineers upstairs.

"Yes, Instructor," Eva says, dutifully scooping up the books. "I'll clean this up now while Ninety-Four goes to look."

After walking past several sections, I quickly sense that I'm on the right track. There's a lot of materials on cyber security—hacking, the deep web, AI super-intelligence—that surprises me considering we're in a hidden, antiquated library. Somehow, the Sanctum remains extremely well-connected with the modern world. Finally, I spot a relatively new hardcover book entitled *FBI Lock Picking: Field Operative Training Manual*. I quickly scan through it, finding that the diagrams and text are shockingly straightforward to follow. This is perfect! I hustle over to Eva, holding up the book to her. "Come on, let's give this a shot."

The two of us ascend the staircase and carefully make our way through the engineering workspaces. The room is bustling with scholars and acolytes by now, and the scholar we saw earlier is fully awake and operating the saw that he slept beside. I'm surprised to see that we don't get as much hostility here as we did from those butchers in biology. It may only be because their attention is diverted; several of them are huddled in the back, gaping at a massive drilling machine that looks like it could tunnel through the planet. What an exciting new toy for them to play with.

Eva and I quickly make it back to the main hallway of the Sanctum (is the chanting getting louder than usual?) and navigate toward the prison. We only pass a few scholars on our way, and the prison is gratefully empty again.

"We need to keep an eye out for that patrolling acolyte," I say, already flicking through the pages of the lockpicking manual.

"I've got that covered," Eva says, glancing out of the door already.

"Okay," I say, exhaling as I grab my tools. When I had done this before, there was never a time crunch or important stakes; it was Aisha and me messing around with the lock on our school's auditorium door when we were bored. This...is different.

I walk to the cell door and whisper through the bars, "Stay quiet, Thanh. We're going to try and break you out." I hear an assenting moan and get to work.

The first step is to identify the type of lock. I peer inside the keyhole, studying its shape and the visible mechanisms. I scan the diagrams in the training manual, glancing back and forth to find the one that's most similar. It looks...like a mortice lever lock. I think I've done a lever lock before; the theory behind it is that there are several levers—the exact number varies by lock—that need to be individually raised to a specific height before the bolt in the back can be fully turned to unlock. I insert one of my turning tools to feel how many levers this lock has—three total, I believe—and then push it against the notch in the bolt. Then, I insert another turning tool to lift the first lever. My hands are shaking from nerves. Thanh is locked in there, with a possible death sentence if I don't—

The bolt slightly turns. I've put the first lever into place! I feel a surge of adrenaline—we can do this; it's coming back to me. I start to raise the second lever...

"Cleo!" Eva whispers. I turn to look at her, crouched by the doorway with her eyes wide. "I think the patrolling acolyte is coming. If he gets closer I'll try to stall him, but I can't promise anything."

Shit. I can't worry about that right now. I focus my attention back on the second lever, slowly raising it...

"Hello," I hear Eva announce, in a voice far too loud to be directed to me. "Instructor Fauna indicated that there were mixed communications about the status of the prisoner's sentence. She asked me to confirm with the guards what you had heard?"

"What?" the gruff voice replies. "How does Fauna not know our plans for the prisoner? She and the rest of the council decided together."

The bolt slightly turns again! The second lever is in place, and I quickly work on the final one. I need to know what's going on outside with Eva, but I'm not good enough at this to multitask. I slowly raise the final lever...

"As I'm sure Fauna knows," the guard continues, "the prisoner will be sacrificed to the heart of the Sanctum in an hour's time. The preparations for the ceremony will commence momentarily—"

The final lever is in place, and the bolt completely unlocks! I look inside to see Thanh's eyes going wide, staring at me and the click of the metal. The cell door will definitely squeal as it opens—I hadn't planned to do this with the guard within earshot.

"Is there a problem here?" another voice asks outside, possibly a second guard.

"No, just some newbie slowing me down. Out of my way, Ninety-Seven!" the first guard barks, and I see a slowly approaching shadow drift toward the prison doorway.

"No wait!" Eva pleads. "You have to listen to..."

We were so close. Thanh's door is unlocked—we just need to swing it open and unbind his hands to free him completely. In the half-second before the two guards enter, I take one final look at the anxious, desperate eyes of Thanh...and I walk away. I feel *Enlightened Rituals* scraping against my stomach—the price I paid for my best friend to be behind bars. I almost bump into the guards on my way out.

"What were you doing in there?" one of them asks.

"Just getting a look at him before the ceremony starts," I say, walking away. They don't bother stopping me.

I meet Eva in the hallway. "We almost saved him," is all I can manage.

CHAPTER 39

"We have to keep trying," Eva says.

I nod, still fixated on the guard's description of Thanh being "sacrificed to the heart of the Sanctum." What horrors does this place have to unleash when it feels threatened?

I take a deep breath. "Thanh's door is still technically unlocked, even though it's closed. We could try another distraction, but at this point I think the acolytes are getting suspicious of us lurking around the prison. Fighting both guards might be possible, but if they yell or sound an alarm, we're all screwed. If the guards leave again, we could sprint in and rush Thanh out. That might work if the opportunity presents itself. My only other option is much worse: once they completely unlock him and escort him to the ceremony, we create a diversion while he's in transit. It would have to be disrupting enough for us to grab him in front of everyone...and then have a foot race to the history section."

Eva glances around the corner to the prison. "I'll stay here and watch for the guards leaving. If I see an opening I'll take it, but otherwise I'll just gather intel. I think you should try and talk with Thomas again."

"What do we want from Thomas at this point?"

"I don't know," Eva says, "but he is one of the guards, and clearly has some resources and connections in this place. It's worth a shot."

"Okay, I'll to find him. But please be safe here; if anyone gets suspicious, just leave. We can rendezvous either here or in the history library."

"I'll be careful," Eva says.

I rush off toward the political science library, hoping to find Thomas at the desk he was occupying yesterday. I scan between the shelves, on the second floor, and in every study nook...but see no sign of him. I jog toward the dining room, but find it empty aside from one scholar sweeping the floors. Maybe he's on guard duty somewhere? Or getting ready for the ceremony? My breathing increases, the sudden time crunch looming over me. I still don't know what to ask even if I do manage to find him. "Hey man, have any get out of jail free cards? Or perhaps a taser for me to assault your colleagues?" He's made it clear already that he doesn't give out any free favors.

I decide to check the men's dorm room next, not knowing where else to look. At first glance it seems empty as well. I shuffle between the bunks, on the verge of turning back when I hear the faintest groan. I peer around one of the bedframes...and see Thomas and a redheaded woman going at it. I quickly duck away into the hallway, embarrassed at catching them. I wonder if that's the girl that he mentioned who's into torture? I shudder at the thought, thankful that I only saw them groping in their robes rather than something more exotic.

Thinking back to that conversation with Thomas, a few more details come to mind. He shared quite a bit when we first met. I wonder...

No. This is such a terrible idea. Like, worse than drunkenly diving under ice to look for a sentimental rock. I try to think of something—any other way of getting Thanh out safely—but come up empty.

Fuck.

I sprint toward the laundry room. It's still empty, and I immediately head for the corner where our belongings are hidden. I grab our wallets and IDs first; if we are leaving within the hour, I don't want any trace of us down here. I wedge them painfully between the wooden script and my stomach underneath my robes, the tightness grating me even more. Next, I grab two more things and hide them in the sleeve of my robe. God, I hope this works.

I rush back to the dorm, barging in deliberately. At this point Thomas and the redhead are just lying on the bed half-naked together, but I pretend I don't see them. I head over to my own bunk. I make it halfway there until I hear a loud squeal and a quick ruffling of robes.

"You said they'd all be gone, Thomas!" the girl shouts.

"They should be!" he yells back. I hear him getting up—guard-mode, activated.

I arrive at my bunk, quickly stuffing my bargaining chips underneath the covers and trying to act casually.

"Who the fuck is in here? You dipshits are supposed to be in the libraries; they made an announcement!"

I emerge sheepishly around the corner. "Sorry dude. I didn't hear that part of the announcement; I was too busy talking about the prisoner."

"Yeah, I get it," he says, agitation slightly waning. "Just get lost, okay Ninety-Four? I'm already late for my shift."

"Of course, yeah," I say. "By the way, when we first chatted you mentioned something about moonshine? How could I get a bottle for myself and Ninety-Seven? Do you have any here that we could have?"

"Woah woah, easy does it. You piss me off and then ask for a *bottle* of moonshine? Do you know how hard it is to make that shit, let alone sneak it around? I'm done with charity for you two."

"It doesn't have to be charity. I could trade something of equal or greater value."

Thomas raises his eyebrows, clearly doubtful that a new scholar could have anything worth this much.

I lean closer, lowering my voice so that his "guest" can't overhear from across the dorm. "You mentioned before how hot your girl is, even with these ratty robes."

"Well...yeah, she is. It's not like it takes us long to rip them off, anyway."

"Right," I acknowledge, "but wouldn't it be nice if she had something on that *really* showed her off? Something special for the both of you, from the modern world?

"Bullshit," Thomas spits back. "There's no way in hell you smuggled anything like that down here. You couldn't get it past the strip search from your first day."

Fascinating. I'm glad we missed that part of orientation. "*If* I did have something like that on me, do you have a bottle of moonshine that we could have? Ninety-Seven and I were hoping to pre-game the execution." My vile word choice has the anticipated effect; Thomas grins like a frat boy who just learned what an ice luge is.

"Dude, that is some wild-ass shit; you two are a total power couple. Alright yeah, I have a bottle of moonshine. If you can pull a lace nightie out of your ass, I'll gladly hand it over."

"Excellent." I quickly reach under my bunk blanket and pull out Eva's bra and underwear.

I am fully aware how inappropriate this is. My defense is as follows: first, this is a life-and-death situation; second, I only had this idea minutes ago, and therefore had no time to clear my actions with the owner of said undergarments; third, I will confess all of these events to her in full transparency once we have returned to safety, and shall rightfully incur any shame, penalty, or dishonor that she deems fitting; fourth and finally, Eva is an incredibly practical woman, and I can imagine her telling me to stop being ridiculous and hand over the damn panties.

The plan works better than I could have imagined. It's not lingerie, per se, but it is a matching set of underwear with some degree of lace on them. To Thomas, they are the Holy Grail, the Mona Lisa, the Hope Diamond; it is the most alluring thing this depraved sexual soul has seen in close to three years.

"Now, I don't know if they'll fit perfectly," I add, "but I think you and your special lady can make something work." I put them back under my covers and wait patiently. "What do you say?"

Thomas is already hurdling across the dorm. He rummages through his bunk, then quickly reappears with a slender glass bottled corked with a clear liquid. I grab it from him, sniffing around the cork and immediately falling into a fit of coughs—my innards reject the mere suggestion of this poison.

"The shit is vile, Ninety-Four, I won't lie to you. But unless you two are sailors, it should last a while. Stuff's *real* strong."

I smirk, swooshing the liquid in my hand before stuffing it under my bed. I hand over the underwear and bra.

"Ninety-Four, you and I are all square in my book. Cheers to a long-standing partnership," Thomas says, shaking my hand.

CHAPTER 40

I can't be sure how much time I wasted in the dorm and laundry room, but at this point I would guess that there are thirty minutes until the ceremony. Which would explain the crowd.

Everyone is surrounding the Nexus. Instructors are standing around the perimeter, with rows of scholars and acolytes staring straight ahead at the blue and gold double doors. All of the students are whispering—murmuring to each other—and it's abundantly clear why: the pitch of the chants has changed. In the two days I've been here, there has been no variation in the flat, endless drone emanating from the Nexus. Now, however, the chant is higher in pitch and pulsating in key. It's raising itself, growing...and coming to life. Based on everyone's reactions, this is new to them as well. Even some of the instructors seem interested, hungry for the coming spectacle.

I need to find Eva. I skirt around the onlookers, searching for her and confident that she's looking for me as well. "Sorry," I say, shimmying past a dense group of students who glance at me strangely. There are now six acolytes guarding the prison. I crane my neck to see over them, but one of them shoves me back into the mob.

"Get lost, newbie. We're working."

I realize that I'm doing exactly what we've tried to avoid for the past two days: standing out from the crowd. I can't help it; my nerves are shot, and every moment we waste feels critical. I leave the group of students and head toward the history section. As soon as I enter, I see Eva just to the side of the door frame, waiting for me.

"I don't know what I expected for security," Eva says, "but there's no way we can get past all of them and the crowd. How the hell are we supposed to get Thanh away now, with..." Eva's voice trails off as I reveal the bottle of moonshine. The cork is already out of the bottle, and a thick wad of torn bedsheet is stuffed inside, soaked, and dangling out like a wick. She's stunned.

I swallow, a lump catching in my throat. "I struck out, too. I couldn't think of anything, and I knew we needed a serious diversion, but then I remembered Thomas had this moonshine. If I light the wick and throw this somewhere in front of Thanh when he's transported, the commotion might be enough for the three of us to sprint out of here." I point to the spiraling ramp in the back corner of the history library. "I'll just...aim away from the crowd so not many get hurt."

"Oh god," Eva mutters, glancing at our only way out.

"I don't know what else to do, and we have to get Thanh out of here."

We hear a loud cheer erupt back in the hallway. Eva's eyes go wide, the two of us knowing that the ceremony is beginning. Without another word, we leave the isolation of the library to rejoin the mob.

The hushed buzzing of the crowd harmonizes with the chants from the Nexus. This place is alive. Torches flicker, voices swell, and bodies press up against each other for the opportunity of front-row viewing. I feel sweat slicking my hand as it clutches the bottle of moonshine in my sleeve. I imagine the Sanctum suddenly ablaze—swarms of students fleeing and fighting each other to get to safety, or to douse their scorched bodies in the laundry tub. How could I ever judge these people? How can I think myself any less savage when I knowingly risked my loved ones' lives for the possibility of acquiring an old book? When I'm willing to let this bottle go for...

A groaning, creaking sound silences the room: the gold and blue doors of the Nexus open before us. The chants are now on full volume, openly projecting throughout the Sanctum and heralding the amazement that lies within. The walls of the inner chamber are covered with tapestries of arcane symbols, and the floor has an ornamental rug depicting a detailed chart of planetary alignments. The room is surrounded with torches that hoist ethereally black flames, casting a haunting, shadowy glow onto the elders. There are nine of them, and all except one have their heads bowed in amethyst-purple robes. The faces of these men and women are ancient and weathered, and their arms are outstretched toward the focal point of the room—the point that all of us are staring at, awe-stricken.

It's a portal. Its appearance is difficult to describe or understand, because it isn't fully material. It is not solid or gas...but liquid. It swirls with some essence—an energy force—that flows with a violet hue to the concentrated matter within it. Eight elders focus their entire selves on this inanimate, pulsating energy, leaving the one remaining elder to address the crowd. He lowers his hood, revealing a small, withered man. He has long tufts of white hair matted down to his shoulders and a full, pointed white beard. His eyes are mismatched—one a sharp yellow and the other a grayed blue—and half of his face seems far more wrinkled and off-center than the other. When he begins speaking, he does not make eye contact with a single scholar, acolyte, or instructor. Rather, his eyes are tilted above us all; he speaks to walls of the Sanctum itself, or perhaps to the greater powers of the heavens.

"We call our home here 'The Sanctum,' as that is what it was created to be. A holy, sacred, and private enclave where one can be free to learn without intrusion, without persecution." His voice is higher than I expected, and ethereally quiet. The crowd collectively leans forward to catch his every word. "The Sanctum is, in every way imaginable, a living and beating heart. It is fragile and it is formidable; it was birthed and it shall ultimately perish. Like all beings, it must be fastidiously tended to; fresh and eager minds cultivate its staggering ingenuity, while disease threatens to lay waste to our institution. On this day, a virus infected these very halls with the intent of revealing us to the unenlightened world. They wish for us to yield progress for their thoughtless squeamishness, to shudder from the truths of the universe rather than revel in them. We live in darkness only so that our minds may be opened to the light, and only because they fear what they would do with the great power we unleash..."

I feel Eva elbow me, and my attention suddenly shifts from the elder's pronouncements. "Look," she whispers fiercely, pointing her head to the side.

There are two students in white linen underclothes, a man in long johns and a woman in a plain chemise. They are whispering, pointing directly at us.

"I think that's the real Ninety-Four and Ninety-Seven," she says, her voice quivering.

The instructor they're speaking to is the severe one from the engineering section. I see a single eyebrow raise as he locks eyes with me, the two still whispering in his ear. I quickly look away, the voice of the elder coming back into focus.

"...for a sickness that has been cleansed can strengthen the body. So, too, will this trespasser strengthen us. His spirit shall be given as tribute to the very heart of the Sanctum, and his memory will forever be a reminder that our secrets must be safeguarded at all costs..."

A gap in the crowd opens, and four acolyte guards escort Thanh forward. He's been stripped down to nothing but his boxers, with bruises and cuts across his body. He has red chafe marks around his wrists and ankles from where he was bound, and when he stumbles, one guard punches him with brass knuckles and laughs. The elder stares at Thanh mirthlessly, a severe pleasure carved into his wrinkled features.

"No..." Thanh, pleads, seeing the portal himself. "I won't tell anyone anything! I'll never say a word! Please, just release me and I'll never—"

As Thanh begs for his life, the crowd finds their own voice as well.

"Fucking spy!"

"Sneak!!"

"Coward!"

They scream at him until their throats are hoarse, until their faces turn red and veins bulge from their foreheads. They spit at Thanh as he walks by, and I see Benjamin and Ninety-One, the skeletally thin scholar who handed me the cracker sandwiches, yelling as well. They're enraged by everything they assume Thanh to be, and justified by the echo chamber of anger around them. He's threatened their existence, just as the elder told them he did. This bloody, pleading, half-naked young man who risked his life to save his friends...is a monster.

My knuckles whiten around the bottle. "Let's go to him now," I mutter to Eva. We bump our way through the crowd, getting as close as we can to Thanh. The engineering instructor and the scholars in underclothes are following us, clearly prepared for a confrontation. That doesn't matter anymore. I reach my arm to one of the iron sconces on the wall, allowing the rag end of the bottle to droop over my sleeve and catch fire. A few faces turn to me with the faintest recognition of what is about to happen. I show as much remorse and hesitation as they do for Thanh.

I throw the bottle.

The glass spins in the air over the crowd, sailing just inside the Nexus before smashing to the ground.

The Sanctum spirals into madness.

CHAPTER 41

An inferno erupts on the ground. The fire quickly catches on the ornamental rug and tapestries in the Nexus, allowing the blaze to climb vertically and horizontally as it engulfs the panicked elders. The asshole from the biology library is burning from the hem of his robes, and frantically pats at them between shrieks. The acolyte who apologized for dirtying the kitchen floors after I scrubbed them tries to vault over a guy on the ground, but she gets tackled by someone else and groans in pain. The women that befriended Eva during meals are openly sobbing, pushing each other forward to hide in the dormitories. Thomas is shoving and snarling at anyone who bumps into his girlfriend—blockading her against the herd in an aggressive display of chivalry. It shocks me how many faces I recognize...

Eva desperately grips Thanh's arm, the three of us trying to blend into the chaos of the crowd. One of the guards—a jar-headed, 240-pound man with a buzzcut—manages to catch up with us, grabbing hold of Thanh's other arm. I throw my full body weight at him, tackling him over someone's ankle and sending us both hurtling to the ground. I haven't been in a fight since the fifth grade, and I quickly remember why: puberty hits people very different. Struggling against the guard is about as effective as tickling a medicine ball. His biceps bulge from the strain of pinning me down, and he leans his weight further up onto my chest to try and choke me. His nostrils are flaring, eyes wide with fury. I look for help but see that Thanh and Eva are busy grappling with others, trying to pull free themselves. Instructors are on their way as well, ready to apprehend us all...until the room is transfixed by the Nexus.

From within the shimmering portal, a hellish red arm the size of a tree trunk reaches into the fiery mayhem. It swings a massive, taloned claw, flinging one of the elders against a burning tapestry. A roar is unleashed—louder and deeper than the center of the Earth—that shudders the stone walls of the Sanctum. Curved horns and the fiery glow of a head bore through the portal, its eye piercing the veil into our shattering world. Everyone loses their grasp of reality—the initial panic of the Molotov cocktail is entirely eclipsed by the mind-shattering deity before us all. Several elders get to their knees, facing the demon and praying in a last-ditch attempt at paying homage.

My senses come back just before the others; I prop both my knees under the horrified guard's chest and fling him off me every ounce of strength I have. I reach for Thanh and Eva, pulling them out of the paralyzed clutches of the acolytes. Many of the scholars are still trapped and fighting their way to safety—smoke choking their screams—but by the time we force our way into the hallway toward the history section, we have a clear path. After another otherworldly roar, I turn once more to see the elliptical portal shrinking to nothing. Just before it closes, the demon's barbed claw grabs a praying elder and wrenches him inside the portal. The old man disappears into oblivion with one final shriek.

We burst through the doors and into the history library.

"This way!" I shout, half a pace in front of Eva and Thanh. The once formidable library becomes a haven as we sprint between the rows of shelves; the stone floors prevent the spread of the fire, and the dense volumes muffle the cries of agony behind us. It strikes me that these books—with all their priceless history and mad ravings—might outlive everyone and everything in here. We will die and perhaps the Sanctum as an institution will fall like the Roman Empire, but these shelves will gather dust for millennia.

We make a beeline for the spiraling ramp that we first entered through, an eternity of less than two days ago. I risk one final glance back, knowing that this will be the last time I see the Sanctum's vaulted ceilings, marble columns, and iron chandeliers. I climb the spiraling ramp—body coursing with adrenaline—and check back to see that Thanh and Eva are still climbing. "We're almost there, hurry!—"

A sudden, smashing pain in my ribs. I turn to see...no.

Wearing tan slacks and a blue blouse with embroidered roses—shocking enough in this archaic world of robes—is Mildred. She's shoving a heavy cart of books into me, her wrinkled face contorted in an ungodly rage.

"You!! I trusted you! You were to be my apprentice—this could have all been yours! But no, you and your little rat friends left this place in ruins! In damnation!"

Mildred rams the heavy cart into me again. I realize that I'm trapped; the tunnel to her office is only as wide as her cart, so I can't get around her. She has me pinned against the sheer drop to the library below, a fall of at least a hundred feet. I grip the other end of the cart—Mildred and I staring down each other—but my feet are at the edge already and I have no leverage. Mildred shoves all her weight into the cart with an ear-piercing shriek...

...and I fall.

My insides jolt, and I'm shocked to see Mildred and the cart plummeting down with me; she overextended herself and couldn't slow her momentum. I reach out my arm and just barely grab onto the ledge of the ramp—the cart slams into me but I somehow hold on. In a last-ditch effort, Mildred claws at the hood of my robe and tries to drag me down with her. The jolt almost shakes my hand loose, the fabric of my robe choking at my windpipe...but the seams tear and the hood rips off my robe. The tips of my fingers strain with every desperate effort I can muster, and I slowly manage to get a better grip on the wall. I hear Mildred scream as she falls, and a loud crash when she and the cart finally plummet to the ground in front of a crowd of acolytes.

"No!" Eva yells, emerging from the ramp with Thanh. I hear shouts from behind them as well, rapidly ascending. The two of them grip me by my forearms and pull. It's an awkward angle and my arms are coated in sweat, but they finally manage to hoist me up. Still gasping for breath, the three of us stumble-sprint down the tunnel just as the others emerge from the ramp.

"We'll fucking kill you! We'll slit your throat Ninety-Four and Ninety-Seven! Traitorous shits, we'll hang you—"

The walls echo with curses and threats, but their verbiage reminds me that they have no idea who we really are. If Mildred doesn't survive that fall—and I can't imagine how she could have—we are three complete strangers known as stolen ID numbers or escaped prisoners.

At the end of the tunnel, the three of us ascend the vent back into the conservation office. I close the vent with a click, and then drag Mildred's oak desk—upending papers, books, and tools onto the floor—over the entrance.

Thanh quickly catches on. "We can remove all the books from one of these shelves, then slide it on top of the vent. When we re-stock it with books, it'll be immovable from below."

"Great idea," I say. Eva and I help him fling all the books off in less than ten seconds, littering the ground with priceless texts. At this point, I couldn't give less of a shit. It's a heavy wooden case, but with the three of us we're able to use our remaining strength to slide it across the carpet. There's banging and more threats just underneath us, but we restack the shelf over them...sealing off the Sanctum.

We slowly shuffle to the other side of the conservation office, distancing ourselves as much as we can from the horrors of the Sanctum. We all look terrible: our faces are coated with sweat and ash, our hair is disheveled, and Eva and I have torn and singed robes while Thanh is bruised and cut in his boxer shorts.

"What do we do?" Eva asks, still glancing warily at the sealed-off Sanctum. "Should we...just walk out?"

"Art and Dot should be out there waiting in the car," Thanh says, still struggling to catch his breath.

"Thank you," I say to Thanh suddenly, reaching over and hugging him.

"Uhh...it was nothing, dude. We were just worried about you both."

"I know," I say, looking at Eva and Thanh. "But I never should have dragged the two of you into this bullshit. It was stupid and reckless, and there's nothing I can say to express how sorry I am, and how grateful I will always be for your help. I'll spend a lifetime making this up to you."

"Do I smell free pizza for life?" Thanh says, raising his eyebrows.

"Absolutely," I respond, and his face sobers when he realizes I'm not kidding. "And that's just a start. But first, let's get out." I glance at a clock on the wall, seeing that it's almost 6:30 PM. "The library is closed and it's dark out; we should be able to leave exactly how we entered without any cameras seeing us."

We exit the conservation office and lock it behind us. Re-entering the dark Rockwell library feels surreal in more ways than I expected. Yes, we look ridiculous wearing tattered robes. There is a tremendous relief of returning to the real-world, and to a place that's felt like home for so many years...but there's also a lingering, sour feeling that home was never what I thought it was.

We rush up the fire escape stairwell, creak the door open, and are greeted by a light snowfall cascading past the campus streetlights. I inhale deeply, my lungs relishing the cool, wintery air. I hadn't realized how desperate I was to breathe something other than torch smoke and mildew.

"All clear?" Thanh whispers from behind.

"I think so. Either of you know the proud owner of a green Honda?"

Eva's face lights up. "That's Dot!"

We jog as quickly as we can to the car, with Thanh rubbing his bare shoulders and arms to stay warm. I wonder if they see us—

"Stop where you are!" a commanding voice shouts.

The three of us freeze, turning to two campus police officers who emerged from behind the building. They stride toward us, one of them muttering into a walkie-talkie without breaking eye contact with us.

Shit. What if they're working with the Sanctum? We know they're well-connected, of course they found us so quickly. I can't believe we...

"What's going on here?" one of the officers asks.

"Soooo sorry, officers!" a voice sings, and we hear two sets of heeled boots clacking against the pavement. Art and Dot! Even on a secret rescue mission, their outfits are as vibrant as ever. Dot chose to wear white fur boots with a puffer coat and boa, while Art has a tailored blue suit with tall, padded shoulders. "We were just picking up our friends for a costume party!" Dot continues, slightly out of breath as she trots over.

The officers raise their eyebrows. "And what are you supposed to be dressed as?"

"She's a runway yeti, obviously," Art says. "And I'm dressed as my favorite Dutch Eurodance artist, Joost Klein. He's an icon." Art wraps his arms around Thanh and me, and already our strange appearance melds into the alibi.

"Should I bother asking what your costume is?" one of them asks Thanh.

He stammers for a moment, but Dot jumps in and winks at the cop. "The body paint is in the car as we speak. All of this is happening at my house, officers, and they're staying the night, so no need to worry about reckless driving or campus disruptions."

"Just go," the officer says. They shake their heads and walk off.

"Dot and I have decided to start an improv troop," Art announces, leading us to the car. "You're welcome to join, or preferably to fund our wardrobe department."

"You two have spent too much time together," Thanh says with a shiver, letting himself in the car. Dot gives him her furry white coat, and he gratefully wraps himself in it.

Once the car doors shut and Dot starts the engine, Art turns to us in the back seat. "Are you all okay? What the hell happened?"

None of us speak. I dig underneath my robe and fish out our wallets, keys...and the *Enlightened Rituals* text.

Eva inhales. "Is that...?"

"It is," I say. I turn back to Art and sigh. "It's a long story."

CHAPTER 42

Dot fully intends to drive us all home, but by the time she arrives at my apartment we've barely covered a quarter of our Sanctum journey. Rather than having her circle my block thirty times, I invite everyone inside.

I flick the lights on and throw my keys and wallet on the kitchen counter. I look around the apartment, not quite recognizing it. So much has changed for me in the past few months, but the tenant who lived here barely resembles me. There are a few remaining mementos from my Kelsie era—the dishware and a toaster we picked out together, the bag of her things stuffed in my closet—but the walls and surfaces are still bare, reminding me of the heart-wrenched, drunken stupor I spent trying to forget her. Tonight, however, the space is filled with a surprising and delightful set of friends, old and new.

I show Eva and Thanh to my dresser so they can pick through whatever clothes they need. Thanh grabs a baggy sweatshirt and a fuzzy pair of red plaid pajamas, while Eva finds a waffle-knit shirt and a pair of gray sweatpants. Kelsie bought the sweatpants for me a long time ago, back when she thought my lack of exercise clothes was the only thing stopping me from jogging with her.

"What?" Eva asks, noticing my glance. "Is it fine if I wear these?"

"Totally," I say, smiling. Life has a funny way of shifting perspective.

Eva and Thanh resume the story in my petite living room while I make tea for the group. I pass around steaming mugs, then pull a kitchen chair next to Eva on the couch. I rest my hand comfortably on her leg as she recounts everything we saw. Her description finally slows down when she mentions the portal...and what came out of it.

"I don't get it," Art says. "A monstrous red arm came out of this magic circle? Like a demon?"

Eva, Thanh, and I look at each other sheepishly, realizing how ludicrous it sounds.

"We don't know," I eventually say. "There were rumors all over the Sanctum that the elders worked on some joint project together. They might have been creating this for hundreds of years. If I had to guess, that's what their chants were doing—maintaining the portal somehow. When I threw the bottle and the place went up in flames, the elders momentarily lost control before things went crazy."

"'Went crazy' is an understatement," Thanh says. "We saw it with our own eyes, and with so many other witnesses that I can't pretend we all lost our sanity. The elders not only discovered the existence of other worlds, but developed the ability to create transferable portals between them. In this case...connecting a demonic netherworld to Brookline, Massachusetts."

Dot smiles at me, lowering her purple gemmed glasses. "Any chance you have something stronger than tea, Cleo dear? Think I'll be Ubering my ass home."

"Anyone else?" I ask.

A round of awkward nods.

I come back with a few relics from my drinking days: half a handle of vodka and a handful of beers. These were toxic to me when I was isolated and grieving, but it feels undoubtedly different now. Alcohol and other substances have been a catalyst for camaraderie since before the written language; tribes would sit by the fire, sharing stories in community and protecting one another from the horrors of the surrounding darkness. Tonight, we fortify ourselves with swigs whenever we consider how close it all was to going wrong—being caught when we first entered, interrogated by the engineering instructor, lockpicking Thanh's prison cell, and confronted by the real Ninety-Four and Ninety-Seven. After sharing, consoling, and comforting...we soon come to laugh again.

"Like, I still can't get over how you threw a Molotov cocktail," Thanh says. "That's some real-life *Call of Duty* shit!"

Art and I look at each other. "Thanh...you swore!"

He shrugs, taking another drink. "I almost died like eight-hundred fucking times today. I'll re-evaluate my habits in the morning."

"Or don't re-evaluate," Dot says, patting his leg. "That whole 'aww shucks, Jiminy Cricket' thing is robbing yourself of the deliciousness of swearing! It's so visceral, so colorful!"

"Meh. I'll consider the feedback."

Art finds my speaker and crafts a playlist of songs we used to listen to in college. Everyone enjoys them, but by the time "Young Dumb and Broke" comes on, Art, Thanh and I are openly sobbing. We wonder how so much time has passed since we were eighteen—how those anxious, bright-eyed freshmen got through it all.

"Do you remember the time those drunk guys had a wrestling match in our dorm hallway at 2:00 AM?" Thanh asks.

"That was right outside our door!" I say. "They used stolen caution tape to create a ring, and for some reason everyone was shirtless, even the spectators..."

Eva and Dot shake their heads, appalled at male dorm living.

"I wasn't complaining," Art says with a grin. "And do you remember in junior year when Thanh's roommate locked him out by accident?"

"You two stood in a bush and hoisted me up through the window!" Thanh says. "I don't know if I ever told you guys, but that really meant a lot to me. You two were always living together and sometimes I felt like the odd one out. But Cleo skipped class to do that for me, and neither of you batted an eye to come help."

Art springs himself over the arm of the couch, landing on Thanh to give him a hug. "We were obsessed with you, babes! Always so mysterious! You'd wear all-black, chain-smoke, and read philosophy books in the heat of August, but also volunteer as a tutor at the local high school? We patiently waited to get you in our clutches, and now we finally have you!" Art tightens his hug on Thanh like a boa constrictor, and I do my best to pry him off.

197

More than any memory, what I can't get over is how we're still this close after all the life changes we've been through. How many apartments, jobs, schools, relationships, and family dramas have we collectively had? Life has given us so many reasons to drift apart, but we're still here, dragging Art off one another when he gets too clingy.

After talking for hours and finishing off the last of the liquor, exhaustion finally kicks in. Eyes drooping, Art orders an Uber for him and Thanh to share.

"Want to share a ride with me, Eve?" Dot asks, opening the app.

"I'll order my own, don't worry. How long until yours gets here?"

"Two minutes!"

I grab Eva's hand, pulling her slightly away from the others. "You don't have to go home tonight, if you don't want to." I say this with a confidence I wasn't expecting. The two of us haven't spent the night together before, but the thought of her leaving just doesn't feel right anymore.

She looks at me in surprise...and relief. "Are you sure you're okay with that? You must be beyond exhausted, and if you want space I..."

"I'm positive. If the Sanctum is searching for us, I don't want either of us to be alone; I'd be worried about you and probably too paranoid to sleep. It's not just a safety thing, though. I...nothing would make me happier than to have you here with me."

"I want to be here too," she says.

We rejoin the group, hugging everyone on their way out. Dot lingers for a moment longer, looking at her friend shrewdly. "You and I have some catching up to doooo!"

"We do," Eva confirms.

Dot giggles to herself and leaves, shutting the door behind her.

It's just the two of us now. Eva and I look at each other, feeling awkward, grateful, hopeful, and desperately tired.

"Do you want anything else to wear to bed? I have other t-shirts or sweatshirts if it gets cold."

She follows me into my bedroom, opening my dresser. "Feels nice to have the favor finally repaid."

"Long overdue," I say, remembering the Rockwell sweatpants and shirt she lent me after the ice incident. "You'll find that my clothes are wrinkled to perfection, but you have full access to whatever you'd like."

She smiles, finally closing the drawer. "The sweatpants I have on are fine. I just wanted to do more snooping."

The two of us are standing in my bedroom. We haven't moved. "I can sleep on the couch tonight—"

"Stop," she says, reaching for my hand. She pulls it to her lips, slowly kissing it. "Can we?"

I hold Eva in my arms. For the first time in what's felt like an eternity, we aren't rushed to pull away from each other. Still, I can't help but kiss her lips, her cheek, her neck, her collarbone as if it's the last moment we'll ever have. I breathe her in with the certainty that I have her now, and that there's nothing else on this earth that I could want.

We shut the lights off, and the two of us crawl into bed under the covers. We lie on our sides, curled together. My arms wrap around her protectively. My cheek rests into the softness of her hair, pressed against the scarlet streak that first caught my eye. It is perfectly quiet in the room and our eyes are closed.

"I don't want this to end," Eva whispers into the darkness.

"It doesn't have to."

CHAPTER 43

Eva and I spend the next two days in a haze of exhaustion. We nurse ourselves back to health with sleep, cuddling, takeout, *Parks and Recreation*, sweatpants, and a vehement refusal to do any house chores, despite the apartment's need for it. We briefly stop by her place to grab a few things, but immediately head back to my apartment; neither of us want her sleeping that close to campus.

By Wednesday, however, our tone shifts. Instead of blissfully, pleasantly rotting, we spend most of the morning lost in our own thoughts. We've caught up on everything our bodies required, which unfortunately prevents us from ignoring the subject anymore. Eva and I are eating leftover Chinese food in the kitchen when she finally breaks the silence, lowering her fork.

"What are we going to do about it?"

I exhale, not needing any more context. "I honestly can't decide."

"Let's talk it out then," she says. "Should we do something about the Sanctum?"

"The 'reasonable' solution would be to call the police, but I think I'm against that. There's no way they would believe us unless we showed them what's down there, and I have no intention of going back. The Sanctum also has high ranking officials across the globe and within Rockwell. If we report something like that, one of their insiders might find out. I can't imagine we'll last long after that."

"I agree," Eva says. "No police, and we don't go back down. What about the conservation office?"

"We left it a mess. At some point the Rockwell staff will wonder why Mildred isn't showing up to work, or will want to open her office for cleaning. When they do, they'll find the place in shambles, raise alarms, and scrutinize security footage across the campus. We...should go back and clean things up, at the very least." Fear creeps into Eva's eyes; our time away from the Sanctum has only made us more terrified of it. "You don't have to come with me if you don't want."

"Of course I'm coming," she says. "I don't want to keep worrying about it, though. Let's get this done tonight."

It's a tense drive over, and the once thrilling experience of hiding in my old study room until the library closes is now an anxious, silent affair. Eventually we hear the familiar sound of the librarian walking through the Rockwell library stacks, shutting the lights off behind them. Eva and I slowly creep through the bookshelves, stopping in front of the conservation office to pause and listen. We hear nothing, but that still somehow increases my heartrate. What if they've set up a trap for us in there?

We don't have a choice, though. This needs to be behind us forever. For the final time I pick the lock with my battered childhood library card, hearing the click. I slowly swing the door open, shining my phone light inside...

"What the hell..." Eva mutters, staring in disbelief.

I swallow, stepping inside cautiously. The conservation office looks pristine. Everything is put back exactly as Mildred had it originally; there are no books and papers littering the carpet, the desk is right-side up, and the bookshelf we dragged is neatly paralleled with the others. I walk to the back of the room, the shadows of Eva's flashlight sneaking up behind me. I crouch down beside the vent, looking down.

"No..." I mutter. The tunnel is entirely gone. Beneath the vent is a thick slab of gray concrete, smoothly finished to look like a natural part of the library basement. I try to use the latch on the vent, but it won't budge forward or backward in the slightest. They've sealed themselves in entirely. As if they never existed.

Eva crawls next to me, staring in disbelief. "I can't believe they would close off the Sanctum."

My mind goes back to the discussion I had with the acolyte when I was scrubbing floors—to the tunnel that leads forty miles north to the

New Hampshire border. They could all still be in the Sanctum working to rebuild, or perhaps there was a mass exodus to get them all to safety. Every surviving scholar, acolyte, instructor, elder...and infant.

My throat catches. For the past few days I've woken up in a cold sweat, dreaming of the fire, the smoke, the screaming, the death of Mildred. At times I convince myself I was innocent, merely defending myself and my loved ones from a dangerous cult. If it were up to me, zero people would have been injured or died; they were the ones who wanted to sacrifice Thanh and ram me off a ledge. Still, a creeping guilt festers. I had always seen myself as the quiet, bookish guy in the background, not making much of a splash on anything or anyone. I didn't know that, when push came to shove, I would be capable of causing such profound devastation. All for the sake of a dissertation.

"Come on, Cleo," Eva says, putting an arm around my shoulder. "It's over, now. Let's go home."

We lock the door and close it behind us, for the last time.

CHAPTER 44

Eva and I gradually resume normal life. She still goes to the University four days a week for her lectures, but never stays longer than necessary and goes to the UPS Store any time the faculty printer breaks. As for my dissertation, I now work from the discomfort of my own apartment. I spread my materials as wide as my tiny table allows while losing myself in the entire discography of T-Rex. I'd grown accustomed to my old routine of commuting, of experiencing the world in a blur of daily ritual. Cooped up in my apartment, the passage of time—the wintery chill, thaw, and relentless spring rain—is a mere strip that I glimpse through my kitchen window. Cars honk in traffic, mail is delivered, Eva comes and goes...but I finally make progress.

I start with the photos that Eva and I had taken when we first arrived at the Sanctum. These texts were definitely cool to read, but they weren't relevant or fruitful enough to be impactful. I spend the remainder of the semester with *Enlightened Rituals*. It is everything I had hoped for, although my initial vehemency to discover its secrets has certainly diminished. I'm no longer fixated on my grade or some obsession to uncover history. Rather, I'm as hyper-focused as ever because my loved ones risked so much to retrieve it, and because there's an opportunity to help real people like Eva and her grandfather.

I still find myself lost in my work, occasionally blinking and realizing that I don't know what time (or day) it is. The sun will set and my apartment grows gradually black, aside from a hazy twilight from the window and the LED rectangle glowing from my laptop.

And then I pour another cup of coffee and sit back down.

CHAPTER 45

"The findings of my dissertation have the potential to refocus modern dementia research," I continue, sweating through the tweed jacket that Art lent me. Luckily, he's smiling in the crowd, as are Eva, Thanh, and Dot. The large conference room is well air-conditioned, but with dozens of eyes on me and my PhD on the line, I'm lucky my hands are dry enough to hold the remote clicker. I've already presented the introduction and methods of my dissertation defense, but it's time to dive into the juicy part. I press the clicker, advancing the slide behind me.

"There are three noteworthy discoveries from the *Enlightened Rituals* text. First, in reference to preparing medicinal herbs, it states the importance of using the entire plant rather than only one section of the roots, leaves, or stems. Modern scientists have focused on the active ingredients extracted from one portion of the plant, but chemical properties in other parts can provide unique interactions with these active ingredients. While modern extracts excel in removing inconsistencies within the plant—which can be caused from numerous sources, such as soil, time of harvesting, weather, and genetic variations—they neglect the chemical balance that nature has already provided, which may limit its potency in treating cognitive decline. In short, modern scientists have been trading effectiveness for consistency.

"Second, *Enlightened Rituals* frequently references the herb Brahmi, which has a known therapeutic impact on memory. It also describes supplementing Brahmi, however, with a second herb known as Ashwagandha. This herb allegedly reduces forgetfulness and provides a calming effect on users. Drug development in modern Western medicine has typically been 'single-target,' meaning that drugs target a specific, simple disease very well by providing the 'key' to the 'lock.' Many chronic and complex diseases, however, can have more sophisticated locks. Have any of you ever been frustrated when your computer logins ask for multi-factor authentication?" Polite laughter from the audience. My face is hot and probably red, but I smile for the first time since this started. I'm finally hitting my stride. "With more complex locks, a single, simple key does nothing. More and more, researchers are noting that complex diseases need to be met with multi-target drugs that can tackle several ongoing issues at once. By coupling Brahmi with Ashwagandha, ancient healers may have been doing just that for hundreds of years.

"Third and finally, *Enlighted Rituals* provides novel, non-invasive means of administering these herbs. They primarily began by turning them into oils." I advance the slide, showing both modern photos and ancient art works depicting these practices. "Shirodhara, shown on the left, is where the healer gently drips medicinal oil onto the forehead of the ailed person. Likewise, Shirobasti is where a leather, funnel-like cap is wrapped around a person's head to create a reservoir for holding the oil in place for close to an hour. The practice of Nasya, depicted on the right, involves pouring the oil into the nose.

"Many of you are probably noticing a theme. Why were so many of these remedies about the top of the head, rather than merely ingesting it orally like a modern pill? Because ancient healers understood the human body as an inverted tree: the head is our roots, the body our trunk, and the limbs our branches extending into the world. Toxins can be sprayed on the leaf of a tree with very little impact, but if they soak into the root system it could harm the entire being. So, too, could it be healed through the roots. In modern medicine, a similar concept is also understood. We want our dementia pharmaceuticals to impact the brain, but unfortunately, we often run into issues with what is called the 'blood-brain barrier.' This barrier plays a vital role in protecting against brain damage and disease, but it can also limit a healing drug's ability to access the brain as well. By testing these novel means for administering medications directly to the head, dementia researchers may be able to penetrate the blood-brain barrier more effectively and thereby increase the efficacy of medications.

"In summation, dementia researchers need to study the effectiveness of treatments that use the whole herb rather than extracts, use multiple complimentary herbs at once, and administer them in ways that better penetrate the blood-brain barrier. Modern Western medicine has often struggled in managing chronic illnesses. It is essential that we look elsewhere—to wisdom across cultures and across time—to fill these gaps in understanding so that we can better serve those who are suffering. I believe such an international, inter-millennia collaboration would showcase the true beauty of human achievement."

The audience erupts into applause.

Waves of relief and disbelief hit me. The public presentation technically doesn't impact my grade—the private dissertation committee defense is what seals my fate—but I'm overwhelmed that my work has culminated into this final display. Everyone in the audience was attentive and engaged, eager to hear the result of thousands of hours that I've poured into this. There's a brief Q&A afterward that goes by smoothly; Eva starts it off by asking a softball question, and the rest are easy as well because most of the audience hasn't read a word of my dissertation.

When the questions wind down, Professor Lewis walks up to the podium as the dissertation committee chair. "That about wraps up the public portion of Cleo Thompson's dissertation," he says, smiling to the crowd as if they were here for him. "I will ask everyone who is not in the dissertation committee to enjoy the refreshments in the lobby outside. Meanwhile, we will proceed with the remainder of the defense."

I remain standing in the front of the room, bouncing in my dress shoes as the blissfully free crowd leaves me and the committee behind. When the door finally closes, it's so quiet I can hear the projector humming above. I swallow, doing my best to smile at the four professors sitting behind an imposing wooden table. All of them are staring at me. The only two that I recognize are Professor Lewis and Professor Blair, which isn't a good sign. I had Blair in undergrad for Medieval European history, and she was an absolute hard-ass; she made a girl cry on the first day of class, and cultivated an aura of fear by employing the Socratic method and asking "are you sure about that?" after you squeaked out your answers. The third committee member can't be much older than me, and by the way he's fidgeting, he might be just as nervous to be here. I wonder if it's the first time he's ever sat on that side of the table, and if he's getting flashbacks to his own defense. The fourth is a much older gentleman with a bushy white beard, bald head, and a dreamy expression as he glances around the room fondly. I wouldn't be surprised if he was on the dissertation committee for Lewis and Blair's defenses, several decades ago.

"Alright, Cleo," Lewis begins, smiling at me. After all these years working with him, I do somehow find his presence comforting on this terrifying occasion. "You provided an excellent presentation, and now we have a few questions for you about your work. Are you ready?"

"Let's do this," I say, instantly regretting the casual response.

And then...the group hammers into me.

"On page thirty-six of your dissertation, you provide a distinction between regional agrarian practices in Southern India, but also indicate that there was open communication between them. Why, then, would you suppose techniques would differ? And were there notable differences in crop yield between regions?"

"How do major Pharma distributors account for the genetic variance in the herbs that they use to create medications? You mention that they trade effectiveness for consistency, but have audits been done on their chemical supply chains?

"Please speak more to your translation confidences. With such an old and localized Sanskrit text, maintaining a high degree of accuracy would be both challenging and necessary, given the specificity needed to detail medical procedures and dosages."

Each question insights a fresh wave of dread. None of them hold back—especially Professor Blair—but I do my best to take deep breaths before answering. It is a shocking realization, but ultimately, I am the expert in the room on this very particular topic. I've dedicated the last four years to my project, and together with Professor Lewis, I have considered most ideas. I can't promise that my decisions have been perfect or that the committee will agree with them, but they have all been thoughtfully considered.

My final question comes from Professor Lewis, and I'm beyond prepared for this one. "Cleo, as you and I both know, the *Enlightened Rituals* text was believed to be lost to history. I speak for all of us when I ask: how did you find it?"

"To tell you the truth, Professor, it started from advice that you gave me. You told me to search for resources so thoroughly that there was 'no stone left unturned,' which made me consider where I was looking in the first place. I had sought out every major library, database, museum, and university. After reflection, I eventually understood my error: I was looking for 'lost' information in places that house everything 'found.' Ayurvedic medicine was discriminated against for centuries, and was therefore practiced in secret. So, I started systematically interviewing Indian ayurvedic practitioners whose families have been doing this for generations. I did a lot of digging. At first, I was merely looking for scraps of information that they might have had, but over time the trail led me to a family who was rumored to have old primary documents. It took me some time to gain their trust, but eventually they allowed me to browse through their personal library. There, I found it. I told them that I wished to use these sources for my work and they consented, but they vehemently refused to be mentioned or credited in my dissertation. I've spent the past three months documenting everything in their library, and I have extensive notes and photos cataloguing it all."

"Excellent," Professor Lewis responds, although his odd smile is inscrutable. "I believe that is all the questions we have at this time. If you'd please step outside, Cleo, the committee will deliberate and call you back in with our decision."

"Thank you for your time," I manage, walking past the committee and out into the hallway, closing the door behind me.

There's one sad, plastic chair waiting for me. I sink into it, lowering my head into my hands from sheer exhaustion. I've done everything I can. It's all out my control now; I just need to be...patient. I've heard horror stories of PhD candidates waiting for their decision for three hours. I chose not to bring my phone with me today in case some alert or alarm went off during the defense, but I'm certainly regretting that decision now. I tap my foot, fidget in my chair, read bulletin messages posted along the hallway...anything to keep myself distracted. How could anyone wait here for three hours?!

I sigh, left alone with a racing mind and restless thoughts. The backstory I had invented for finding *Enlightened Rituals* came to me a few weeks ago, and I cursed myself as soon as I thought of it. It demonstrates dedication, outside-the-box thinking, and consideration of the culture that developed these healing techniques. In short, it's exactly what I *should* have done. I've spent years struggling to find resources, and somehow I convinced myself that the best course of action was to risk our lives by sneaking into an occult library? Of course I might not have found *Enlightened Rituals* by interviewing ayurvedic practitioners, but I'm certain I could have learned a great deal. I've been so fixated on this being wisdom of the past that I failed to consider how history never really goes away; it's implications, lessons, and traditions are carved into generations that live among us today. Somehow, I have to make this right. I don't know how, but—

I startle to reality—the door beside me swings open and Professor Lewis steps through, stone-faced. "At this time, the committee would like you to return and hear the results of your defense...Doctor Thompson."

I enter the room, fending off tears as every professor in the room shakes my hand and congratulates me on my outstanding work.

I've done it.

CHAPTER 46

Having received minimal feedback from my dissertation committee, I spend the week making edits and reviewing my paper one final time. After uploading the document to the ProQuest portal and quadruple-checking that my file formats are correct, I have my mouse hovering over the "Submit" button. Nearly shaking, it takes several seconds before I can finally...make myself...click.

I exhale, shocked at the realization that it's actually done. I feel an immense relief that it's over, but also a surprising sense of loss as I close my laptop. Four years of my life have been spent nurturing this dissertation, and it has been one of the only consistent through-lines I've had. What am I supposed to do now? What have regular civilians been doing on weekends and late nights when I've been cooped up in a library? Should I go frolic in a park or something? I try to remind myself that this was only ever meant to be a stepping-stone; that the purpose of an education is to equip me tools to enter the world and make an important impact.

There is, however, one final thread that I need to take care of before I can move on: what to do with *Enlightened Rituals*. My first thought is to bring it to a museum, until I realize that that's exactly what caused this mess in the first place; colonizing nations have been destroying and stealing precious artifacts for centuries. Flying it all the way to India would be a nightmare; if the TSA found it in my bag, I could only imagine how long my interrogation would last. The easiest answer is for me to keep it, but that doesn't feel right either. This isn't my knowledge to hoard, and although I would cherish it to a sickening degree, I wouldn't be putting it to good use.

Ultimately, I take inspiration from my lie. I open my laptop back up and Google "ayurveda healers near me." I look through countless websites and reviews, ignoring the ones that seem to be run by white people encouraging other white people to try their new smoothie cleanses. Eventually, I come across one that has only eleven reviews, but they're all five stars and many of them are written in Hindi. Their website looks like it was last updated in 2007, but it's still open and it's operated by an older Indian couple, Aakash and Sunita Nigam. I read through their credentials, bios, and more glowing customer testimonials. There's nowhere to make an appointment, however, and the phone line I call provides the automated message that their voicemail is full.

Challenge accepted.

The next day I ask Art if I can borrow his car, and he graciously agrees in exchange for filling his gas tank. I take off at around noon, securing the eight-hundred-year-old text in my backpack and buckling it in the passenger seat. I glance nervously at it as I cross the bumpy, indented train tracks. I hear the familiar *bing-bing-bing* behind me and smile; the red-and-white candy-striped bar lowers seconds after I cross, and I cruise past the commuter rail. It's strange not to be a passenger on the narrow, linear iron rails for once—I take a left turn and then a quick right down a winding street, enjoying the freedom.

My GPS says I've arrived at Eternal Healing and Wellness, and I manage to find parking close by. The small building I'm looking for is tucked between a Dollar Tree and a Spanish market. I open the door and almost run into an elderly woman on her way out. She's speaking rapid Hindi over her shoulder, and while I struggle to translate the quickness of native speakers, it sounds like every form of "thank you" that I know. The clinic waiting room is small but cozily decorated, with plush furniture and plants surrounded by a warming incense. Aakash and Sunita are both at the front desk, and they greet me as I enter.

"Hi, my name is Cleo. I don't have an appointment, but I was hoping to have a conversation with one of you if you're available? It shouldn't take much of your time."

"Of course!" Aakash says in a thick accent. He's wearing a yellow button-down shirt with brown slacks, and there's a bright smile beneath his thick, graying mustache. "Please, follow me."

Aakash leads me to a cramped beige office in the back. There's a large bookshelf on the left, a locked case of medicines on the right, and plaques and certifications filling up the remaining space. He takes a seat behind his desk and gestures for me to use the chair across from him.

"I am Dr. Aakash Nigam. You may call me Aakash, if you like. It is a pleasure to make your acquaintance."

"You as well! Thank you for seeing me on such short notice. I'm Cleo Thompson. I..." I glance around the room desperately. I tried to rehearse this last night with Eva, but it always came out clunky. "I...love your bookshelf. I'm a recently graduated doctorate student who researches ancient Sanskrit texts, particularly ayurveda. I believe I've read through of few of these in my studies."

"That is wonderful!" he replies. "Absolutely wonderful. The study of ayurveda is five thousand years old; the more we can bring it to the world, the better."

"I couldn't agree more," I say. "Do you read those books on your shelf a lot? Or any of the older Sanskrit texts, like the *Charaka Samhita*?"

Aakash is absolutely beaming. "Your pronunciation is phenomenal, young man, I must say. Yes of course, I have studied the *Charaka Samhita* and other sources extensively, and will continue to do so. Knowledge is a lifelong pursuit. To me, each of these texts are worth their weight in gold."

I exhale. Part of this cloak-and-dagger on my part is not only awkwardness (which is abundant), but also to get a vibe for who I might be giving *Enlightened Rituals* to. I desperately want it to go to someone who will use and cherish it, and I believe I've found that someone.

"I completely agree with you, Aakash," I say, taking off my backpack and unzipping it. "I actually came in here because, during my studies, I found a very old text that contains ayurveda teachings. I've gotten everything that I need from it, and I was hoping to give it to someone who would continue to learn and study from it to improve their care in ayurveda. Would you be interested in having it? I'm not asking for anything in return; I just want to make sure this is in the right hands."

Aakash looks at me with the kindest smile, almost on the verge of tears. "What a beautiful thought. As a part of my certification, I am not ethically allowed to encourage patients to provide gifts, or to treat them with any beneficial treatment as a result. Seeing as you are not a patient of mine, it could be possible. At the very least, I would be most pleased to see this historical text."

I pull out the wooden covers from my bag and fan out the palm leaves on the center of his desk.

Aakash's mouth drops open.

CHAPTER 47

A few weeks after submitting my dissertation, I receive an email from Professor Lewis asking me to meet him on campus. The once ordinary request sets off a thousand alarms. Does he have concerns about my paper that will prevent me from graduating? More suspicions about where I found *Enlightened Rituals*? Or is he somehow aligned with the Sanctum, and this is a trap? Of course I don't have much of a choice; if I don't go, everything I've endured for the last four years will have been for nothing.

The university campus is beautiful this time of year. The sun shimmers off the green lawn, lilies sprout beneath budding maple trees, and swathes of white and pink mums are in full bloom. Much like the plant life, Rockwell's students begin to emerge as well. The long, dark winters of huddling inside and bracing against the cold are gone; the grass is filled with students sunbathing on beach towels, laughing with friends, and reading for their upcoming exams. Today is one of those rare, picturesque days when college life is exactly what they had imagined.

It always feels criminal to enter the dark, crusty Ancient Studies department when the weather is so perfect. I've been committing this crime for years, though, and the thought that this could be my last time is a slap to the face. Rockwell terrifies me after everything that happened in the Sanctum, yet still I feel an aching nostalgia at the thought of losing it. Slightly out of breath from the stairs, I walk up to Professor Lewis' office and knock.

"Welcome and enter!" I hear him sing. I roll my eyes and let myself in.

Professor Lewis is behind his desk, grading a large stack of exam papers. "Cleo! Shut the door behind you, if you'd be so kind. Please, have a seat."

215

My heart pounds in my chest. I do as I'm asked, trying to read the glimpses of undertones in his voice. "Good to see you, Professor. I know things get busy this time of year."

"That they do," he says, gesturing down at the exams with a look of resigned martyrdom. "But I consider this far, far more important. Your dissertation, Cleo." He clasps his fingers together, looking at me across his oak desk. I wait for him to continue, but the pause drags on for what feels like an eternity.

"Are there issues with it, Professor? Did the submission go through okay?"

His gaze hardens for a few seconds longer before cracking into a hearty laugh. "Issues?! I've already submitted it for international awards! I contacted press and pharmaceutical representatives to come speak with the university!" I look at him in relief and disbelief, which only makes him laugh harder. This was all just his usual dramatics? "Most faculty will go their entire careers without generating work as novel and groundbreaking as this, and you've managed it as a student. This is going to be what finally puts our department on the map! I *knew* you would rise to the challenge, and together you and I are going to be the rockstars of the department, the university...hell, all of academia!"

"That's fantastic news! I can't believe it, I...I couldn't have done this without you, Professor."

Professor Lewis smiles. "I'm glad you feel that way, Cleo. My own academic achievements, while undoubtedly extensive, have been outshined only by my devotion to mentor the next generation of scholars. With a few additional years of collaboration between the two of us, there's no telling what we'll be capable of."

I laugh politely at the mention of additional years, but Professor Lewis continues in seriousness. "What I mean to say is that I've had a few conversations with the university's finance and human resource departments. Faculty teaching appointments for next fall are already set, and as you know, it is common practice to have PhD graduates begin their careers teaching at other institutions. As a *research professor*, however, you would be able to remain at Rockwell University in a grant-funded position that has no teaching responsibilities. Your sole concern would be furthering the work we've begun here. It's an offer that would make any of your peers, should word get out..." he says, peering at the closed door, "quite jealous. The starting salary would be $130,000 a year, though between you and me, if you played a little hard ball and counter-offered, we wouldn't be able to say no," he adds with a wink. "So, shall I get the paperwork started?"

I plaster a smile over my nerves. Jobs like this are impossible to get. Every PhD student would want one—including myself, a few short months ago—at any university. And at an institution as prestigious as Rockwell? Forget it. Both the opportunity and the salary would be life-changing; I wouldn't have to worry about housing or moving ever again. It's just...

"I'm beyond words at the moment," I say truthfully, and he laughs. "It's an incredible offer; I'd just like to take a few days and think everything over, if that's okay?"

"Of course, my boy! Thoughtfulness with such critical decisions is one of the many qualities we look for in our faculty here. Just don't tease us for too long!" he says, laughing again. I try joining him, praying the rest of my face gets the memo. After a few brief pleasantries, I manage to excuse myself.

I exit the academic building while attempting to control my breathing. I pass by the carefree students on the lawn again, wondering if they know how limited their time is here. What lengths would they go to keep this feeling forever? I pass the columned façade of the library, but the very sight of it makes my skin crawl, urging me to walk faster. I shake my head, cutting through a side path toward the student dorms.

I pass a young couple—god they're so young; did I look like that when I started here?—holding hands on their way to the dining hall.

That's where Kelsie and I used to go at least, when we walked together on this same path. And here's Clark, our old brick dorm building. I remember how exciting it was at that time, the idea of living under the same roof as my girlfriend, even though we were two floors apart. I look for the plants that always used to be in her window, but see a large tapestry there instead. Of course the tenants and everything they brought would change, but I haven't been to this part of campus in years. My memory is still vividly frozen in place, and every difference in buildings, decorations, and landscaping brings an unexpected pang. It takes me a moment to realize that I'm not mourning the loss of Kelsie or dorm living...merely the passage of time. I was so happy here—so happy to *be* here in those early days, that it felt like a dream I would startle awake from.

I pass the dorms as well, wandering aimlessly until I make it to the edge of campus. I find a small dirt path that transitions to a wooded trail. I've only been here once before during the day, and I forgot just how beautiful it is. The trees curve inward, forming a green archway overhead that billows softly in the wind. Sunlight streaks in small rays, shifting and swaying with the breeze and spotlighting low-flying birds and fluttering insects. A narrow, sturdy bridge creaks underfoot as I cross a stream. A deeper, quieter calmness washes over me with each stride.

My pace hasn't slowed since I left Professor Lewis' office, but I finally rest here in front of the lake. I stare across the shimmering surface, a flood of memories from Kelsie, Eva, and Rockwell coming to mind. I've drifted here in moments that marked the beginning of the end, the end...and new beginning. "And they all revolved around some stupid geode," I think to myself, laughing. It meant so much to me at the time, but now...I think I've outgrown it. After everything that's happened this semester, I've outgrown a lot of things.

I reach down, picking up a rock and weighing it in my hand. It's cool and solid to the touch, and feels grounding in a way that surprises me. I twist back and throw it far across the lake—splashing into the surface. I smile, watching it ripple the water in ways I hadn't expected.

EPILOGUE

It's a Friday night and the sunset is fading into a warm lavender. Eva and I are lounging on the balcony of our new apartment, enjoying a few glasses of wine and some top-tier people-watching. Her tanned legs are stretched lazily against the railing, but her eyes are locked in on two pedestrians.

"They are absolutely a couple," she says again. "Do you see the way he's holding her backpack? And look at the body language—they both keep laughing and turning to face each other. They're practically fawning!"

I smile, squinting my eyes at them again. "They're definitely close...I think they're just friends, though. Part of me thinks he might be gay."

"No way! You've just been spending too much time with Art; he thinks everyone is gay."

"True. I'm assuming you don't recognize either of them from your courses?"

She shakes her head. "It's early enough in the semester that they might be, though. The lecture halls at Ashland are a lot bigger than I'm used to, so it's easy to forget all their faces."

We live three blocks away from Ashland University, where Eva recently began her new teaching appointment. So far, she's loving it; her department is small and collaborative, and she's already been given more opportunities to teach advanced courses in her area of research. The university also has the added benefit of being established within the last sixty years, which makes it far less likely to have a cultish underbelly.

Eva finishes her wine and wiggles the empty glass in front of me. "Need anything?"

"Yes please!" I say, handing her my glass to refill. I lean forward in my Adirondack chair, presenting my forehead for a kiss.

"Such a silly man," she says, dutifully complying before going inside.

"Love you! Also, can you check if the mail came today?" I don't usually expect anything good, but Kathy should be responding to me soon. Despite my general aversion to Rockwell University, I can't help but stay pen-pals with my favorite librarian. She and I share a muffin bond for life.

It was hard to turn down my job offer at Rockwell, and harder still because Professor Lewis didn't handle the news very gracefully. I don't think he's used to being told "no." Some of the awards that he mentioned fizzled away, and a few of them were mysteriously awarded under his own name. Beyond academia, my dissertation did make a bit of a splash in the pharmaceutical world. I received several emails from major pharma companies asking me to work for them. Some of these companies have even sent extraordinarily generous gifts to accompany their offers. The hilarity of this and Lewis' ego has only solidified my resolve to change my career direction; there's a lot of good to be done in the field of dementia care, and it doesn't need to be accomplished by profiteering from the sick.

That said, I made sure that the bribe and award money didn't go to waste. After everything I put him through, I decided to give Thanh most of the funds—totaling about thirty thousand dollars—so that he could pay off some student loans and help his mom out. He went nonverbal for close to a minute, and only spoke again when I asked if this at least partially repaid his suffering in the Sanctum.

"Are you kidding? I'd take a day of torture for thirty grand any time!"

Always so sentimental.

I had planned to spend the summer applying to jobs until my eyes bled, but somehow I managed to fall into one. I checked my email one morning and saw a lengthy, formal message from Aakash. He said he and his wife had Googled my name after we spoke, and they found my email address in the university directory. They had read through *Enlightened Rituals* and my dissertation and were eager to discuss. I was nervous when I arrived, but after hours of conversation and many cups of tea, we all felt an immediate connection. This niche history that I've obsessed over has been everything they've practiced and lived. Likewise, the rich traditions that they brought with them when they immigrated to the United States are being embraced, studied, and championed by someone a world away from its origins, simply for its own merit.

After that day, I started coming over frequently. It began as mere social visits, but soon I was asking more about how their practice was doing. Customers would come in periodically—always well-attended to and grateful after their appointments—but the traffic was sparse to say the least. Sunita admitted that they both struggled with the "business" side of things. She had taken a free course at the library about web design, but technology was not her strong suit.

It's funny how my brain works. I had always assumed I was interested specifically in history, but more and more I'm coming to understand that my interest might simply be...interest. I love getting lost in a subject, whatever that might be. That very night, I found myself researching strategies for marketing a local business, establishing a social media presence, and creating websites. I watched videos, listened to podcasts, and read books. I interviewed Art about how he developed a social media following, and he even recommended a friend of his in graphic design who could make a brand logo. I felt guilty for spending so much time on this when I should have been applying to jobs, but it was vastly more interesting and felt like I was doing something meaningful for people who deserved the help.

With their permission, I began overhauling the 2007 website that Sunita had lovingly attempted. I brought it up a decade in presentability, reorganized the tabs, made sure the links worked, and created a field for people to book online appointments. I also finally cleared out their voicemail, and was gratified to see that they had received several new ones the very next day. Within a month word began to spread, and Aakash told me they had more bookings than ever. They needed help managing inventory, scheduling appointments, filling out paperwork, and continuing their social media presence. If I stayed on to help, they agreed to pay me as much as they could, and even more as the business grew. Plus, Aakash offered a unique employment benefit: I was allowed full access to their ayurveda library.

I accepted the position, and I can firmly say it is one of the best decisions of my life. I feel valued here, and the more I learn about our clients, the better I appreciate the impact that these ayurvedic practitioners have on those who need it most: women whose pain isn't taken seriously by the traditional healthcare system, chronically ill people whose insurance won't cover their inflating prescription costs, racial and ethnic populations who have been openly mistreated for centuries and no longer trust western medicine. Every day I get to see care, community, relief, and gratitude on the faces of our customers, and it continues to remind me why we bother learning anything in the first place: because knowledge is only as important as its application.

I startle from my thoughts as Eva plops the mail on my lap. "Did I miss anything noteworthy?" she asks, glancing over the balcony.

"Yes, actually; a dachshund walked by and she was wiggling her butt in a really fierce, regal way. It was a sight to behold."

"Ugh, that's the last time I get you anything!" She props her legs up again, closing her eyes blissfully.

I quickly flip through the stack of mail, ignoring several sales flyers. Alas, nothing from Kathy. I had hoped she would...

At the bottom of the pile, I find one letter that catches my eye. The envelope is completely blank—no address, return address, or stamp—and is secured with a thick wax seal embossed with a runic symbol. My eyes widen; an immediate jolt of panic hits me for reasons I can't quite articulate.

"Eva," I say, and she startles upright. Something about my voice must have alerted her, because she's already leaning over my shoulder to study the envelope. Hands shaking, I break the wax seal and pull out a thick, tri-folded letter:

Dear Cleo and Eva,

This letter comes to you from a fellow alumnus. While technically you did not graduate from this academic institution, your brief time here—perhaps only Ninety-Four or Ninety-Seven hours in total—was the most momentous in all of the institution's grand history.

We are pleasantly surprised by the discretion with which you have conducted yourselves following your untimely departure. We have closely monitored each and every one of your movements since you left (including those of your close compatriot, who was formerly incarcerated), and were ready to quell any rumors that were spread to those who had not received such a classified education. Any indication of indelicacies on your part would have been met with the swiftest retribution.

I write not to reminisce of our alma mater, which has relocated and undergone significant leadership changes. Rather, I seek your service in a matter of importance. The two of you have proved yourselves to be of the highest caliber of academic young minds, undoubtedly resourceful, fanatically curious, and, above all else, judiciously protective of clandestine information. The opportunity that I offer is not that of student or instructor; rather, you would be singularly tasked with a research assignment of special interest to us.

THE SCHOLAR'S SANCTUM

This opportunity is completely voluntary. You will not be subject to maltreatment of any kind should you not respond. If you are interested, I have provided precise meeting instructions for the three of us to convene.

While I can imagine a healthy degree of hesitancy, there is one point that I wish to make abundantly clear: what you witnessed in our alma mater is far from the endless knowledge you believed it to be. That was but a taste of our enlightenment—a singular book in our vast shelves.

This position would provide you with the truths of the world.

Sincerely,

One

Did you love *The Scholar's Sanctum*? Then you should read *Inferis*[1] by Chris Delude!

2

There are worlds below us.

Of course, Tim Fischer isn't aware of that when he accepts a house-sitting position in upstate New York. All he knows is that he needs a change from his soulless job and wasted life spent alone. His friends Sophia and Lawrence visit him in New York for a pleasant afternoon hike, where they run into the gorgeous, unhinged gas-station cashier that Tim can barely speak to. The four of them find themselves in awe of the scenery. No, not the picturesque landscape of New York wilderness—the undiscovered civilizations that lie in hidden caverns.

They've stumbled farther than they meant to. They're trapped—helplessly lost and in danger—until a geeky hermit living under the earth offers to guide them through a labyrinth of tunnels to an entirely new world. Panoramic skies illuminated by floating violet creatures, death-worshippers hunting for their lives, a forest sorceress guarding the secrets of nature...every lethal step is the journey of a lifetime. In Inferis, Tim finds love, happiness, strength, and himself. If only he can find his way out.

About the Author

Chris Delude is a public health researcher, administrator, and advocate. In his free time, he is the author of the novels *The Scholar's Sanctum* and *Inferis*. Chris lives in Boston, Massachusetts with his brilliant wife, Margaret.

For more information about his writing and future project announcements, visit: www.chrisdelude.com